Kudos for *FLYING HIGH*

"Jim Healy uses his years of service with the FBI to put together an accurate portrayal of how this elite organization functions. *FLYING HIGH* has it all: intrigue, romance, thrills and an exhilarating climax. Along the way, the reader can see how the FBI utilizes all legal methods available to solve crimes and thwart criminal elements such as the Mafioso." —*John Wagner*, FBI Special Agent in Charge, Retired

Retired FBI agent Jim Healy has successfully transformed his many years of chasing the mob into a delightful novel that covers stories of love, comedy, and intrigue, based on actual events he experienced during his long career. A must read that will keep you turning pages to the end. —*Edgar E. DeLong*, LCDR USN (Ret), author of *Navy Mustang*

Jim Healy's new novel FLYING HIGH (pun intended I'm sure), doesn't wait for the reader to catch up to the story; rather, it plunges him or her into the crisp writing of this page-turning narrative, punctuated by Healy's ear for dialogue and language, and old fashioned and suspenseful story telling ability. The reader, in the midst of the story, just hangs on; and it is a fun and pleasant ride laced with humor and at times, dark irony. While this book is not about the FBI per se, many characters in it, from those in the Mob to Special Agents, are informed by Healy's substantial experience as an FBI agent and executive.
—*I.B. Wells*, Retired FBI Agent in Charge and author of *Women of Summer*.

Flying High:
FBI vs. THE MOB

A SPECIAL AGENT DEL DICKERSON NOVEL

To Charleen,
a lovely lady
in all ways.
Love,

Jim

Jim Healy

DISCLAIMER: *FLYING HIGH* is a work of fiction, based on a wide variety of characters encountered during the author's 32-year FBI career. Any resemblance to actual persons, living or deceased, is coincidental and unintentional, and merely reflect the author's imagination.

Dedication

FLYING HIGH is dedicated to the men and women of the FBI who often labor in unheralded anonymity while nobly defending our Nation from its enemies, foreign and domestic.

Acknowledgements

Deep appreciation is extended to my exceptional editor, Sandy Robinette, whose wealth of historical knowledge proved invaluable in accurately portraying the real-life experiences of the men and women of the FBI.

Special thanks are also conveyed for the support and encouragement of my extraordinary teacher, Lauran Strait, President of the Hampton Roads Writers, and her stable of exceptional writers, including Jeff Andrews, author of *The Freedom Star*, and Mike Owens, author of *The End of Free Will*.

Thanks, too, to my mentor, Ed DeLong, a cherished friend whose fantastic life is vividly chronicled in his hair-raising autobiography *Navy Mustang*.

Foreword

Former Special Agent Healy recounts the dangers and the surprises of the life of a Special Agent with the deft touch of a master story teller. After hearing oral histories of hundreds of agents, I know he is telling the true story of the job, the adversaries, the danger and the camaraderie of the FBI.

—Sandra Robinette, former Administrator of the Society of Former Special Agents of the FBI Oral History Heritage Project.

Chapter One

The Mountains

G od, I need a man, Kerry Vita muttered, striding from the small rustic cabin into crisp mountain air. Low forties, she guessed, watching her breath vaporize. She raised the zipper of the dark-blue jacket that hugged her curvaceous figure, and pulled the jacket hood over cropped raven hair. Shouldering a white canvas bag holding easel, palette, paints, and canvasses, she hurried down the narrow path leading to her favorite painting site. The twenty-five-year-old ivory-complexioned woman glanced up at the milky contrails of a high-flying jet darting through random cumulus clouds. Up, up, and away, she thought, sort of like me.

With a flick of her right thumb, the pristine stillness was shattered by the intrusion of a country-western ballad flowing from the compact transistor radio she'd found in a cabin drawer. One station, girl. Get used to it. A slight smile parted her generous lips as she thought of the vibrant music she was accustomed to, and the rapt audiences roaring approval. *There's A Broken Heart For Every Light On Broadway* came to mind, and a shadow of sadness clouded her classic features as she thought of Jeff. Now, there was a man! What a damned waste! A grimace of determination firmed her delicate jaw. I owe you Nicky, you bastard, and I won't forget.

The golden rays of the morning sun sliced through towering pine trees and highlighted the view of the snow-clad mountain peaks miles away. Thoughts of New York, Jeff, and the past, even Nicky the bastard, evaporated as she propelled her energies into a life-long avocation. Thanks, Mom, for the talent, and rest in the peace you never enjoyed on earth.

The warmth generated by her energetic preparations so steadied her hands that her first brush strokes were firm and fluid despite the chilled atmosphere. The long-range vista forming on her canvas held her full attention for over an hour, until the engine drone of a small airplane slowly orbiting above the massive valley penetrated her consciousness. She looked up at the intruder with annoyance. *Can't a girl even enjoy some peace and quiet out here?*

She tried to refocus on her painting, but kept shifting attention to the small plane that now bounced around from the unpredictable updrafts characterizing the valley. Concentration broken, she guessed it was time for a smoke. *Except you gave that up, too,* she reminded herself. She collapsed into the old deck chair she had installed in the mountain-side clearing and resumed her study of the bobbing aircraft that had steadily gained altitude. Momentarily closing her eyes, she thought of the circumstances that brought her to this place. She also listened to the echo of the plane's laboring engines, and pondered the nature of the people aboard. *I wonder what your stories are.*

The Sky

"Is this what you guys do on a day off?" shouted the jumpmaster to the parachute-clad young man perched near the open door of the King Air.

"Beats fishing," FBI agent Del Dickerson shouted back with a grin, adjusting the straps of his multi-colored chute. "Of course, my fiancée thinks I'm crazy, and my bosses aren't too keen on the risks, but if it's good enough for President Bush 41, I guess I'm in good company."

Jesse, the crewman, shook his head. "His wife isn't too happy about it either, I understand."

Del nodded. "But his survival skills are legendary. I hope I'm as lucky."

"The winds have really picked up," Jesse cautioned, "and Magic Valley is notorious for surprises. Sure you don't want to put this off a day?"

"It's my last day here. Then I'm back to the office. Today is now or never."

"Never isn't a bad option sometimes."

The muscular, sandy-haired agent looked reflective, gazing at the wiry skydiving instructor and then at the broad valley below. "I appreciate your concern, but I've established a rather bizarre reputation for doing goofy things. Weird incidents seem to happen to me, and people around me." Mental images flashed through his mind, like the time he stumbled into a Knoxville chop-shop and broke up an interstate auto theft ring. And the time he was kidnapped with a potential father-in-law and forced in the man's presence into a sexual act with their captor's comely girlfriend in an effort to effect their escape. He smiled at another recollection of the time he became an instant hero when he shot a pit bull attacking the Mississippi governor's granddaughter outside the state mansion. He grinned. "No, I'm ready to go, unless you insist to the contrary."

Jesse shook his head. "It's marginal, but I'd probably do it."

Del raised his right thumb. "That's good enough for me. Let's go." He moved against the strong wind pressure rushing through the open cabin door, while the jumpmaster radioed the impending jump to the pilot.

"We'll wait till we level off at 10,000 feet. Remember the location of the handle of your emergency chute, and keep aiming for the designated landing zone. And good luck. I'll see you back at the airport."

Del nodded understanding, sensed the plane leveling, saw the green light flash, felt the firm thump on his shoulder, and leaped forward into space.

The City

Nicky "The Nose" Vincente screamed obscenities at the two swarthy thugs cowering before him in the cramped, smoke-saturated office of Brooklyn's Bossa Ristorante Italiano. "What the fuck good are you two pricks if you can't find one scrawny broad?"

Louis Milano, known as "Loose Louie," due to chronically defective bowel controls, made the mistake of correcting his employer as he envisioned the exciting contours of the missing woman. "She never looked scrawny to me, boss."

Vincente glared. "You fuckin moron, all you think about is pussy. If I say she's scrawny, she's scrawny."

Loose Louie gulped. "You're right, boss, scrawny." He was relieved to hear his partner divert attention.

"We looked everywhere, Nicky, all the places she used to hang at. She just disappeared without a trace."

The ambitious, fortyish member of the embattled Gambino crime family shifted attention to Salvatore Rinalti, also known as "Sulfur Sal" for his expertise in disposing of bodies of adversaries in drums of sulfuric acid. He adjusted his black-rimmed glasses on his prominent nose and snorted disbelief. "No one just disappears without a trace, unless, of course, you practiced your specialty." His scowl was momentarily replaced by a glimmer of grudging admiration. "What are you doing to find her?"

"We got all the boys checking their sources," Loose Louie assured. "It's only a matter of time."

"It's been almost a month already. I'm losing patience." He glared at the two hirelings who watched the rapid movement of their leader's eyebrows that twitched spasmodically when he was agitated. "If you'd completed the job when you whacked her old man and the boyfriend, we wouldn't be in this fuckin mess now."

"She must have been tipped," Sulfur Sal parried. "Slipped out a back window or something."

"With the fuckin book," Vincente reminded.

His lieutenants looked uncomfortably at the floor, then each other.

Vincente continued fulminating. "Now I gotta go to another fuckin meeting and explain that my two hot-shot soldiers can't find one scrawny broad."

"Right, boss, a scrawny broad," Loose Louie quickly agreed, again mentally undressing the traffic-stopping figure of the missing woman.

Vincente took off his glasses and placed them atop a case of imported extra-virgin olive oil stacked next to his desk. He wearily rubbed his blood-shot brown eyes that had immediately crossed when the glasses were removed. "You guys are living on borrowed time," he hissed. "I don't know how long I can hold off the boys from replacing you."

The message was deathly clear. Sulfur Sal blanched and croaked, "They won't have to do that, boss. We'll find her."

Loose Louie shuffled his feet nervously. "I gotta go to the can."

Chapter Two

The sun warmed the day dramatically, and Kerry removed her jacket, comfortable now in black, fleece-lined sweat pants and a snug white, cable-knit turtleneck. Having absorbed her limit of country-western music, the radio was silent, reinforcing the ethereal beauty of her isolation. The pulsating mountain winds brought recurring movement to the surrounding trees, delivering a symphony of muted sounds with intriguing rhythms. They prompted thoughts of her recent adventure as a member of the Greenwich Village group *Angels Three* and their constant quest for a new beat. Put the sounds of nature to work, she thought, before returning to reality. She sighed. I'll never be able to go back.

As recollections prompted recall of some of the group's more popular numbers she found herself humming aloud. Though often compared by the club's promoters to Norah Jones for her sultry voice and deft timing, some admirers proclaimed that all Kerry had to do was stand there, so striking was her enchanting facial blend of Italian and Irish features. Her clinging, low-cut gowns, barely constraining her voluptuous figure, prompted a pleasant bonus for the club operator who reported bulging receipts whenever her group appeared. The memories caused Kerry to close her eyes and momentarily relive a happier time when she was able to lose herself in her music. Submerging into an almost trance-like state, as her body moved to the stimulating electricity of Jeff's drumbeat, she would envision their eventual round of abandoned lovemaking. The simmering eroticism communicated to the audience frequently required bouncer intervention to evade the grasp of over-stimulated fans. It had been a glorious year, and their wedding date was set.

Jeff's parents were hoping that marriage would encourage their talented son to apply his engineering degree to a more stable career, with his music a happy diversion. The future seemed guaranteed until the horrendous night when the contract on her father was executed. Tears formed as she relived the horrifying events, vivid images appearing of the bullets ripping into her father's body at the door of her apartment. Then Jeff was pushing her into the bedroom with the small briefcase her father had arrived with. "Run!" Jeff had shouted as he retreated to tussle with the two thugs. As she climbed through the third floor window and scampered down the fire escape, a fusillade of gunshots resounded from the front of the apartment. Total silence followed. While she slipped through the deep shadows of the alley, she saw two burly heads outlined in the window, muffled curses emerging.

Kerry's tears were flowing freely now, and she slumped into the deck chair, allowing the pent-up emotions to erupt. Dad, I loved you, but you knew what you were doing. But Jeff! He was never involved with the Mob. The tears increased.

It was several minutes before the torrent ceased, and she reflected on how she fled to the Queens apartment of her deceased mother's sister, a former nun who was now teaching mathematics in a city high school. Former Sister Agatha, now known as Ms. Mary Agnes O'Brien, wasted little time in applying her scholastic prowess to Kerry's plight after they jointly reviewed the contents of Carlo Vita's briefcase. "I always liked Carlo," she consoled, "but we knew of his Mafia ties when your mother married him, against all of our families' advice. I know she loved him, and he treated her well, but there was a lot of heartache over never knowing if she'd be a sudden widow. Just when it looked like he was retiring from the rackets, your mom was diagnosed with leukemia, and you know all too well how fast she went. She didn't have a whole lot of happiness in her life, Kerry, except for you." The former nun touched Kerry's arm gently. "You brought her great joy. You're my favorite niece, you know."

Kerry laughed. "I'm your only niece."

"Let's not bother with details," her aunt smiled. "I love you like a daughter. And you're clearly in danger. BIG danger. Obviously, the book in your dad's briefcase is important enough to get people killed. I'm not sure what it means, but there are large sums of money listed with names of businesses and corporations, and countless individuals. I recognize some of the names from media coverage. Some are in politics."

"Yeah, I noticed. What should I do?"

"You can go to the police, or better yet, the FBI. Maybe they'll know what it all means."

The younger woman frowned. "I suppose so, but what happens to me while they figure it out? Those creeps planned to kill me too, and they're going to be even more determined now that I've got this stuff."

"I think you should go to the authorities with it ASAP."

"But if they put me into protection or something I won't be able to settle the score. I owe Nicky Vincente big time."

"Remember, 'Vengeance is mine, saith the Lord.' Besides, how do you know he's responsible?"

"Dad worked for him. And I heard one of the goons say 'Nicky sent us.' There's no question in my mind."

"You're not the gun moll type, Kerry. I know your mom kept you away from violence and weapons. I bet you don't even know how to shoot a gun."

"I can learn."

"You can also learn to slow down and think. Staying alive is the primary concern now."

"You've always been so analytical, Aunt Agnes. You're probably right."

"Go to the FBI."

"Maybe eventually. I need time to think now." She paused and searched her aunt's eyes. "Do you still have that mountain cabin you inherited from Uncle Ed?"

"Yes, bless his soul. He made it big on Wall Street, but forgot that they've always made more whiskey than the Irish can drink."

"He sure tried, but he was always so jolly. I remember the gifts he gave me when I was a child."

"Ed was a kind man, and generous, leaving me the cabin so I would always have a place if I left the convent. Haven't had much time to use it, but, yes, I still have it."

"Can I use it, Aunt Agnes? Just for a little while, till I get over the loss of Dad and Jeff?"

"And while you plot retribution?"

"I promise I won't plot retribution while I'm in your cabin."

Mary Agnes O'Brien chuckled. "I told that sister of mine that she'd be creating a monster if she mingled Italian and Irish blood. Okay, for a while. And it's our secret. No one else is to know."

"That's the way I see it, Auntie. Your Irish blood is pretty smart."

***

Kathryn Vinson occupied a window seat on westbound United flight 629 out of LaGuardia airport the following morning. Despite the oversize casual clothes and large slouch hat, she still looked like a seductive version of Norah Jones.

Chapter Three

The pilot of the King Air looked worried. "Damn, Jesse, it's not even Friday the thirteenth. My luck's better then."

"What is it?" the jumpmaster yelled, tightly gripping a cockpit stanchion to remain upright in the aircraft that began bouncing around like a Ping-Pong ball.

"Crazy thermals," George Starke grunted, "plus a loss of power in the starboard engine. Oil pressure's dropping fast, and I'm afraid I'm going to have to shut her down. It all started just after that guy jumped."

Jesse looked serious. "He said that unusual things happened to him, and people around him."

The pilot briefly shifted his concentration from his array of gauges. "Is he still in sight?"

Jesse shook his head. "No, lost him in the clouds shortly after he jumped."

"Shit," the pilot muttered. "What else can go wrong? Does he know what he's doing?"

"I hope so," the jumpmaster replied. "Claimed to have had wilderness survival training."

"That's good."

"Not really. He left the survival packet behind, under his seat."

"Double shit. Any other good news?"

"Well, we at least know who he is, and who to notify. He also left his credential case and badge behind."

"Good Lord, he sounds like a royal screw up." "That's sort of what he told me. Guess I should have listened better." The pilot afforded more attention to the sputtering engine. "We'll never make it over the south ridge to get back to the airport with one engine. We'll have to put down on that small emergency field on the valley floor. Maybe the guy will be waiting for us with a cold beer. That's where he's heading, isn't it? He has the GPS we loaned him, right?"

Jesse looked more uncomfortable and pulled the pencil-sized global positioning device from his jacket pocket. "Found it on his seat."

"Jesus Christ," the pilot moaned. "In business for less than a year and we're on the brink of losing a plane, a company and a Federal Agent."

✶✶✶

Breathtakingly beautiful, Special Agent Del Dickerson judged as he dangled in the harness of his swiftly-moving parachute some 7,000 feet above the broad canyon floor, intermittently seen through rapidly closing clouds. The southern tip of Lake Tahoe was occasionally visible. Gee, I wish Anna could be here to see this. Warm thoughts momentarily engulfed him as he pictured his fiancée, Anna Chen, in San Francisco. I also wish I could see the ground a little better.

Rapidly shifting winds prompted him to scan his surroundings closer. The result surprised him. The southern snow-capped mountain range he was headed for seemed to have shifted considerably westward. And the northern peak that looked like Fidel Castro's beard now looked to his east. And the long ridgeline defining the western perimeter appeared to have shifted south. Oh well, you can't get lost these days when you have a GPS. He patted his jacket pocket confidently. He patted it again. Damn, must have slipped out when I jumped.

Dismissing his momentary alarm, he recalled his happy years in the Boy Scouts. "Be Prepared" flitted through his mind as he reached for reassurance from the survival pack tucked at the small of his back. Hmm, must have lost it somewhere too. Well, you just have to make do, Dickerson. You've been in tight spots before. He looked around more intently, somewhat alarmed to see the valley floor fading in the distance. He was surprised to see his proximity to looming mountains and clusters of sturdy trees that appeared to be moving quickly in his direction. He began frantically pulling on his parachute harness.

***

Kerry resumed her painting, and was again engrossed in her work when she heard the sputtering engine of the small silver plane that had been circling earlier. When she looked up she thought she saw an object dropping from behind the aircraft, and spotted what appeared to be a ballooning parachute. Studying the object, she saw it was getting larger, speeding in her direction. She put down her brush and watched with fascination as the parachutist loomed ever larger. Maybe someone dropping in for dinner was her initial whimsical thought. Then a chilling afterthought. Could they have found me out here? She paid close attention to the descending object, recalling folklore anecdotes about the far-reaching tentacles of the Mafia. No, that's being paranoid. She concentrated on the fast approaching figure dangling below a multi-colored canopy, seeing a white-clad helmeted body suddenly whiz over her head at about two hundred feet in a direct line with a nearby grove of trees. The object immediately disappeared from her vision and she strained at the horizon, hoping to spot a lucky parachutist who had somehow cleared the tree line. She scanned the empty sky. Nothing. No sounds but the recurring whisper of wind-swayed tree limbs.

God help the poor soul, she silently prayed, hurrying toward a nearby clearing with a broader view of the adjacent range. She gazed out at the irregular mountain ridges, seeing nothing but the natural beauty of acres of towering jack and sugar pines, Douglas firs, and quaking aspens. She was turning to leave when a wind gust shifted the lower branches of a tall pine, revealing a glimpse of red and yellow cloth a hundred feet or so above the ground. Focusing her sight across a shallow ravine, Kerry saw the branches move again, revealing even more of the multi-colored fabric. She hurried in that direction.

Chapter Four

"Good landing," Jesse Williams complimented the pilot who also breathed a sigh of relief as the King Air finally braked to a halt just short of the end of the bumpy emergency runway.

"Our luck held. I hope it also did for our jumper. Any sight of him?"

"No sign of him or his chute. You know those shifting upper and lower winds can blast you way off course. Guess he won't be providing the cold beer. Hope he didn't end up in Lake Tahoe."

***

The moments before the blackout had been exhilarating. The parachute lines didn't respond as they were supposed to, and the powerful cross-wind currents had Del racing horizontally at an astonishing pace. His goggle-covered eyes had bulged at the green wall of trees that seemed to be accelerating in his direction. Good Lord! was his last conscious thought.

***

It took Kerry almost fifteen minutes to traverse the rugged terrain, slipping sporadically on the traces of snow that covered portions of the ground. Finally reaching the base of a tall pine tree, she studied the multi-colored parachute dangling from a sturdy limb. Drooping in a harness about twenty feet above the ground was a man-sized body, which swayed periodically with the recurring wind gusts. She saw no other movement, but thought she detected slight chest contractions.

Looks like he's alive, but how do I lower him to the ground? As she pondered possibilities, a stronger gust of wind moved the limb upward. When it settled down, the parachute rigging slid slightly downward, moving the boot-clad feet marginally closer to the ground. She watched, intrigued, as the procedure repeated every few seconds until she was within reach of the dangling feet. At the next drop of the branch she grasped the person's ankles and yanked, prompting a ripping sound and a free fall of weight that pinned her to the spongy ground. Tough way to land a man, she laughed as she wriggled free of the body. After rolling the body face up, she removed the scratched plastic helmet. Not a bad-looking guy, she concluded, feeling for a neck pulse. He was breathing shallowly, but she could see no major wounds, just an assortment of abrasions on his hands. His left foot, however, pointed in an awkward direction. Gentle slaps on his cheeks produced no reaction, so she grabbed a handful of snow and rubbed it on his face. A slight muscular twitch resulted, but the man's eyes remained closed and he remained dormant.

While deliberating what to do, Kerry felt the chill of the early afternoon air, and wished she hadn't left her jacket behind with her painting gear. It's about a half-mile back and another quarter-mile to the cabin, she estimated, looking again at the unconscious man. I've got to get you to a shelter, she said aloud. You'll freeze to death out here. But how? You must weigh close to two hundred pounds. Think, girl, Kerry ordered herself.

***

It was clearly not Happy Hour in the back room of Bossa Ristorante Italiano, as Nicky "The Nose" Vincente made profanely clear. "You fuckin assholes have me in deep shit now," he roared.

"But we got a full-court press going to find the broad," Loose Louie countered. "You know, the scrawny one."

Vincente glared at his legman. "You being a smartass? You used to think she was some hot body."

"I reconsidered, boss, she's really scrawny." He could feel his unpredictable sphincter muscle contract.

Vincente snorted, "A couple of real pros—couldn't find a fuckin virgin in a convent."

Sulfur Sal's eyes brightened like an illuminated bulb. "Funny you should say that, Nicky. We got the name of Carlo's sister-in-law out in Queens. She's an ex-nun. Never had the time of day for him, so she might be willing to help us. We'll tell her we're holding something valuable for his daughter, and maybe she'll tell us where she's hiding. We're going to see her tonight."

Vincente looked unimpressed. "Don't get into the habit," he jested.

Sulfur Sal laughed loudly. "That's a good one, boss."

Loose Louie looked puzzled. "Huh?"

★★★

"Just a cracked hydraulic line," George Stack reported when he finished his examination of the failed engine. "Ernie can fly in a replacement part and some fluid within the hour and we'll be out of here."

Jesse frowned. "That's all that's wrong?"

"Yeah, these are fragile but wondrous birds when everything works."

"<u>When</u>, everything works," the veteran skydiver mumbled. "<u>Everything</u> has to work when you bail out of a plane – no place for when."

The pilot nodded at his business partner. "Yeah, when a plane engine falters, you have the option of jumping, crash landing, or limping down with one engine like we did. When your parachute fails, what's your option? Hope our jumper's chute didn't fail," Starke murmured.

"Couldn't have," Jesse declared defensively. "I packed it myself."

"Then let's not pay attention to those reports of no sightings. I'm sure we'll hear any minute that he's safe and sound, relaxing in some rich dame's Jacuzzi."

"Sure hope so. That was my favorite chute."

***

Jesse's chute would never be the same when Kerry finished. After analyzing the circumstances, she applied what she considered Aunt Agnes' analytical skills to devise a means of transporting her weighty drop-in guest. Following a spirited tugging match with the parachute fabric, she had managed to dislodge most of it from the stubborn tree branches. Employing the small penknife she carried in her pocket to open painting materials, she cut out several sections of nylon material and layered them for multi-thickness. Atop this she laid a cushion of pine needles. She then tied lengths of the sturdy parachute lines to two corners of the makeshift sled and with a burst of energy rolled the inert man onto it. Regaining her breath, she fashioned a Y-shaped tow line at the end where her passenger's head rested, and cushioned his head with bundled parachute fabric. Encouraged by a slight moan, she gained enthusiasm as she saw her conveyance take form. She looped some of the remaining cord around the body to keep it in place and stood back to assess her creation. Hope you're worth all this trouble, buddy. You turn out to be a messenger from the mob, I guarantee this will be your last ride.

Chapter Five

Special Agent in Charge Chuck Reynolds closed his eyes in disbelief when his assistant finished reporting the details of the telephone message from the Carson City, Nevada, airport. He turned to look out the window of his corner office on a top floor of the FBI offices on Golden Gate Avenue. San Francisco Bay glistened in the rays of the afternoon sun, and famed Coit Tower stood in its white stone majesty on a nearby hill. "Why me?" he moaned. "Why, with fifty-five other Bureau offices, did I get saddled with the guy?" He swiveled back in his brown leather chair to face his aide. "I only have a month to retirement, Phil, and I thought we had him under control. Six months of ulcer-building escapades, and now he's missing. Am I being punished for the sins of my past life?"

Assistant Special Agent in Charge Phil Whitman nodded understanding. "Well, as you recall, we got him when he graduated with honors from the Language School at Monterey. He speaks Korean like a native. But I know it's been rough, boss. He's like that guy Joe Bffst, or something, you know—the guy who walks around with a black cloud overhead."

"Only the rain falls on people nearby," Reynolds noted. "Dickerson never gets wet."

"You're right, Chuck, but he has stumbled into some major situations."

The senior official looked skeptical. "You mean when he uncovered the kick-back scheme in the Mayor's office that had the Mayor screaming Federal meddling until we convinced him he could make political hay by claiming credit?"

"Yeah, and we did get several convictions in Federal court."

"Okay, I concede that one, but how about the ruckus with the gay and lesbian coalition when his informants sidetracked their parade through Chinatown? We were picketed for a week."

"It prevented a riot, you remember."

"All right, he's due some credit, but I'm still pissed that his inquiry into that Chi-com espionage ring got me subpoenaed before a Congressional Committee. Damned near got me jailed for refusing to identify our informant."

"Isn't that the price of leadership, boss?"

"Yeah, I know. I'm just letting off steam. Do you think something bad could have happened to him? He's really a pretty likeable guy, even if he is a pain in the ass."

"I'd say, with his track record, he's fine and dandy, but we sent some agents out to help with the search."

"Keep on it, Phil, and let me know what develops. Has anyone notified that lovely Amerasian he's engaged to?"

"Anna Chen. I'm sending Malloy to tell her. They're good friends. They worked some big cases together. Remember the Bureau special code-named SHARKS, when we bagged a bunch of crooked congressmen and senators? Del was working undercover in the investigation, met Anna, and helped her escape the clutches of that scumbag from Massachusetts."

"Whoa, Phil, aren't we suppose to show more respect for our elected leaders?"

"Sorry, boss. You're right. I tend to lose control when I think of all the people he's screwed. 'Honorable' scumbag."

"That's better. Go on."

"Well, as I recall hearing, she got badly injured in a car wreck, and Del helped nurse her back to health. She later worked with him in a couple of other sensitive Bureau investigations, including the commie spy case at the Language School. They have quite a history. I tell you, the guy has phenomenal luck. And he attracts women like bees to honey. He doesn't look like a Hollywood pretty boy, but he's got something. Maybe it's the mothering instinct. Whatever it is, I wouldn't mind a dose of it."

"And explain the attraction to your wife and daughters?"

Whitman smiled. "No, better leave well enough alone."

Reynolds shook his head. "Why anyone would go skydiving instead of spending time off with Anna defies logic."

The assistant nodded agreement. "He is different. He's a Yale graduate, you know."

∗∗∗

Kerry thought her arms were leaving their sockets when she tugged her heavy load uphill. Thanks to patches of snow that made the ground slippery, progress was fairly easy on the level areas, and rather exciting downhill when she almost lost her tow a few times. Winded and wearied, she reached her painting site in about a half-hour and stopped for rest. Her passenger remained comatose, faintly breathing and occasionally moaning. Sections of the bottom of her homemade sled had ripped or worn through, but she guessed it sufficient enough to complete the journey. The harness lines remained secure, their imprint pronounced on her aching palms. She bundled her painting equipment in her canvas bag and tied it to the sled. She looked at the dormant figure. *Off we go, brother. It's the home stretch.*

The gradual rise of the trail to the cabin increased the strain, and Kerry began to question if she could make it. Rounding a curve in the path, she saw the cabin's shake roof and impetuously shouted "hallelujah!" The returning echo of her own voice sounded eerie, prompting a laugh. *I guess I can always talk to myself if I get lonely.* Glancing at her passenger, she thought she noticed his lips slightly quiver. She moved closer and shouted into his ear. She then sang a few bars of *God Bless*

America, but detected no more movement. Maybe he's not from America, was a random thought as she resumed her task. Darkness was quickly approaching when she managed to drag her bound guest into the cabin. After a momentary rest, she pulled him into the main bedroom and deposited him alongside one of the two double beds. Near exhaustion, she collapsed on her bed and closed her eyes.

✳✳✳

Henry Wilhelm wasn't about to let the two thuggish-looking men into his building, much less proceed to the apartment of Mary Agnes O'Brien. His years on the New York City Police Department enabled him to spot Mafiosa before they spoke. When they did, the husky building superintendent was determined they would not be disturbing the nicest tenant in the building. Not only did he feel protective of the genteel lady, but since his wife died he had entertained illusions of a golden-years' romance with the attractive, fair-complexioned woman. No way will they bother her, he swore, until the taller visitor mentioned they had news that a family member had passed and left holdings worth a small fortune. Only then did the retired sergeant agree to see if Ms. O'Brien might be in. He was surprised when the woman promptly agreed to see the men, assuring Wilhelm that she felt totally safe so long as he was in the building.

Warmed by the confidence, Wilhelm guaranteed he would remain within earshot if she needed him.

"You're a fine gentleman," she said with conviction.

To insure her evaluation wasn't misplaced, Wilhelm pocketed his old service revolver and escorted the visitors upstairs.

In her apartment, Mary Agnes O'Brien turned on the concealed tape recorder and thought, let's see what you two misguided souls can tell us. You can't be any tougher than my seventh grade students.

Chapter Six

When Kerry awoke she saw total darkness through the window. The large red numerals of the bedside clock read 7:12 PM. No wonder I'm hungry. When she switched on the bedside lamp she suddenly remembered she wasn't alone. Scurrying off the bed, she examined her new companion, who appeared to remain unconscious. Well, you don't look hungry, but I'm starved, so we'll think about what to do for you after I've eaten. No offense, but a girl has to look out for herself.

The large rustic kitchen was well equipped with cooking essentials, and the supplies Kerry had hauled up the mountain in the rented Jeep Cherokee offered a variety of choices, the simplest being a frozen DiGiorno pizza supreme.

Fast and filling, while I figure out what to do with what's-your-name. She laughed aloud. Wonder what your real name is? Joe, Bill, Igor, Angelo. She stopped smiling at the last possibility. Italian? Mob? No, that's being paranoid. Yet, I'd better be careful. She uncorked a bottle of Kendall-Jackson cabernet and decided to apply Latin logic.

Feeling more confident after finishing the pizza and half the bottle of wine, she concentrated on her situation. Only Aunt Agnes knows my location—and she will never tell.

They had agreed to only communicate with an initial call from Aunt Agnes, utilizing a secret prefix known only to them. Kerry would then call back from a public phone in a nearby community selected at random. The Jeep had been rented under the stage name Kerry had temporarily used before hitting it relatively big with her band, and her identification in that name was known to few—like her slain boyfriend.

That loss moistened her eyes, and she felt compelled to take another gulp of wine. Fortified, and feeling somewhat relaxed, she proceeded to focus attention on the mysterious stranger.

***

"Oh, do you think he is all right?" Anna Chen asked with alarm when contacted at the Pier 39 gift shop on San Francisco's Embarcadero where she worked.

"I'm sure he is," Special Agent Mike Malloy said with feigned conviction, gently steadying the fragile shoulders of the petite Chinese-American woman. "You know how resilient he is. You two survived a storm on the Chesapeake Bay, didn't you?"

She nodded. "And the shooting in Buffalo. He does lead a charmed life, but how long does good luck last?"

Malloy tried to sound encouraging. "He has you to come back to, Anna. With that incentive, I'm sure he'll turn up any minute."

The attractive woman with exotic good looks blushed. "You are always so kind, Mike. Marie is a lucky woman."

Malloy was reminded of his new bride, Special Agent Marie Stanley, temporarily assigned with him to the San Francisco office pending their testimony in a major fraud trial. Maintaining her maiden name made it easier for them to avoid complaints of nepotism from anyone who didn't know of their remarkable achievements as an undercover team. "She's a gem," Malloy agreed. "I'm the lucky one. And she thinks you and Del are tops. She'll be mighty upset if we aren't still assigned here when you and Del walk down the aisle, so think positive. We don't want to upset Marie, do we?"

Anna managed a warm smile. "I'll communicate with my honored ancestors if you will invoke the fabled luck of the Irish."

"Deal," Malloy agreed, squeezing her hand firmly and kissing her cheek. "I just hope Murphy's Law doesn't get in the way."

On his way back to the office, Malloy passed close to San Francisco's famed Chinatown, prompting recollection of what Del had told him of Anna's background. Born to a Taiwanese seamstress and a U.S. Army sergeant, who had been shipped back to the states without his family, Anna had lived in hopes of finally traveling to America and reuniting with her father, whose early correspondence had abruptly stopped. Her resolute mother had sacrificed to send Anna to a prestigious school operated by Catholic nuns, ever hopeful of eventually joining her sergeant. When Anna was in her early twenty's she was hired as an interpreter for a U.S. congressional delegation. While purportedly studying defense matters, the Senator heading the study directed more attention to his vivacious Amerasian aide, culminating with an invitation to accompany him back to America as a personal assistant, vowing to use his influence to find the missing father.

Malloy snickered as he recalled hearing about how the unscrupulous politician virtually enslaved the trusting woman, installing her as his mistress in a Georgetown townhouse, several safe miles from his wife and children.

Bastard, Malloy muttered, recalling the sordid details of the abuse of Anna, who the Senator kept assuring he was doing everything possible to find her father, despite knowing that the man was dead. He repressed an urge to smile over the knowledge that the Senator was killed in a violent auto accident while fleeing arrest by the FBI. Anna, he remembered, who was his hostage, had been critically injured and barely lived. Quite a history, Malloy concluded, pulling into the Bureau garage. They're both survivors. I'm betting on Del turning up.

✶✶✶

The mountain winds and dropping temperature made Kerry glad she still wore her boots. She was also grateful for the living room's wood-burning stove. Its heat barely reached the bedrooms, however, and she was aware of the chilly drafts around her ankles as she gazed down at her guest. Have to get "Skydiver" off the floor, she decided, chuckling inwardly at the impromptu name. Why not? Better than "him." Now, the trick is to get "Skydiver" on the bed.

***

The two goons reminded Mary Agnes O'Brien of truant school-boys as they shuffled into her apartment and introduced themselves. Both in their early forties, she guessed, five-ten to six feet tall, with thick black hair and bushy eyebrows.

Loose Louie, the shorter of the two, with a pudgy, pasta-enhanced appearance, whipped off his hat immediately, followed by Sulfur Sal. The taller, thinner man displayed a perpetual half-smile, emanating from a knife-scar near the right side of his mouth. Aromas of garlic and olive oil seeped from their rumpled suits. Gold watches and bracelets encircled beefy wrists emerging from dark-colored silk shirts. Both seemed nervous in the presence of a distantly remembered authority figure.

"Please sit down," she said, pointing to a wide leather couch front-ed by a coffee table, centered with a large crystal decanter and three glasses.

"Yes, Sister," Loose Louie mumbled.

The former nun laughed. "I'm no longer a nun, Louis. Ms. O'Brien will do."

Loose Louie nodded. "Yes, Sister."

Sulfur Sal spoke up. "We told the super downstairs we had information for you about a rich relative who recently died."

"And who might that be, Salvatore?"

Rinalti reddened slightly. "No one's called me Salvatore in a long time."

"Would you like me to call you something else?"

"Oh, no, that's fine, Sister. Reminds me of my mom, God rest her soul. She just passed last year."

"You have my sympathy, Salvatore. I'll include her in my prayers. Who did you say the wealthy relative is?"

"Carlo Vita, an old friend of ours, God rest his soul, too. We hear he was murdered by some gangsters."

"Oh, how sad. I didn't have much contact with him, but I'm sorry to hear of his death. He was married to my recently deceased sister. Do they know who did it?"

"I don't know, but I'm sure the police are working hard to find out," Sulfur Sal replied in a solemn tone.

"Yeah," Loose Louie interjected, "I'm sure the police will find those vicious killers. There's too much violence out there. A law-abiding citizen don't stand a chance these days."

Rinalti shot his partner a "shut up" look.

Mary Agnes interrupted. "Please forgive my manners—would you gentlemen like a drink or something? I have some nice Chianti in the decanter."

"That would be nice, Sister," Sulfur Sal responded. "I mean Ms. O'Brien. Takes a while to get used to it, you not wearing one of them black things and all."

"You mean a habit?"

Rinalti blushed, recalling Nicky Vincente's joke. "Yeah, that's it. I went to Saint Cecelia's until the fifth grade."

"I thought so," she said, pouring three glasses of wine. "To the success of your mission," she toasted. "And how can I help you regarding Carlo?"

"Well, he left a lot of money, and we're trying to find his daughter. We think she's his only heir."

"A lot of money," Loose Louie added, after draining his wine glass.

Mary Agnes refilled it, as well as Sulfur Sal's. "How much is a lot?'

"We really don't know the total amount, but it's a lot," Sulfur Sal replied, finishing his second glass of wine. His glass was promptly refilled.

"Do you know how we can find his daughter?" Sulfur Sal asked.

The ex-nun smiled sweetly. "What's her name?"

"Kerry."

"Oh, the singer. I thought she ran off with a drummer."

"Yeah, but he got killed, too."

"Oh, how horrible. Is Kerry all right?"

"We hope so," Sulfur Sal said, taking another gulp of wine and trying to regain control of the conversation. "We thought you might be able to help us find her—to tell her about all the money."

"Yeah, lots of money," Loose Louie chorused, finishing his glass and holding it out while it was refilled.

The ex-nun looked serious. "You can be sure I'll tell her about your visit if I hear from her. Who did you say has the money?"

"Nicky," Loose Louie blurted.

Sulfur Sal's murderous glare warned he had said too much. "A friend of ours," he quickly said. "But if you hear from her you can contact us." He handed her a grimy business card bearing his name and a telephone number with a Brooklyn area code. "You ain't heard from her lately?"

"Oh, it's been some time, Salvatore. Would you like some more wine?"

"No, I think we've had enough, Sister."

"Yeah," Loose Louie said, struggling to his feet. "Can I use your bathroom?"

Awaiting Loose Louie's return, Sulfur Sal looked at the near-empty decanter. "We don't normally drink much."

"That's good," Mary Agnes said. "You don't want to get into the habit."

Chapter Seven

"Skydiver" was finally sprawled out on the double bed across the room from Kerry's. Deciding it was better than isolating him in the other bedroom, she would know when he regained consciousness. She could also keep an eye on him, in case he became a danger to her. Using all her strength, she had maneuvered his limp form off the floor and onto the bed. The effort had surfaced fleeting reflections on the last time she had grappled with a male body, and a sense of loss descended when she thought of Jeff, followed by a renewed determination to even the score. Then she remembered her promise to Aunt Agnes. Okay, I'll wait till I get outside to think about you, Nicky, you bastard.

Her struggle had prompted a few low moans from the dormant man, and she renewed attention to his left leg, that not only looked misaligned but swelling. She gingerly removed his boots, then decided to conduct further examination to see if there were any other apparent injuries. Painstakingly, she removed his white jumpsuit and unbuttoned his thick red Pendleton shirt. Using a pair of bandage scissors from the first-aid kit she found in the kitchen, she cut open his tee shirt, revealing nothing noteworthy, other than a well-muscled upper body. She paused as she looked at his blue jeans and weighed her assumed responsibility. Recalling scenes from the ER TV series, she cut away the jeans, feeling minor embarrassment until she uncovered his legs. Diverting her gaze from his snug shorts, her eyebrows rose at the sight of the object strapped above his right ankle. The handle of a small gun protruded from a brown leather holster.

"God," she gasped, as the man's body moved slightly and he emitted another low moan.

39

***

As Mary Agnes concluded replaying the taped conversation and finished her initial glass of wine, a satisfied smile emerged. *You boys should have stayed in parochial school. They teach you to think.* She evaluated the information they had imparted, especially the urgency of their search and, more importantly, the identity of their leader. *I think he's the one Kerry referred to as "Nicky the Bastard." She does have a descriptive vocabulary. I'll call her tomorrow. Meanwhile, I need to thank Henry for looking after me. Maybe he'd like a glass of wine.*

***

"Nicky the Nose" Vincente was clearly disappointed with the report from his glassy-eyed lieutenants.

"You sure she don't know where her own niece is?"

"No way, boss, we really grilled her."

"Yeah," Loose Louie chimed in. "We put her through the wringer. She was almost crying when we left."

"You didn't mess her up, did you? Those church folks have a strong lobby."

"No, just put the fear of the Lord in her," Sulfur Sal guaranteed. "She'll call us if she hears from the broad."

"The scrawny broad," Loose Louie added.

Vincente directed a cold glare. "You're beginning to irritate me, Louie. Knock off this scrawny broad shit."

"But . . ." Loose Louie began to protest.

"He will," Sulfur Sal loudly promised, with a withering look at his partner.

"The clock is running," Vincente reminded. "The boys want results, not excuses."

"They can count on us," Sulfur Sal was saying when Loose Louie jumped up and raced out of the room.

Vincent looked startled. "Where the fuck is he going?"

Sulfur Sal shrugged. "You know his problem, boss."

***

Special Agents Michael Malloy and L. Marie Stanley were headed for a meeting in the Carson City, Nevada, Resident Agency, a branch of the Las Vegas FBI Division. Although they were temporarily assigned to the San Francisco Division, awaiting their continually deferred testimony, the search for a missing colleague faded territorial lines. The search party also included representatives of the Sacramento Division that covered South Lake Tahoe, as well as Las Vegas agents. As they hummed along I-80 in the beige Bureau Ford Taurus, they exchanged anecdotes of their bizarre experiences with the missing agent. "He's always landed on his feet," Malloy remembered, "like the time he rescued the drunken lobbyist from the Potomac River and gained access to that inner circle of crooked congressmen."

Marie smiled. "And the time in Jackson when he literally caught the bank robber with his pants down when you guys hit the front door and the subject bailed out of the john window and landed right at his feet. Yeah, he's led a charmed life. Hope it continues."

Malloy reached over and squeezed her arm. "Speaking of charmed lives, I haven't done so bad. I got you, didn't I?"

"Hmm, just like a chauvinist male. I thought it was me who got you."

They exchanged smiles. "I concede, Marie. You have the power."

The recent bride blushed slightly at their private joke. "I enjoy sharing the power."

Malloy smiled. "We're still on our honeymoon, aren't we? Maybe we should stop and rest."

Marie laughed. "Rest! Is that what you call it now?"

"You know what I mean, Lola."

"I'm sure I do, dear, and, I like it when you call me Lola."

"It's an alluring name, and I'm still a little ticked the Bureau changed your official name to L. Marie."

"Guess they had their reasons," she murmured, recalling the stimulating circumstances under which she had met Mike. "I was thinking of the night we met."

Malloy diverted his eyes briefly from the road to look at the tall, beautiful brunette. "I get excited every time I think about it. You sure got my attention."

The fair complexion of the former Radio City Music Hall Rockette reddened noticeably as she recalled the desperate financial circumstances that had prompted her to perform an exotic dance at a Jackson, Mississippi, law enforcement farewell party. "I shouldn't have done it, Mike."

"It's history. You were desperate to save your horse ranch. And, it did lead to us." He patted her arm affectionately.

"Oh, Mike," she sighed, "I'm so fortunate to have your love."

He brightened. "Does that mean we can stop?"

She punched his side playfully. "We do have an assignment to help find a lost friend."

"He'd understand."

"Not if we didn't show up for a couple of days. I know you."

"Spoilsport."

She traced her delicate fingers around his neck. "Let's find him in a hurry, honey. Step on it."

Chapter Eight

Kerry had succeeded in gingerly removing the small chrome-plated revolver from "Skydiver's" ankle holster and concealed it under her lingerie in a middle drawer of the old oak dresser. The only identifying data she could see on the gun were the words Smith & Wesson, stamped into the short barrel. She decided against trying to open the weapon, remembering her loved ones who had died from their deadly potential. *Aunt Agnes was right, I know nothing about firearms.* Resolve firmed her jaw. *But that can be corrected, Nicky, you bastard!* She forced herself to remember her promise to her aunt. *Okay, only outside.*

A thorough search of her surprise guest's pockets produced nothing but forty-two dollars cash, and a receipt in the amount of $240.00 "for services rendered." The listed establishment had been obliterated by moisture. "Damn. This isn't getting any easier," she muttered to the still form. *And now I'm talking to myself.* She redirected attention to the swollen area on the front of his leg, midway between ankle and knee. It bulged like a red tennis ball, but the skin was not punctured. *Wish I knew more about medicine, but I guess the leg is broken. Maybe I should make it look like the other one and point the foot in the same direction.* She smiled at the thought and giggled, recalling various dance partners with "two left feet." *Leave it as it is and strike a blow for the sisterhood?* Then the seriousness of the situation evaporated her fantasy and she concentrated on the challenge. *Okay buddy, I have to set it. For better or worse, I'm your doctor, nurse and maid. Boy, are you in trouble.*

Kerry retreated to the kitchen and collected a package of ace bandages, a roll of wide adhesive tape, and an assortment of cooking utensils. Back in the bedroom she centered two long-handled wooden spoons vertically on either side of the swollen knot, holding them in place at the top and bottom with ace bandages. She then manipulated the foot in an effort to set it in the proper position and wrapped the limb tightly with adhesive tape.

"Skydiver" moaned, and mumbled a few unintelligible sounds that Kerry strained to hear. Placing her ear close to his mouth she heard a few strange sounds with a peculiar musical cadence. After waiting and listening intently, she heard no repetition so she twisted the foot slightly. Her patient grimaced and uttered a stream of anguished words. To an ear attuned to the multi-cultured tongues of the "Big Apple," they sounded clearly oriental. My God! What do I have here? He sure doesn't look Asian. Kerry stood stunned, pondering the significance of her discovery when she saw her patient shift his body slightly on the bed. Her eyes widened as she looked at his midsection and saw his jockey shorts expanding upwards. His breathing rhythm also seemed to increase. "Holy, Moly," she exclaimed as she watched the tent-like phenomenon continue to rise.

She looked up imploringly. I take back my irreverent prayer request, Lord. She raced towards the kitchen for a glass of cold water.

***

George Starke, President and Chief Executive Officer of Blue Sky Airlines was in spirited conversation with his partner and Chief Operating Officer, Jesse Williams. The third member of the firm, mechanic and student pilot Ernie Adams, was still checking the plane.

Starke and Williams had just returned from an exhaustive aerial search in the other half of their aircraft fleet, a Cessna 182. "You'd think we would have spotted the chute somewhere," Starke bemoaned. "You're sure of the direction he was headed after he jumped?"

"Come on," Williams replied testily. "You know better than that. He went where the wind took him."

"Yeah, but he could direct himself if he knew as much as we thought he did about skydiving."

"Not in that wind. It picked up like crazy after he jumped. You know how it knocked the plane around."

"We shouldn't have let him go."

"Your 20-20 hindsight is improving, George. Too bad it wasn't working before that hydraulic line busted."

"Touché, Jesse, I shouldn't be blaming you, but what the hell good is a brother-in-law if you can't pin all your shortcomings on him? Sorry."

"Hey, no problem. I'm feeling just as bad. We both have our life savings in this baby, and losing a Federal agent somewhere out there isn't going to be good advertising."

"Maybe they don't want the bad publicity either. When are they due?"

The jumpmaster looked at his watch. "About twenty minutes from now. A search party is flying up from Las Vegas to coordinate things with us, the Air National Guard, and all the other folks who have been notified."

Starke looked hopeful. "The FBI's supposed to be expert in finding people and things. Let's hope they maintain a good batting average."

"Yeah, I've got my fingers crossed that we find the guy. And I'd like to get my chute back in good shape. It's my lucky one."

✳✳✳

The remnants of Jesse Williams' parachute were piled in a corner of the kitchen, destined for the trash barrel until Kerry deliberated the significance of the concealed weapon and the strange language of her mystery guest. Reaching a quick decision, she cut lengthy sections of the strong canopy cord and went to check "Skydiver's" status. She was relieved to see his underwear deflated, and that he seemed to be resting comfortably. Pieces of cord dangled from her right hand as she contemplated her actions. A glance at the bedside clock, and a feeling of near exhaustion, convinced her. It's almost two in the morning and I need to get some sleep without worrying about my roommate getting up and strangling me. She proceeded to knot the cord sections together into a makeshift rope and then looped the line loosely around the man's body several times, pinning him to the bed á la Gulliver's Travels. Relieved that he had moaned only slightly during the procedure, and was breathing normally, she placed a thick, down-filled comforter over him and moved wearily to her own bed. Removing her sweater and sweat pants, Kerry crawled beneath the covers, too tired to don pajamas. And I didn't brush my teeth, she sighed, closing her eyes.

Chapter Nine

The ringing bedside phone startled Kerry awake. The clock read precisely seven AM as she moved her arm from below the snug warmth of her thermal blankets into the room's chilled air. Recalling that Aunt Agnes promised to call exactly on the hour, she cautiously answered "hello," and was relieved to hear their agreed recognition code. "Nun plus," she heard her aunt crisply declare. "Call me as agreed." The click was distinct. She glanced again at the clock, remembering their agreement that she would return the call exactly two hours later, which she calculated would be noon in New York—lunch break at the school. As she swung out of the high bed, and felt the stimulating coldness of the bare floor, she noticed her companion still on his back, snoring softly. She randomly wondered if an unconscious person could sense the cold. Dressing quickly in a pale-blue warm-up suit, she visited the bathroom and then moved to the main room where she restocked the wood-burning stove with compressed-wood pellets and fanned the lingering embers into a robust blaze. The immediate outpouring of heat felt restorative, as did the quick breakfast of cereal, toast, orange juice and coffee. She checked her watch, estimating the amount of time it would take to drive a safe distance from the cabin and find an appropriate telephone. Just time to check my roomie.

Walking back to the bedroom she noted it was heating up. Don't want to freeze you stiff. While she saw he was still torpid, her eyes couldn't avoid noticing a pronounced elevation of the comforter around his pelvis area. Good Lord, I've got to get out of here. Sure glad he's tied down.

***

The search party was completing its briefing session in the main, and only, hanger of Blue Sky Airlines, the tiny corner office being too small to hold more than three people at a time. This group was considerably larger. Mike Malloy and Marie Stanley had joined two agents from the Sacramento Division and two from Las Vegas who had arrived in a leased FBI plane. Nevada and California Highway Patrol planes were also parked on the runway apron, along with a Cessna from the Nevada Air National Guard. Counting the FBI plane and the Blue Sky aircraft, a squadron of six planes was assembled for a thorough aerial grid search. Sectors of the rugged mountainous terrain had been assigned, and an agent with maps, powerful binoculars and a Bureau-band radio would accompany each pilot. All secretly hoped they would gain the company of the beauteous woman agent whose loosely-fitted pantsuit couldn't conceal the reality of a striking figure. One agent would remain behind at the airport with Jesse Williams to coordinate the search, and a coin-flip was agreed upon as the most democratic manner of deciding who would end up with the least exciting job. Damn democracy, Malloy thought as he lost the flip and tried to balance husbandly possessiveness with professional equality while watching his bride depart with the beaming Air National Guard pilot. "Good luck," Malloy and Williams bid as the search party embarked, everyone hoping for success, and avoidance of an exhaustive ground search.

***

Faint sounds seemed to have been echoing off and on in the remote recesses of his subconscious for some time, like a recurring distant call for a child to come home for dinner. And then there was that fleeting beacon of light, swiftly obscured by a cloud-like film. But now the sound was loud and constant—a car motor starting nearby. Del's eyes blinked open momentarily, closing almost immediately from the

unaccustomed light. They opened again slowly, and the fuzziness began to disappear. The sound of the engine evaporated and he stared at
the exposed log rafters, then around the rustic, pine-paneled walls.
Where am I? He felt pain in his left leg and tried to move his foot. It
felt somehow restrained. The thick white spread reaching his chin tick-
led and he raised his right hand to scratch. The hand moved only
slightly. He tried to sit up, but achieved little upward movement. *Like a
seatbelt,* was a random thought. *What's going on?* Recollections began
to clarify, and he suddenly visualized a mass of green branches approaching at break-neck speed. *The jump! The overpowering winds.
The sudden oblivion. I must have survived, unless heaven is a lot different than advertised.* He shivered from the lingering cold and chuckled. *Not hot enough for the other place.* He said a silent prayer of
thanks to St. Anthony, the patron saint of miracles. *You're working
overtime, my friend. But just where am I, and how did I get here?*

"Hello," he called out, startled at the dry cackle of his voice. "Hello," he called again louder. Receiving no response, Del tried to raise his
body again, managing an estimated inch or two of slack. *Tied down
somehow. Why?*

Now fully alert, he moved both hands to the limits allowed by the
restraints and felt his fingers touch bare skin. He tried to raise his
knees, but quickly abandoned that effort on his left side when a sharp
pain ensued. Gingerly moving his right knee, he achieved a bit of upward movement. Aided by the fingers of his tethered hand, he was encouraged to see the cover begin to move sideways. Repeating the effort,
Del soon had the material sliding to the right. With intensified zeal, he
watched as it slowly slipped to the floor. His bindings were immediately visible, and he recognized the parachute cording, replete with somewhat amateurish knots. *But why? Maybe they don't want me to fall out
of bed. Maybe. And maybe they aren't nice people. Lots of maybes, Del.*
He became aware of the room's chill, and wondered about his minimal

clothing. The crudely splinted leg offered hope. Someone must be trying to help. "Hello!" he called out once more.

Chapter Ten

It was ten minutes before nine by the time Kerry located what she considered a safe coin-operated telephone outside a convenience store in a tiny mountain community several miles from the cabin. The phone was out of sight of the lone storekeeper who seemed more interested in watching a televised soap opera than serving customers. From her standpoint, it was perfect. She purchased a few kitchen supplies and had a handful of change when she called her aunt's school-lounge number in New York City. Mary Agnes O'Brien's authoritarian voice was instantly recognizable and Kerry delivered their password, a racy song title from Kerry's early band days that she once thought would make the former nun blush. "Or Gas 'Em," she enunciated.

"I'm glad you articulate well," her aunt laughed. "How is it going?"

"Kind of goofy, Aunt Agnes. Would you believe I have an unconscious, good-looking, half-naked man tied down on one of your beds? But before I tell you the story, tell me if you've heard anything from you know who."

"Well, I believe I'd rather hear more of your adventure, but I'll make my report short and cryptic. There are a lot of people nearby. I had visitors who work for your father's old employer. They made it clear he is the responsible party. Also, the item you have must be very important. Guard it carefully. They want it back, desperately, but have no idea where you are. We'll keep it that way. End of my report. Your turn. I can't wait."

Kerry laughed and proceeded. "I'm relieved that they didn't seem to know where I am, because I had the wild idea that the parachutist I rescued from the tree could have been sent by them." She briefly recounted the circumstances of her discovery. "But I don't know who he is, only that he looks Caucasian but speaks an oriental language. He didn't have any identification on him, and I searched him thoroughly."

"It sounds like it, Kerry. You said he is half naked."

"I had to check for injuries. I think he has a broken leg."

"Oh. And you say he's unconscious?"

"Well, not completely. He mumbles oriental words occasionally and, how do I put this? ... He periodically has, ah, erections. Big ones."

"My, my, you do seem to have an exciting life, Kerry."

"Oh, and he had a gun in a pouch near his ankle."

"Holster."

"Yes, that's the word. How do you know so much about such things?"

"I read a lot. You said <u>had</u>?"

"Yes, I took it and hid it. I really don't know what to do about him. I should probably notify the authorities, but then people will know where I am."

"His loved ones are probably looking for him, Kerry. I think you need to notify the authorities. And I think you should contact the FBI about the book. It has to be very important."

"You're probably right, Aunt Agnes. Maybe he'll come to and make it easy, but what if he is a bad guy? I'll think about it."

"Do that, my dear, and if I learn anything more, I'll call you, using the same system and code word. Meanwhile, if you need to reach me, call me at home after six PM 'Big Apple' time. I'll be sure to recognize you by your unique recognition signal."

Kerry smiled as she remembered the raucous reaction of club audiences when she concluded the funky tune about exterminating bugs by shouting the final lyrics, 'You can Stamp 'em out, OR GAS 'EM!' "Maybe I shouldn't be embarrassing you like this, Aunt Agnes. Perhaps I should use another intro?"

The ex-nun's voice sounded whimsical. "No, your vocabulary is dictionary proper and I've heard the words before. As I told you, I read a lot." Kerry thought she detected a muffled laugh.

***

The quiet of his surroundings elevated his senses and he concentrated on his situation. *Well, you learned how to tie and untie knots in the Boy Scouts, Del, so get to work.* He was cheered by the discovery that one of the knots was within reach of his right fingers and it was loosely tied. A few minutes of intense effort had it undone and he quickly found himself unraveling lengthy amounts of cord from around his body. With increasing freedom of movement, he was soon sitting up in bed unrestrained. Shifting his gaze from his splinted and bandaged left leg, he discovered that his small revolver was missing. *Hmm, lost in the jump? Or have I fallen into hostile hands?*

With eerie silence continuing to reign in the cabin, Del decided to explore. Swinging his legs to the side of the bed, he stepped on the floor. His scream was loud as he fell flat on his face. The pain in his left leg was biting, and he lay motionless for several seconds until the trauma faded. *Has to be broken.* He looked around the room and spotted a broom standing next to a pile of leaves, twigs and pine needles. Next to the pile were muddied remnants of a multi-colored parachute that was immediately recognizable.

Dragging himself across the plank floor, Del employed the inverted broom as a rudimentary crutch and was soon thumping around the room in search of whatever could help him define his host. Or was it captor? *Friend or foe?* Puzzled, he glanced through the open doorway at an apparently uninhabited living area, then decided to concentrate on the bedroom. Two jackets that appeared to be in light, feminine colors hung from wooden pegs next to the door. A slight scent of perfume radiated. He next directed attention to the large oak dresser and was about to search it when he felt an overpowering bathroom summons. Hobbling awkwardly, he located one off the hallway, to the left of the bedroom door. From his performance he estimated that it had been several hours since he had last used such facilities. Light brown beard stubble reflected in the oak-framed mirror further attested to the time lapse, but the day and date calendar of his wristwatch had apparently ceased working when he crashed into the trees. How long have I been here? One day, two days? He rubbed his beard stubble again. Feels like a 24-hour growth. He chuckled aloud when he viewed his reflection. Hope jockey shorts, a Pendleton shirt, and tattered tee are fashionable here. The bathroom counter and medicine chest held minimum items, including a barely used tube of Crest and one pink-handled toothbrush. There were also a few female cosmetics and one medicine bottle containing a prescription he thought he recognized as a cold remedy. It was written for a Kerry Vita, filled at a New York City pharmacy. The name and city sounded remote bells.

Returning slowly and awkwardly to the bedroom, he began his search of the dresser, discovering nothing but a small assortment of feminine clothing until he got to the lingerie drawer. He was just learning that the owner was a 36D with a tiny waist when he uncovered his gun. One mystery solved. It felt reassuring back in his ankle holster.

Some slacks, sweaters and sweat pants filled the bottom drawer, except for a large manila envelope bound with an elastic cord. The old ledger book inside the envelope gained his immediate attention, especially the numerical figures aligned alongside lists of names that looked surprisingly familiar. Some were media-prominent individuals, including well-known political names, plus a number of business and entertainment establishments in the New York area that were featured frequently in the press. Although no dollar signs accompanied the listed numbers, Del's investigative experience convinced him that he was viewing heavy-hitting collection and payoff records. Flipping the pages, he saw dates ranging from several years ago to just a few weeks back. What gained his special interest was the name inscribed on the inside cover of the book: Carlo Vita. Mental bells began clanging like a fire alarm.

Now fully alert, he recalled the recent organized crime seminar at Quantico where the various New York Mafia families were discussed. The name of Carlo Vita had been mentioned as a key mob record keeper. The medicine bottle with the same last name sprang to mind. No, Del, that's too coincidental. But a New York drugstore, too? Stranger things have happened, was his sobering thought. He felt himself perspiring as he held the book in deep thought. Then he heard the groan of an automobile engine struggling uphill. A glance out the window provided a fleeting glimpse through the trees of a slow-moving maroon SUV.

Deciding his course, Del closed the drawer and hobbled back to his bed where he stashed the ledger between the mattress and springs. He crawled onto the bed, covered himself with the comforter, tossed the broom towards the pile of debris and lay back to see what would happen next. When he heard the approaching footsteps a few minutes later, he closed his eyes and tried to remain motionless. He also tried to remember if he had flushed the toilet.

Chapter Eleven

The dejected air search crew was back in the Blue Sky Airlines hanger, completing its review of the unproductive mission. "Damn, thought for sure someone would have spotted some trace of my chute. It's so colorful. My favorite, you know."

George Starke nodded to his jumpmaster. "We know, Jesse. We were all hoping."

"No pun intended," the California Highway Patrol pilot interjected, "but it's like he disappeared into thin air."

"There are a lot of deep ravines with surging waters," the Nevada Air National Guard pilot remarked ominously. "And Lake Tahoe isn't far away."

"But not finding a trace could be looked upon as hopeful," Marie suggested with an encouraging smile.

The men looked at the stunning woman agent, a visual diversion all of them had enjoyed during their time together, and Starke spoke up. "There's always hope, and we won't stop being on the lookout, but as far as continuing an active air search goes, I think we've about run the course. We've covered areas far beyond the logical parameters. It looks like an intensified ground search is the best approach now."

The pilot of the FBI plane said that he and his observer would continue their air search as long as light lasted. "Maybe we'll have some dumb luck. I hear our missing colleague is known for coming out smelling like a rose."

Malloy chuckled. "He holds a patent on Houdini-like stunts. I'd bet on him surviving," he said, keeping his crossed fingers concealed. "So, let's start a detailed terrain search, beginning in the center area that was his most probable landing zone, and work outward from there." He looked at Starke and Williams. "We're relying on your expertise in such matters."

Starke nodded. "Jesse and I have gone over the wind and drift data a dozen times—it's our best estimate." He held up a chart with several areas outlined in red.

"Two dozen times," the jumpmaster corrected. "We want to find your buddy as much as you do." He handed out a marked chart to each searcher.

"We know that," Malloy said. "We'll start the ground search first thing in the morning, using the maps you've provided. A group of agents is coming in from surrounding offices."

"You'll have a lot of isolated areas to check out," Starke noted, "heavily wooded sections, with a cabin here and there. It'll take some time to get to them, but they're pretty much good folks living around here. If they've seen anything, they'll help. Now, where do we stash you folks tonight?"

The FBI pilot and observer said they would fly back to Las Vegas for the night and be back in the morning. The other pilots looked at Marie, then at each other. Malloy nodded toward the woman. "My wife and I will spend the night here, if George and Jesse can rustle up some cots or sleeping bags."

"We didn't know you were married," the surprised Nevada Air National Guard pilot attested with a slightly reddening face.

"We don't advertise it," Malloy said.

"I would," the California Highway Patrol pilot murmured with an admiring smile.

"We're really sort of newlyweds," Marie volunteered, blushing slightly.

"Well, damn, we need to celebrate then," Starke proclaimed, pulling a bottle of J&B scotch from a cabinet drawer. "Beer's in the cooler. Go get some, Jesse."

"Right, everyone needs their spirits lifted after a day like this."

"I'll get the cups," the Nevada Highway Patrol pilot declared, looking wistfully at Marie and slapping a congratulatory palm on Malloy's shoulder. "You lucky dog."

As they toasted the bride and groom, the congregation took temporary refuge from their underlying quest. Marie accepted sedate bridal kisses from the mellowing group, then paused and raised her cup. "To Del, our irreplaceable, irrepressible, missing link. May it be your good fortune that our good fortune is finding you."

Jesse Williams, known to grow sentimental from the mere scent of an open beer bottle, looked misty eyed. "That's so profound."

The party drank up and planned the next day's challenge.

***

Kerry deposited the bags of groceries in the kitchen, listening for any sounds from the bedroom. Complete quiet prevailed. Wonder if "Skydiver" will ever wake up. She went to look.

Lying motionless with closed eyes and controlling his breathing, Del heard the soft approaching footsteps. He felt a slight breeze on his face and detected a faint but intriguing perfume scent. He pictured her standing over his bed, and wondered if she would notice anything different. Wonder what she looks like.

Several seconds passed before he heard her move away, the sound of footsteps fading as she apparently left the room.

Del opened one eye cautiously, moving it from side to side to insure he was alone. He heard country western music echoing from a distant part of the cabin. A dim shaft of light could be seen through the open bedroom door, and a glance at the parted window curtain revealed that early afternoon shadows were arriving. Soon he began smelling enticing cooking aromas and realized that he was famished. Senses sharpened, he thought he heard a cork popping. Next, he heard a husky voice singing a recent pop hit. It was so professional, he initially thought it was from a radio, until the melodic voice started and stopped again, repeating the spirited lyrics. He fought the temptation to crawl toward the seductive sounds and scents.

In the kitchen Kerry was submerging her concerns in a favorite pastime. Nothing like pasta and wine to raise a girl's spirits. Well, not quite. She thought of the virile-looking young man in the next room, then laughed aloud. With my luck, he'll turn out to be gay. She sampled the marinara sauce. Needs a little more garlic. Wonder if my mystery guest would like my cooking? Do people get hungry when they're knocked out? She filled her plate and sat down at the round oak table. Raising her glass of merlot, she tipped the goblet toward the bedroom in a silent toast. Here's to the odd couple—a stone-cold guy and a red-hot gal. She giggled and drained her glass.

Chapter Twelve

While Loose Louie and Sulfur Sal continued their intimidating but unproductive visits to everyone Kerry had been associated with in her old haunts, Nicky "The Nose" Vincente was collecting information from the family consigliere, Anthony Conn, Esquire, whose baptismal certificate recorded him as Antonio Alberto Contini. Vincente was drawing heavily on a thick Monte Christo while listening attentively to the lawyer's telephonic report on the results of the public record check his office staff had conducted. Vincente puffed harder with heightened excitement when he heard that Kerry's aunt had inherited a remote mountain cabin in California. "I knew that fuckin broad was holding out on Louie and Sal. Those numbnuts got snookered again. Betcha that's where the bitch is hiding."

"With the book," Conn frigidly reminded, contemplating the extent to which it incriminated him. "You need to get it back. Quickly."

"I'll get right on it, you can bet your ass."

"Who are you going to use? Do you want me to engage the services of some colleagues out there?"

Vincente snorted. "Colleagues? I like the way you fuckin lawyers talk. No, we don't need no 'colleagues.' Louie and Sal can handle it. They do good work when you keep the job simple. I'll make sure they do it right this time."

Conn didn't argue. "It's your tail, Nicky. The boss won't tolerate any more screw-ups. He was even talking about using Sal's specialty on all three of you."

Vincente almost swallowed the remains of his cigar. "Consider the job done, Tony. Tell the boss he can count on me." The phone almost slipped from Vincente's sweaty palm as he concluded Conn's call and frantically punched Sulfur Sal's phone number.

∗∗∗

Kerry felt relaxed as she finished her dinner, mildly surprised that she had consumed half the bottle of wine. Solitary drinking's dangerous, they say. Maybe "Skydiver" will wake up and join me. She giggled. Maybe he's a Mormon. She giggled again. Get a grip, girl, I think you need a cold shower.

Del heard the approaching footsteps, which sounded somewhat uneven. He closed his eyes and soon sensed he was being observed up close before the footsteps proceeded to the other side of the room. His visitor was softly humming a tune that sounded familiar – an old show tune, *Some Enchanted Evening.* He almost burst out laughing.

The rustle of clothes was the next sound he heard, followed by the soft clunk of shoes hitting the wood floor. Then he heard what sounded like elastic faintly snapping and a slightly audible "ah." Retreating footsteps were the next discernible sounds and when he estimated his roommate was exiting the room he cautiously opened his right eye. He wished he had opened both eyes, and sooner, as he watched the disappearing back of a classically rounded, naked female body of stimulating proportions. Any concern that his eyes might not be fully communicating with his brain evaporated as he noted an immediate signal of arousal. Wow! was his mental declaration as he heard the shower water running and wondered what to do next.

∗∗∗

Hmm, thought I flushed the john this morning, Kerry mused, stepping into the shower. Not like me. Maybe I'm going native out here in the woods. Oh well, this shower feels great. The Dove soap lather felt sensuous as she rubbed it over her body. She closed her eyes, remembering the last time she and Jeff made love, with his exploring hands delicately finding and igniting every sense. Oh, Lord, I miss you, honey. Her tears joined the flow of water while she tried to dismiss the past. She shifted thinking to her current dilemma. What to do with the guy. He might need serious medical attention. And Aunt Agnes is probably right about loved ones searching for him. Well, we'll worry about that later. She stepped from the shower and grabbed a large white terrycloth towel. Drying vigorously, she began feeling stimulated and felt her nipples hardening. Two erasers, she recalled Jeff calling them. She looked at her reflected image in the full-length door mirror and studied her damp, close-cropped ebony hair. She looked down at herself. Almost as curly. The reflection of her hips caught her attention, and her eyes then shifted upwards to her full breasts. Pretty well proportioned, as long as I watch the pasta. She patted her flat stomach and spread her fingers on each side of her narrow waist. Still have the hourglass, until the sands of time start to shift. She began to feel a tingling sensation in her groin area. You're getting in bad shape, girl. Think about something else. Kerry thought she had succeeded and was brushing her teeth when an old Toni Tennille hit came to mind and she started to hum the lyrics. *Do It To Me One More Time.* She wrapped the large towel around her body and headed for the bedroom.

Del heard the bathroom door open and prepared to close his eyes. His bare-footed hostess moved faster than he had anticipated, however, and his eyelids were just blinking shut when she glided through the doorway. He heard her abruptly stop. A faint aroma of soap and perfume floated over him. He could hear her light breathing as she hovered over his face.

"Are you awake?" She asked softly.

He kept his eyes shut, debating what to do.

"I could swear I saw your eyes blink," she muttered, moving her face closer to his.

He held his breath. God, she smelled good.

"I want to help you," she said, touching his face lightly. "You might need medical attention. Can you hear me?"

Del decided it was time to end the charade. Opening both eyes, he found himself staring inches away into two startled dark-brown eyes. "Hello," he said.

Kerry screamed and jumped backwards, unhinging the large towel that dropped to the floor.

"Who are you?" they shouted at each other almost in unison, as Del continued to stare with fascination at the curvaceous naked woman.

Chapter Thirteen

The Carson City, Nevada, FBI Resident Agency was selected as the command center for the search. Mike Malloy was designated coordinator. He and Marie drove over early in the morning from the Blue Sky Airlines facility, and search areas were assigned to teams of assembled agents. The FBI plane would continue its aerial quest, but the main thrust would be the land search. Detailed maps and radios tuned to a secure Bureau frequency were distributed. "A steak dinner on me for the team that finds him," Malloy promised. "Keep the command center apprised of your progress, and good luck. He's a cat with nine lives. Think positive." Reflecting on the escapades his young colleague had survived, Malloy privately wondered how many of those fragile lives remained.

***

Vincente was issuing his orders to Loose Louie and Sulfur Sal in characteristically obscene terms. "This is the last fuckin chance you pricks get. Screw this up, and you're fish bait. Capisce?"

Milano and Rinalti nodded understanding. "We'll take care of the scrawny broad this time," Loose Louie guaranteed.

Vincente stared at him. "You being a wiseass again?"

Loose Louie felt the surge of increased perspiration staining his dark green silk suit. "Hell no, boss," he quickly assured. "Me and Sal know how important this is. We won't let you down."

Sulfur Sal joined in. "Consider it done, boss. That was some good luck finding out about the cabin."

Vincente sneered. "That wasn't luck, you dumb shit. It took brains, of which I wonder if you two have half of one between you."

"Huh?" Loose Louie muttered. "What did he say?"

Sulfur Sal looked at his puzzled partner. "The boss just pointed out that we need to act smarter."

Vincente jeered, "What I did was call you stupid assholes."

Sulfur Sal gulped. "You're right, stupid assholes."

Loose Louie displayed a hangdog expression. "Gee, that don't sound very nice."

Vincente stood up. "Okay, maybe I'm being too hard on you guys. Just get the fuckin job done. All you have to do is whack one broad and bring back the book and everyone will be happy."

Loose Louie brightened. "We can do that—just whack one scrawny broad."

Sulfur Sal grabbed his partner's arm and hurried out of Vincente's office.

***

Kerry stood paralyzed with shock, momentarily unmindful of her nakedness as she returned Del's open-eyed stare.

He raised his head from the pillow, asking again, "Who are you?"

Suddenly aware of her nudity, Kerry blushed and reached for the towel. "Who are <u>You</u>?" she demanded.

"I'm Del Dickerson, and I'm not going to hurt you." He sat up, causing his blanket to slide to the floor, revealing that he was no longer bound.

"How did you get loose?" she gasped.

"It wasn't hard," he replied, beginning to swing his legs over the side of the bed.

The site of her muscular guest unfettered and moving in her direction, prompted her to jump back and drop the towel again. Terrorized that she may have been found by the mob, she screamed again and fainted, slumping to the floor atop the damp terrycloth.

Oh my, Del thought as he stepped from the bed to aid the dormant woman. Forgetting his injury until his splintered left leg touched down, a lightning bolt of pain surged through his body and he toppled to the floor. On the way down, the left side of his head struck the edge of the steel bed frame, and he again blacked out, sprawling face down atop Kerry.

Within seconds Kerry regained consciousness to find a heavy head resting motionless on her abdomen in what might be interpreted as an obscene position.

"What the hell do you think you're doing?" she yelled, grasping his head with both hands and vigorously pushing it aside. The effort flipped his body over, and Del lay face up, emitting a series of low, plaintive moans as his eyebrows began to flutter. "Oh," he groaned.

Kerry jumped to her feet and leaned over the reviving man whose eyes suddenly blinked fully open. "Who in the hell are you?" she reiterated, "and what are you up to? How did you get loose? I want some answers. Now!"

Del continued efforts to focus his eyes, gulping involuntarily at the provocative sight. "I told you, I'm Del Dickerson. How did I get here, and who are you?"

"Me first, mister. It's my place, and the name's Kerry."

Del managed a slight smile as he looked up. "Well, at least I sort of know where I am, and your first name – a pretty one, by the way – for a pretty woman."

Color washed back to her face as she was reminded of her nakedness. She quickly refastened the towel about her, noticing with alarm the expanding bulge in his shorts. "You some kind of sex pervert?" she demanded, "because if you are, I've got a gun." Then she saw the small revolver back in his ankle holster and stood frozen. "How long have you been awake? Have you been faking this all along? What's going on?" Her voice hovered on the edge of hysteria.

"Please relax," Del pleaded, speaking quietly in a soothing tone. "I'll do you no harm. I don't know how long I was knocked out, but I just came to a little while ago. Last thing I remember I was flying toward a bunch of trees."

"That's where I found you."

"Then I owe you a lot. Did you wrap my leg too?"

"Sure, who else? Do you think I've got a jolly band of elves doing the work around this place?" Her voice displayed renewed assertiveness. "I think it's broken," she added.

"I think you're right, and I thank you for your help. What day is it?"

"It's Thursday. I found you yesterday."

He shook his head. "I've got to call my employer – let them know I'm okay. Where exactly are we?"

Wariness suddenly returned. What if he was sent by the mob? "You're in a mountain cabin in California."

Del frowned, "Gee, I thought I was in Nevada. Where in California? May I use your phone?"

"It's not working," Kerry lied. "Who's your employer?"

Del remembered the book he found, and felt suddenly cautious. "The government."

"That what your doing with the gun?"

"Yes, I'm a Federal law enforcement officer."

Her disbelief was apparent. "Ha! What branch of government jumps into mountain-top trees?"

Del grinned sheepishly. "None intentionally. I'm an FBI agent."

Kerry laughed aloud. "And I'm Queen Elizabeth."

"No, really, it was my day off."

"You serious? Where's your badge?"

"Afraid I left it behind."

"Don't you have a card or something with your picture on it?"

"Credentials. I'm afraid I left that behind too. I don't have anything to identify myself."

"And your foreign language. How do you explain that?"

"Korean. Yeah, does seem a little out of character. But there's a simple explanation."

"I'm listening."

"The Bureau tests all its new agents for language aptitude. Somehow, I scored high and they decided I should attend the Defense Language Institute in Monterey. It's run by the Army, and they work the hell out of you. I put in sixteen months of toil and sweat, and ate a lot of Korean cuisine—Gimbap, Japchae, Kimchi, plus tons of rice. They really immerse you in the culture. Anyway, I survived, surprising a lot of people. When I graduated they needed a Korean-speaking agent in San Francisco, and that's how I ended up here. End of tale."

Kerry had regained full composure, "You tell a smooth story, Del, if that really is your name. But I'm not fully convinced." She studied her supine guest who was grimacing in agony. Perspiration covered his brow.

"The leg really hurts," he said. "Do you have any aspirin?"

Kerry paused. "I might be able to find something." She moved closer. "And I might help you into bed again, but not while you look like Machinegun Kelly." As he looked up questioningly, she quickly grabbed the pistol from his ankle holster and yanked it free. She beamed a triumphant smile. "Now that makes me feel better." She waved the gun nervously in his direction. "So tell me who you really are."

Del groaned again. "Del Dickerson, FBI. And please watch where you point the gun. It has a hair trigger."

Kerry pointed the pistol up toward the ceiling. "You mean this thing?" she started, when a .38 caliber slug exploded from the weapon and put a neat hole in the cedar shake roofing.

"Shit!" she yelled, dropping the gun and clasping her ears. "I didn't know it was loaded."

Del laughed despite his pain. "That's what they all say. Believe me, it's a real gun, with real bullets. Let's leave it on the floor so neither of us receives an unwanted aperture. I'll settle for a pain pill and help into bed."

Still stunned from the explosion, Kerry remained uncertain. "Stay where you are and I'll see if I can find a pill. Meanwhile, let us not be led into temptation." She kicked the gun under her bed and headed for the door.

Del watched the retreating form minimally covered by the clinging towel, again stimulated by the sight. "Yes," he sighed, "lead us not into temptation."

Chapter Fourteen

Loose Louie and Sulfur Sal exited New York via the Holland Tunnel and were headed west through New Jersey in Nicky "The Nose" Vincente's 2010 Lincoln Town car—black, of course, with shiny chrome wheels. Loose Louie was at the wheel, listening to Sulfur Sal snoring loudly in the reclined passenger seat, a satisfied smile on his face after stopping by Madame Lee's Oriental Cultural Palace in lower Manhattan's Chinatown.

Sulfur Sal had delayed their departure by over an hour while being "culturally revitalized" by his favorite disciple of Madame Lee, a vivacious 18-year-old illegal alien from mainland China, who either brought a treasure of ancient healing techniques with her, or had learned an astonishing variety of East Coast treats in record time. Whatever, Sulfur Sal was blissfully dreaming about the merging cultures while Loose Louie squinted at traffic signs that guided him on Pulaski Highway to I-95 and then onto I-280 which would eventually put them on I-80 for their trip West. He glanced at his relaxed companion and vividly recalled their pre-departure briefing. "Bring the bitch back, dead or alive" was Vincente's profane message, focusing his baggy eyes on Loose Louie. "The scrawny broad, the one you like," he chuckled. "Or don't bother to bring her back," he added. "All I want is the book and proof she's dead. Bring me her right tit," he laughed, looking intently at Loose Louie. "It's the left one if you're standing in front of her," he sneered. "This is your last chance, you know, even if you are my brother-in-law."

"We know," Milano and Rinalti chorused, before listening to Vincente's rationale for sending them cross-country by car. "It'll take longer, but it'll make it harder to trace you. No plane records, no gas receipts—pay cash, no gun checks of your luggage." Vincente's scowl returned. "Thanks to you fuckups, we don't want the western families to know what happened back here, or we would have given them the contract. They could have provided the muscle and guns, but then it wouldn't be our secret, would it, boys?"

"No, guess not, boss," Sulfur Sal ventured to say.

Vincente then erupted from his controlled emotional state. "All this because you jackasses fucked up a job. Don't let it happen again!"

Their promises had been profuse, and had increased when Vincente handed them $5,000 in 100 dollar bills. "Don't blow it," he laughed, shaking the light coating of cocaine powder from the currency. "Take turns driving, and keep moving," Vincente instructed, "and don't get arrested. Some of those assholes out there like to stick it to wise guys from the big city."

Reflecting on the warning, Loose Louie looked at the speedometer on the big Lincoln's dashboard. Shit, 85! He slowed and glanced at the 65 mile per hour speed limit sign. Too late, he groaned, seeing the rearview mirror image of pulsating red and blue lights of a fast-approaching vehicle. "Shit happens," he groaned, elbowing Sulfur Sal awake. "We got trouble."

✳✳✳

The FBI search party was back in the Carson City command center, rehashing the negative results of their day's search. "Didn't know there were so many thick woods and secluded cabins," Kevin Winslow observed, pointing to the map of the sector he and his partner had searched. "We've got a long way to go."

The Bureau pilot nodded agreement. "The area is so thickly wooded it's hard to see much of the ground. We were hoping we would see signs of his chute. Sorry to report no luck."

"We didn't do any better," Marie reported, "but we have a lot of uncovered ground." She strained to sound hopeful.

Malloy's dark brown eyes surveyed the group. "I know it's discouraging, but let's proceed on the premise that no news is good news. I tell you, Del is like a bad penny when it comes to turning up. We go at it again tomorrow at first light. Okay?"

The searchers tried to sound upbeat. "Maybe his good luck charm will help," Marie announced. "His fiancée, Anna Chen, is arriving tomorrow, and hopefully she will bring the mystic of the Orient. They've shared some near-death experiences. She insisted on coming."

"Hey, I met her once when I was assigned to San Francisco," the Bureau pilot volunteered. "She's a real china doll. I'd like to have her looking for me. Makes you wonder why a guy would leave her behind in California to jump out of a plane in Nevada."

Malloy smiled. "I told you, he's different."

* * *

Kerry provided Del with two Advil tablets she found in the medicine cabinet, after replacing her unstable towel with a thick sweat suit. "Ready for a lift into bed?" she asked, studying him with wariness.

"I'd sure appreciate it. Sorry to be so much trouble, but this floor is kind of hard."

"Just no monkey business," she warned, helping him up onto his good leg and propping him against the side of the bed. "That's the easy part. Getting you onto the mattress is a little harder, but I did it before."

Del was surprised at her strength and looked with gratitude into her sparkling dark brown eyes. "I can't thank you enough. You've been very kind. I'm in your debt."

"Save the soft soap. We're not there yet."

"I'm confident," he said as she placed her hands under his arms and lifted while he pushed off against the floor with his right foot.

The common efforts propelled him abruptly onto his back, and with her arms trapped under his, their bodies were momentarily pinned together on top of the bed. "Let me go," she yelled, springing backwards when he lifted his arms. "You did that on purpose, didn't you?"

"No, but it was kind of nice. You're a very appealing woman, you know."

"Let's get something straight, mister. I might be your temporary nurse, but that's all, and until I'm convinced you are who you claim to be, you're sort of my prisoner. I've got the gun, you know."

Del shuddered, looking up at the roof. "No argument. I'm your prisoner."

"Good. I'm glad you realize that."

Just a Prisoner of Love, Del crooned.

"Stop that," she said, her eyes unable to avoid surveying his well-toned muscular body. Suddenly aware of the recurring sensations beginning to stir within, she wondered if the heat she felt had reddened her face.

"Please don't take offense, Kerry. I assure you I'll behave. Scout's honor."

"You were a Boy Scout?"

"Eagle."

"Didn't they teach you not to jump into trees?"

Del sighed. "They didn't have a skydiving merit badge. Guess they should have."

"You're a strange bird. What's the matter? You look like you're going to cry."

"Sorry. It's the left leg. I think it's out of whack again."

She looked at the misdirected foot. "Yeah, it does look out of line. I'll try to straighten it out if you want."

Perspiration covered his forehead. "Please, it hurts like hell," he winced.

She gently realigned his splinted leg and placed a pillow under his knee.

"That's better," he wheezed, "you're very compassionate. I'm most fortunate to have fallen into your hands."

"You might change your mind when you taste my cooking. By the way, are you hungry?"

"Starving. Cardboard would taste good right now."

She released a small smile. "My cooking's a bit better than that. Hold on, I'll see what I can find."

"Kerry, you truly are an angel. I'd sure like us to be friends."

"We'll see," she replied, heading for the kitchen.

Chapter Fifteen

"Prick," Loose Louie groused as he pulled back onto the highway into fast-moving traffic.

"Could be worse," Sulfur Sal comforted, reading the list of fines printed on the back of the traffic summons. "Eighty bucks, unless you want to go to court."

"And I was nice to the bastard," Loose Louie continued. "Yes sir, no sir, yes sir, all that shit, and he still gives me the fuckin ticket."

"Nicky warned us to watch our driving. He'll be pissed if he finds out about it."

Loose Louie's bowels were suddenly energized. "You won't tell him will you, Sal?"

"Hey, we're partners aren't we? You know I'd never rat. Just like I know you'd never mention my stop in Chinatown."

Loose Louie glanced right and nodded. "Right, we gotta stick together."

"Just watch your speed, Louie. I gotta get back to my dream. You'd never believe what she was doing to me."

Loose Louie checked the speedometer again and set the cruise control at exactly the posted speed limit. He recalled his dialogue with the trooper and frowned with displeasure, muttering aloud the officer's name. "Reggino – what's this country coming to? No fuckin respect anymore for a Paisano."

***

Kerry had cautiously propped Del up with pillows behind his head so he could eat the linguini with clam sauce that he was zealously devouring.

"Slow down, or you'll get sick," she said. "You act like you haven't eaten for a week."

"Seems like it," Del said, twisting another fork full of pasta against his spoon. "And it's so tasty, it's hard to resist. You're a great cook." He smiled with gratitude. "You deserve a medal. You just saved an agent's life."

"You're good with words, sure you're not a con man rather than a G-man?"

"You still aren't convinced, are you?"

Kerry looked serious. "I've been fooled before."

"Just call my office. They'll verify it, and I need to let them know I'm okay."

"I told you, my phone is out of order."

"Can't you go next door or something?"

"Ha!" she laughed. "Next door is miles away. We're deep in the woods."

Del nodded, recalling the view just before his crash into the tree. "Yeah, I sort of remember. But sure wish I could get word out. My people are probably worried."

Kerry thought of the phone on her bedside table, and wondered if she looked as guilty as she felt. "I can go down the mountain and make a call for you tomorrow."

"That would be great. You're a doll. And thanks again for the delicious dinner. Do you suppose I could have another glass of that fine wine?"

She smiled. "That fine wine is from the vineyards of Ernest and Julio Gallo, but I guess you could have another glass, providing you promise to behave yourself."

He raised three fingers of his right hand and opened his mouth to speak.

"I know," she interrupted, "Scouts Honor. I was a Girl Scout once. I know all about you guys."

Del beamed. "See, we have something else in common."

"What do you mean, something else?"

"Well, we're both young, we both like pasta and wine, and we're both in a remote cabin out of contact with the world and wondering about each other."

Kerry looked curious. "What are you wondering about me?"

He studied her dark eyes briefly before replying. "What a lovely young lady like you is doing out here in the woods all by yourself?"

She stared back. "That's a long story."

"I'd like to hear it," he said, nodding his head in the direction of his splinted leg. "I've got a lot of time."

Kerry stood up. "I'll get your wine."

"I don't mean to pry, Kerry, but I am a good listener, and I think you're a special person who could use a friend."

She paused and looked at her guest. Damn, you're looking better all the time and you're saying things I like to hear. Do you have any idea what you might be starting?

"I'll get your wine," she repeated.

Chapter Sixteen

Special Agent Marie Stanley stood alone at the bottom of a narrow mountain trail that rose at a thirty-degree angle from the twisting black-topped country road she had followed for a half hour from the valley floor in a car loaned by a local agent. Educated by the previous day's experiences, the searchers recognized they had a surprisingly large number of locations to check out and decided to divide the two-agent teams to double their production. Radio contact would be maintained, so any positive developments could be immediately communicated and the forces could converge on a hopeful site.

The dirt and gravel side road Marie studied was blocked several car lengths off the main road by a heavy chain with a massive padlock. A prominent sign nailed to a nearby pine tree clearly proclaimed: "NO TRESPASSING."

Situated below the sign was a small wooden box bearing a telephone symbol. As Marie moved closer she saw a smaller sign below the box that read "Phone For Instructions. Dial Nine." Picking up the handset of the old rotary instrument, she followed directions, glancing around at her surroundings as it rang. It was then that she noticed another sign nailed to a tree on the opposite side of the road: "SUNNY-GLOW SLOPES."

"Hello," a masculine-sounding voice answered after several rings.

Momentarily startled by the sound of another human voice in the remote wilderness, Marie finally replied. "Hello, my name is Marie Stanley and I'm looking for a friend who might be lost in these woods. I wonder if you could help me. Perhaps you've seen a stranger around. I have a photograph of him."

There was a prolonged pause before the unexpected reply. "You have a nice voice. What do you look like?"

She paused, puzzled by the odd inquiry. "I'm a woman, looking for a friend who is lost. What's important is what <u>he</u> looks like. Can you help me?"

She thought she heard a snicker. "Yeah, I think I'd like to try. Wait there. I'll be right down."

As the phone clicked, Marie wondered what she had run across, debating whether she should leave and return with a partner. No, that's wimpy. I've been trained to deal with weirdos. Besides, I've got baby. She patted her black leather shoulder purse housing her Glock automatic.

Almost ten minutes elapsed before she heard footsteps coming from the direction of the narrow road that turned abruptly a short distance from the chained entry. Shortly thereafter a bearded man dressed in a long white robe rounded the bend. Marie guessed him to be in his early forties, weighing about a hundred and sixty pounds and standing about five-foot-ten. Light brown hair hung close to his shoulders, and dark brown sandals adorned his bare feet. He displayed a deep tan on his thin face. A Biblical character was her initial impression.

"Welcome to Sunnyglow Slopes," he greeted, roving eyes surveying the full-figured woman in the tailored pantsuit. "You look good in blue."

What kind of squirrel do I have here she wondered, pondering her approach. Better not mention FBI. It could spook him. "Like I said on the phone, my name is Marie Stanley and I'm searching for a lost friend who may have parachuted into these woods. Here's his picture. Have you possibly seen him?"

As the man moved closer, Marie inhaled the strong scent of marijuana. "Parachute you say? Like from an airplane?" He took the photo into his calloused hands.

"Yes, he parachuted out of a plane two days ago, and may have drifted into this area."

"Nice looking guy. Your boyfriend?"

"No, just a friend, Mr. …"

"Simpson, Charlie Simpson. Just call me Charlie."

"Did you see or hear anything that could help us, Charlie? Like a plane overhead, or a parachutist, or anything?"

"Have lots of planes flying over our place," the man replied with a smirk. "Maybe some of our guests saw something. Want to come in and ask them? Seems I recall one of them mentioning seeing something strange falling out of the sky the other day."

Marie's pulse raced. "Did they say what it was?"

"No, I really didn't pay much attention. Thought it was just Julie's imagination. She gets that way sometimes."

"Can I talk with Julie? It's really important, Charlie."

He surveyed her figure again and released a crooked smile. "How important?"

"Very important. It shouldn't take long."

"My guests value their privacy. I hate to disturb them."

"Please, I won't bother anyone for more than a couple of minutes." She flashed an ingratiating smile. "You look like a helpful man."

"Well," he drawled, "if you insist, but you'll have to follow our camp rules."

"Certainly. Just tell me what to do."

His eyes sparkled. "Take off your clothes. This is a fresh air sunshine camp. What some folks call a nudist colony."

Chapter Seventeen

Kerry was carefully piloting the Jeep Cherokee down the curving mountain road, recalling the events of the previous evening. They had stimulated her mind to a point where she had experienced a rare sleepless night, and something was gnawing at her subconscious. Something hadn't seemed right when she was dressing in the burgundy-colored running suit she had pulled from the bottom drawer of her dresser. She dismissed the thought and stifled a burgeoning yawn, redirecting attention to her unusual guest. She had joined him with a glass of wine while they talked, and he had presented a fairly convincing story that he was, in fact, an FBI agent, despite his lack of identification. She had remained wary in discussing her family background, but did disclose that she was from New York City, and had been a band singer. She ignored his subtle probes for more personal information, but acknowledged she was mourning the loss of loved ones. Pouring them both another glass of wine, she began to get weepy and accepted his extended hand of solace until she concluded that his expressions of sympathy were tempting her to fling herself into his comforting arms. "Time for bed," she had abruptly announced, moving away. "Do I have to lock you in another room, or tie you down again?"

Del smiled gently. "I've told you, and I repeat, I'll do you no harm. You've been too kind. Besides, I don't move around very well, you know."

"Well, I'm exhausted and need to get some sleep if I'm going out tomorrow to make your phone call, so I'll take you at your word. But, don't forget, I've got the gun, and I know how it works."

He shuddered, looking at the ceiling. "I know. I'll be good, but I do have one more favor to ask."

"Yes?"

"I need to go to the bathroom."

"Oh, yeah, I can imagine. You want a pan or something?"

"If you'd bring me the broom in the corner, I think I can use it as a crutch."

She looked enlightened. "So that's how you got around to find your gun. Pretty clever. Guess you were a Scout."

He nodded acknowledgement and with her assistance proceeded to maneuver his way awkwardly out of bed and onto the inverted broom. She could still hear his thump, thump, thump as he left the room, and visualized the sight of the perspiring muscled form in the snug jockey shorts. During his absence she changed into flannel pajamas and crawled beneath her bed covers, remembering first to disconnect the bedside phone. Don't want him to think I'm a liar.

She was just slipping into welcomed slumber when she heard the thump, thump, thump of her returning roommate. His laboring form was discernible in the dim light of the bedside lamp. She stifled the inclination to rush to help as he struggled back into bed, emitting a series of low moans as he settled down. Several seconds passed before he quietly spoke. "Good night, lovely lady, and thanks for everything."

She feigned sleep as she repressed the urge to leap out of bed and bestow a good night kiss.

✶✶✶

As Kerry approached the same store where she had made her call the previous day, she was relieved to find it as lightly patronized as before. One old Chevy pickup truck was parked near the entrance. Pulling up, she saw an elderly couple in jeans depart the store and climb in the truck. After they drove off she entered the store and saw the same clerk, again absorbed with the flickering picture on a small TV set.

She purchased a few essentials, including a toothbrush for her patient, before retreating to the outside pay phone to call the number Del had informed her was that of the San Francisco FBI office. She had been told to ask for Mr. Whitman, the Assistant Special Agent in Charge.

When a business-like female voice announced "FBI," Kerry stammered, "Mr. Whitman, please."

"Who may I tell him is calling?" the operator inquired.

"Just a person with information about one of your agents. A guy who calls himself Del Dickerson. Do you have someone by that name?"

"Let me put you through to Mr. Whitman."

Kerry felt nervous. "No, just tell him the guy is okay. I've got to go."

"Wait, where is he? Is he all right?"

"I told you he's okay. I can't talk any longer."

"Don't hang up," the operator was pleading when she heard a sharp click.

✳✳✳

In the San Francisco FBI office, the operator informed Assistant Special Agent in Charge Whitman of the call. "The tech guys are trying to trace its origin."

"Hot damn!" Whitman exclaimed. "Our bad penny has turned up."

Minutes later he listened to the report from the Technical Surveillance Supervisor. "Call came from a pay phone at a rural store near Echo Summit in El Dorado County."

"Bingo," Whitman said. "Get the search party leader on the line."

✳✳✳

Why didn't I tell them more, Kerry questioned herself as she wheeled the Jeep back in the direction of the cabin. It sounded like they know him, even if the woman didn't say so. It sounds like he's legitimate, and he probably has a wife or girlfriend worrying about him. I should have asked him last night. She frowned, trying to identify the elusive thought that had been bothering her all morning. Unsuccessful, she refocused thoughts on Del. Do I want to keep him for myself? Is that it? He is quite nice, besides being good looking and having a great build. She felt a tingling sensation in her groin that refused to be ignored. Oh, God, it's been a long time.

As the Jeep bounced ever closer to the cabin she tried to divert her thoughts. But, the lingering idea that had been hovering like a rain-filled cloud suddenly burst forth as she was comparing the color of her sweat suit with that of the Jeep. The drawer! That's where the ledger book was stashed with my sweats. It wasn't there this morning! "Son-ofabitch!" she yelled aloud, stepping on the gas.

Chapter Eighteen

The bug-splattered Lincoln Town Car purred along at the posted speed limit, plus five, that Sulfur Sal declared was a cop-free pace. Alternating turns at the wheel, and stopping only for food, restrooms, and gas, the pair had just left Lincoln, Nebraska, near the end of their second day on the road.

"My ass is numb," Loose Louie grumbled, "and I gotta go to the can."

"We just came out of a rest area. Didn't you go then?"

"Didn't have to then. Besides, the stalls looked dirty."

"Shit," Sulfur Sal snorted, "you look like a pig and smell like a goat and you think the crapper ain't good enough for ya?"

Loose Louie frowned. "That wasn't very nice. You don't smell so good yourself."

Sulfur Sal stared at his sulking partner. "At least I know enough to go when I can. Want me to stop on the side of the road?"

"No, but don't waste time getting to the next stop. I don't wanta have an accident in the car."

"Geez, I'm trying to figure out the best way to whack the broad, and I gotta worry about you crapping in the car."

"I know how to whack the broad," Loose Louie promised, "but I might have a little fun with her first. She really ain't scrawny like Nicky thinks."

"First we gotta find the cabin," Sulfur Sal reminded. "I hear they don't got street signs up in the hills."

"We'll find her," Loose Louie assured, envisioning the curvaceous woman who was becoming more voluptuous in his mind with each passing mile. "Speed up a little, Sal. I'm beginning to feel a strong urge."

"Keep your horbones under control until we finish the job. Think of something else."

"Okay, how about a good Italian meal? Haven't had one since we left the 'Big Apple'. Suppose anyone out here in the sticks knows how to cook?"

"Don't know, but I seen a sign a ways back advertising Angelo's Italian Bistro. It's in Grand Island. Check the map."

Loose Louie studied the AAA map. "Here's Grand Island, just up the road. Maybe it's like Coney Island. They got good chow there. Let's stop. Veal parmesan's almost as good as nooky."

"Yeah, but we can't waste much time. Nicky said to keep moving."

"But he dint say not to eat. We'll need our strength to finish off the broad."

"All right, keep your eye out for Angelo's."

"It don't come out."

"What?"

"My eye. I ain't gonna give away my eye for a plate of pasta."

"Of course not, dummy. That's a figger of speech. It's like saying keep an eye peeled."

"I ain't gonna peel it either."

Sulfur Sal turned to look at his partner. "Ya serious? Ya gotta be a complete moron."

Loose Louie flashed a lopsided grin. "Just pulling your shank."

"My what?"

"Your leg, numbnuts. One of your figgers of speech."

Sulfur Sal groaned. "Here I am, in the middle of nowhere with a complete idiot who thinks he's a comedian. What did I do to deserve this?"

"Missed the fuckin book in Brooklyn."

"Me? You was there too."

"Yeah, we're in deep do-do. That's a figger of speech too, smartass."

"Shit," Sal grunted.

"Right. Let's find Angelo's."

***

The parking lot in front of Angelo's Italian Bistro was empty, except for two dusty pickup trucks with rusted fenders.

"We musta beat the rush hour," Loose Louie said, heading for the green and red door that bore a cardboard OPEN sign.

Sulfur Sal frowned. "Don't look too hot to me."

"Can't ya smell the marinara sauce?" Loose Louie said, pushing through the door.

"Looks kinda empty. Maybe the food's not so good."

"Who can ruin Italian cooking, Lou? And look at the red and white tablecloths. Has to be genuine Italiano. Bet it's a hidden treasure. Here comes the waitress."

"Welcome," the young black girl greeted. "Glad to see you. It's been a slow day. Sit anywhere you like."

"She don't look Italian to me," Sulfur Sal muttered as they moved to a table near the door.

"Maybe she's Sicilian."

Sulfur Sal shook his head. "See her name tag? KIASHAWA. Here she comes."

"We have some nice specials today, gents—a tasty appetizer, and the chef's special entrée, Prairie Cacciatore. They're heavenly."

"What's the appetizer made of?" Loose Louie asked.

"Sautéed rabbit ears. Sort of tastes like calamari. Our chef has a magical touch."

"I think we'll skip the appetizer," Sulfur Sal said. "The cacciatore really good?"

The waitress nodded. "Out of this world."

"That's what I'll have," Sulfur Sal said.

"Me too," Loose Louie added. "And a bottle of Chianti."

"Gee, sorry. This is a dry county. How about a Pepsi?"

The pair looked at each other when the waitress departed. "No wine! Sautéed rabbit ears!" Sulfur Sal growled. "What kind of a fuckin place did you take me to?"

"Yeah, that's a bummer. But you was the guy driving."

"You was directing. Never shoulda listened to ya."

They were still trading insults when Kiashawa returned with their meals.

"At least the marinara looks good," Sulfur Sal said.

Loose Louie nodded and grabbed his utensils. "And lots of it."

"Kind of tough," Sulfur Sal said, chewing on a piece of meat.

"And stringy," Loose Louie said through a mouthful.

Sulfur Sal gulped some Pepsi. "Tastes kind of funny too."

"Eat some more of the marinara sauce," Loose Louie was suggesting when the waitress reappeared.

"By the way, how did you hear about us?" she asked.

"Saw your sign on the highway," Sulfur Sal answered.

"Oh, I didn't know it was still up."

"Yep, caught our eye," Sulfur Sal said. "Thought we'd like to say hello to Angelo."

"Don't think that's possible. He's dead. Passed away a couple of months ago."

"Oh, sorry to hear that. Was it sudden?"

"Yeah. Happened right here, after he ate. At first they thought it was a heart attack – he was all excited about a big argument he had with the chef. But the doc said it was something he ate. Business has been pretty slow since then."

Loose Louie put down his fork. "Something Angelo cooked?"

"No, Charlie's done all the cooking for a couple of years. Really talented. How do you like your meal?"

"It's kind of different," Sulfur Sal said. "What did you call it again?"

"Prairie Cacciatore. It's Charlie's secret recipe."

"Ah . . . what kind of meat is in his recipe?" Sulfur Sal asked.

"He won't tell me. Maybe he'll tell you. He's kind of temperamental. I'll go get him. He likes to meet customers – make sure they're enjoying his cooking."

"What the hell ya doing to me?" Sulfur Sal demanded when they were alone. "This stuff tastes like crap. Ya screwed me again."

"Don't taste great to me either. Ya don't have to eat it. Have some more bread."

"That's stale too. And the parmesan cheese smells rotten. What a disaster."

"Tell that to the chef. Here he comes."

"Him?"

"Yeah, the little guy with the big white hat."

"He's a chink."

"I think ya guessed right for a change. Say something in Chinese. Chop-chop, or something. He looks mad. And, what's that in his hand?"

"Kiashawa say you ask about favorite recipe?" the unsmiling cook asked.

"Well," Sulfur Sal said, "we was just wondering. The meat tastes a little unusual."

"Yeah," Loose Louie chimed in, "our taste buddies ain't used to such fine dining."

"You no like?" the cook said, moving closer.

Loose Louie's sphincter muscle contracted. Shit, that's a meat cleaver in his right hand!

"What's wrong with it?" the scowling cook demanded.

"Nothing, nothing, Mr. . . ," Sulfur Sal sputtered, "and we really gotta be going," he said, standing up. "Great meal. We'll see you again some time."

"You insult Charlie Wong," the cook said in a near shout. "You no like dog? I cook all day, and you come and dishonor me."

"Dog!" Sulfur Sal exclaimed.

"Ugh, I'm gonna be sick," Loose Louie yelled. "Where's the crapper?"

"Get out!" Charlie Wong screamed. "After you pay check."

"I ain't paying nothin' for this shit," Sulfur Sal shouted, heading for the door.

Loose Louie felt a disturbance in his trousers as he hurried behind his partner and piled into the Town Car. Sulfur Sal already had the engine running.

"Come back and pay," Charlie Wong yelled as the car backed and turned toward the street.

"Step on it," Loose Louie urged, about the same time a loud thud sounded as the meat cleaver struck the front passenger door an inch or so below the window.

"Keep going," Loose Louie bellowed, raising a middle-finger salute to the irate chef who was jumping up and down in the parking lot of Angelo's Italian Bistro.

"Ya crazy loon, ya damned near got us killed back there," Sulfur Sal screamed as he steered the black Lincoln screeching onto Interstate 80.

"Me?" Loose Louie retorted. "He threw the fuckin axe at me. Yur the guy that insulted his cooking."

"Cooking! Ya call that cooking? Why I ever let you talk me into going there I'll never know. Gotta get my head examined. Ya must like eating prairie dogs."

"I like dogs," Loose Louie said. "Just don't like eating them. I loved Lassie."

"Prairie dogs ain't like Lassie. They're more like moles and rats."

Loose Louie groaned again. "Rats! I think I'm going to be sick."

"Well, open the fuckin window. I ain't stopping. That chink might be following us."

"It won't open, Sal. Charlie must have messed it up with his chopper."

"Well, don't puke in the car. And what's that smell?"

Loose Louie looked contrite. "Ya know my problem. When Charlie waved that tomahawk . . . well, ya know, accidents happen."

"Keyriste! Yur an accident," Sulfur Sal yelled, opening his window. "This is unbelievable. I shoulda let that chink kill us both. Put us outta our misery. Thank God there's a rest stop coming up. Get cleaned up in a hurry. We're falling behind."

"I'll make it pronto, Tonto."

"Tonto?"

"Yeah, the Lone Ranger's faithful sidekick. Sort of like us."

"Ya mean you think you're the Lone Ranger?"

"I always liked cowboys. We oughta see a lot of them around here. Think I'll get one of them big hats. A white one."

Sulfur Sal snorted as he pulled into the rest stop. "Okay, white hat, get going."

"Door won't open," Loose Louie said. "The chink musta screwed it up. I'll have to slide over to your door."

"And mess up the whole front seat," Sulfur Sal shouted. "I'm going outta my mind."

"Better hurry," Loose Louie urged, watching Sulfur Sal leap out before him.

***

"Whew," Loose Louie said a few minutes later to his partner who leaned against the car hood puffing on a cigarette. "Everything's okay now, and did ya see what Charlie did to the door? His fuckin axe was stuck right by the lock. I pulled it out and the door works now."

"Yea, with a big gash in it. Nicky's gonna be royally pissed. I shoulda used it on you. I bet they'd call it a mercy killing."

"Geez, that don't sound very nice. Thought we was compadres."

Sulfur Sal took another puff and shrugged. "What choice do we have? Let's go."

"I'll drive for awhile," Loose Louie said, climbing into the driver's seat. "Let ya get some rest. Might improve your altitude."

"Stop using big words if ya don't know what they mean. It's attitude."

"No, smartass, it's altitude. The higher it is, the thinner the air. Affects yur brain. I read that in the tour book."

"I give up," Sulfur Sal said, closing his eyes.

Oh Give Me a Home, Where the Buffalo Roam, Loose Louie began singing off key several minutes later.

Sulfur Sal's head jerked up, his eyes showing alarm. "What's that noise?"

"It was me singing. Doncha like music?"

"Sounded like a cat getting castrated, and I was just starting a dream about a session with Ming Lee in Brooklyn. Ya messed up a hot date."

"Ya was snoring. Sounded like a subway train going off the track."

Sulfur Sal stared at Loose Louie.

"Watcha lookin' at me like that for?" Loose Louie asked.

"Just figuring what size barrel I'm gonna need to put you outta yur misery."

Loose Louie's laugh sounded hollow. "Ya really wouldn't do that to me, would ya Sal?"

Sulfur Sal's eyes narrowed. "One more of them home on the range songs and I'll be measuring you. Capisce?"

Chapter Nineteen

Marie stood stunned, gaping at the be-robed man. "You mean even a visitor has to undress?"

Charlie Simpson displayed a lingering leer. "If they want to come inside. Our guests would be uncomfortable if someone was concealing something."

"How many guests do you have?"

"About a dozen right now. They come and go. Have a lot more on weekends."

"Men and women?"

"Yeah, but no kids. This is an adult camp." His eyes continued to gleam as he emphasized adult.

"Total nudity?" Marie probed.

Simpson's eyes continued to roam over his visitor's body. "No, not total. You can wear shoes. But no socks," he chuckled. "We strive for maximum exposure to the sun. You can bring a purse, though."

Marie thought of the Glock automatic in her purse and pondered the situation. Above and beyond the call. Probably a bum steer anyway. Yet, what if this Julie did see Del? It could be a matter of life and death. Maybe I should ask Mike what to do. No, I'm trained to make independent decisions. Didn't cover this in training school, other than stressing the need to be assertive and take the initiative.

Simpson's impatience was becoming apparent. "Make up your mind, lady. I've got to lead an exercise session in a few minutes. You coming in or not?"

Marie recalled her times on the stage as a Music Hall Rockette, and her brief undercover role as an exotic dancer. Not like the merchandise hasn't been exposed before. She looked into Simpson's eyes. "Yes, I'm coming in."

"Why don't you move your car to the wide spot up the road?" Simpson suggested, unlocking the heavy padlock and lowering the chain. "Some folks might want to come or go and we don't want to block the entrance."

Marie drove the white Chevy Impala to the designated area, watching in her rearview mirror as Simpson refastened the chain. She also noticed when she finally stopped that the paved county road was no longer visible.

She was about to covertly radio her location to the command center when Simpson walked up to her lowered window. "Car looks kind of official. You a cop or something?"

"No, I'm not a cop," she laughed.

"Didn't think so. You're too good looking. You can leave your clothes in the car." He looked at his watch. "We need to get going."

Marie exited the car as Simpson continued to stare. "Do you need to watch me undress?"

"Ha, not used to the free life are you? You'll be surprised how fast you adapt. Okay, I'll be up the road a bit. But hurry it up."

Two minutes later, Marie turned a corner of the path and almost ran into the bare back of her host. He turned to face her, holding his white robe in his right hand.

He visibly gulped when he viewed the trim, provocative body of the naked woman standing before him. "Wow!" he exclaimed, eyes bulging. "You're the best looking woman I've ever seen."

Marie wondered if she looked as flush as she felt. "I thought you were used to seeing naked bodies?"

"Never seen one like yours," he stammered, "but you're right, we don't let such things get us excited. Mind over matter, you know. It's just that none of the others look like you." His breathing seemed labored.

"You said you were in a hurry," she reminded, trying to keep her eyes elevated.

"Oh yeah, we are running a little late. Why don't you go ahead of me."

"But I don't know the way."

Simpson was visibly perspiring despite the cool air that had Marie feeling goose bumps. "Right," he finally said, taking another thorough look before turning to lead the way. "Follow me," he croaked.

"Kind of chilly," Marie said.

"We're heading for a hot pocket over the hill," Simpson replied. "It's why we call it Sunnyglow Slopes. Our special valley. Only gets cold at night. You'll be plenty warm," he added in an ominous tone.

As she followed the tanned skinny frame of Charlie Simpson along the car-wide path bracketed by towering pines, Marie noticed tattooed wreaths circling both of his upper arms and both ankles. She had also noticed when he turned that he was a mere boy when compared with her husband. However, her brief glance revealed that "boy" was struggling for a place in the sun. The feel of her pistol-laden purse slapping rhythmically against her bare thigh provided minimal comfort as she proceeded on her bizarre search.

Chapter Twenty

Kerry's mind raced as she swerved into the final narrow lane leading to the cabin. He knows who I am. Why didn't he tell me he took the book? Could he really have been sent by the mob? The woman at the FBI never did say he was an FBI agent. Maybe he changed sides, and that's why they're anxious to find him. No, he wouldn't have asked her to call them if that were true. Damn. This is confusing. Don't let your imagination run wild, Kerry. She slowed down and scanned the area around the cabin, relieved to find that everything seemed the same as when she left. The purse next to her caught her attention and she felt better by remembering she had placed Del's pistol in the bag that morning. She was also comforted to remember that she had disconnected the kitchen phone and placed it and the bedroom instrument in the living area closet.

Well, we shall soon see what you are all about, Del. And you seemed so nice. To think I was ready last night to fall into your arms.

***

From his bed, Del heard the approaching car and smiled, hoping Kerry had reported his whereabouts and that he would soon be reunited with Anna and his associates. He also thought of the kindness of his hostess, and how much he owed her. Her beauty also could not be ignored, nor the sadness of spirit she exuded. She seems to need a lot of comforting. It's the least I can offer.

***

"You dirty rat!" Kerry exclaimed as she burst into the bedroom.

"That's a famous James Cagney line," Del spontaneously responded. Then he saw she wasn't smiling. "What is it? You're serious, aren't you?"

"You're damned right I'm serious, Mister. You haven't been honest with me."

"What do you mean? Didn't my office confirm who I am. What happened?"

"You didn't tell me you took the book."

"Oh," he said, falling back on his pillows from his raised position, "didn't even think about it."

"Sure," Kerry shouted, "like you don't know what it is. You're either for real or a damned good liar. Where is it?"

"It's safe, Kerry, and I'm really not sure what it means, but I suspect it indicates you have some dangerous knowledge that certain people would like back."

"We sure agree on that, but how do I know you're not one of the people looking for it?"

"If I was, don't you think I would have taken off by now, after disposing of you, of course."

"Maybe you would have if you hadn't broken your leg. How can I believe you?"

Del tried to sound consoling. "Didn't you call my office?"

"Well, yes, but they never said you were an FBI guy."

"Did you talk with Phil Whitman?"

"Not exactly, I hung up before he came on the line. I was scared." She looked close to tears.

"You did tell them I was okay, didn't you?"

Kerry was crying softly now. "Yes, and I do want to believe you, but I'm so confused. They killed my dad and Jeff, and I'm out here all alone and I don't know where to turn." Her tears increased and her body shook spasmodically. "Damn, what should I do?"

"Come here," he whispered, "let it out. You'll feel better."

She was soon sobbing loudly in Del's comforting arms.

Chapter Twenty-one

Spirits in the command post soared after the call from the San Francisco FBI office. "Finally got a break," Malloy beamed. "We now have a focus point for the search," he told the other team members who had been called back for a strategy conference. "We'll all be moving in that direction shortly."

"Where's Marie?" one asked.

Malloy's look dimmed. "I've been wondering the same thing. I radioed her, but she's off the air. I'll keep trying. She was in sector 46 at last word." He pointed to the giant map attached to the wall. "She should have radioed her location before she went out of service."

"Maybe she's in a dead spot," a local agent said. "You get them sometimes with all the hills and valleys around here."

"Yeah, it's probably something like that," Malloy agreed tersely. "Hope she didn't run into trouble. I'm going to personally check out her last known locality when we finish here."

"She seems pretty capable of handling situations," the local agent said in an encouraging tone.

Malloy tried to look optimistic. "Yeah, she's always been resourceful."

***

The tall, naked, true brunette was preparing to employ her resourcefulness during a vigorous ten-minute uphill climb behind her sun-roasted escort. As they crested a ridge, a wide clearing of trees opened, and the trail began sloping gradually downward to a large saucer-shaped basin bathed in brilliant mid-day sun. Marie was surprised how

warm it felt in the depression. An outer circle of small log cabins surrounded an elevated rough-hewn wooden stage that was covered with
an open-sided canvas canopy. Lounge chairs and air mattresses scattered around the grassy clearing were largely occupied by an assortment of naked bodies, some of them puffing on wooden pipes.

"We have a visitor," Simpson announced loudly, turning several
heads in their direction. Four of them appeared to be male, Marie concluded from their beards and mustaches, to say nothing of the intense
attention they offered the arriving pair. When they sprung to their feet,
little question remained, although Marie had to restrain a laugh over
their qualifications. Three were short and paunchy; the fourth, string-
bean thin. None remotely compared with her husband, she thought,
suddenly wondering what he would think of her exploration.

"Whee!" the string bean whistled. "Can I initiate her, Charlie?"

"She might not want to be, Willard. Besides, I found her and have
first rights."

"You always do, Charlie," the string bean complained.

"I'm the group leader, right? Besides, we're scheduled for conditioning exercises now."

Spurred by the obvious interest of the men, an odd assortment of
women directed attention to the newcomer who now stood uncomfortably alongside Simpson in the center of the sun-drenched circular
yard.

"This is Marie," Simpson introduced. "She's looking for a man."

One of the women, an overweight brunette with dyed blonde hair,
snickered. "So are we."

Two of the women put down their pipes and assessed Marie, as the
woman agent counted bodies. Seven women was her tally, and soon all
were standing except a listless appearing redhead who remained reclined on her side on an oversized air mattress while continuing to puff
on her pipe.

"That's Julie," Simpson informed Marie. "I'll introduce her after our afternoon exercise."

"Can't I just talk to her now and get out of your hair?"

Simpson released a slight smirk. "Can't interrupt our camp routine. Our guests could get upset. It won't take long, and it's really very beneficial—great conditioning."

"For what?" she made the mistake of asking.

Simpson's eyes twinkled and he glanced at the large air mattress dominating the platform. "For our worship service. We glorify the function of the human body."

Marie's stomach muscles flexed. *Good Lord, this is worse than I thought. I must have stumbled into some weird sex cult.*

"All right," Simpson ordered, "form the usual circle and follow me."

Marie watched with fascination as the sun worshipers complied, men and women alternating places and grasping their neighbor's hands as Simpson ascended the stage. When he reached the center everyone raised their hands skyward and shouted "Sun Goddess!"

One totally kinky ring, Marie concluded as she surveyed the collection of unattractive bodies that began to perform basic limbering up exercises under the direction of Simpson. The men seemed to range in age from thirty to fifty, and the women at a slightly younger average. Upper-body silicone enhancement appeared to be a standard feature of the women, with one exception, a thin, mannish-figured brunette with a butch haircut who hovered protectively close to Julie.

When the group completed a series of routine exercises, Simpson descended the stage and called out, "Now it's time to concentrate on spiritual uplifting. Think of your innermost desires," he said, picking up a large plastic bottle and dispensing a palmful of liquid into his hand. He then proceeded to slowly rub it over his body in a sensual manner, pausing periodically as he gazed up at the sun. "Oh spirit of life," he chanted as he moved from one guest to another and dispensed a portion of liquid that Marie thought smelled like coconut oil. As each participant rubbed the oil over their bodies they gazed up, chanting, "Glorify us, oh mighty Sun Goddess."

Turning, they slowly oiled each other's backs with lingering hands that caressed, cupped, and stroked.

Watching bug-eyed, Marie was transfixed by the pervasive eroticism of the event, not surprised to see its effect on the men who were evidencing pronounced states of arousal.

"Time for private contemplation," Simpson declared, watching the men grasp the hand of a nearby woman and hurry toward the surrounding cabins. Julie seemed to be the subject of a tug of war between Simpson and the mannish-looking woman, who eventually surrendered and rushed off with a squat blonde with bulging hips.

As Simpson and Julie stood together, glistening with body oil, he held out the bottle to Marie. "How about some. We can make it a threesome."

Marie couldn't ignore his aroused condition and was ready to reach into her purse when Julie's glazed eyes abruptly closed and she slumped to the ground.

"Damn," Simpson muttered, making no move to aid the crumpled body. "I told her not to smoke so much. She'll probably be out for an hour."

"Shouldn't you do something to help her?" Marie asked.

"Nothing to do," Simpson shrugged. "Happens all the time. She'll be ready to go when she wakes up." His eyes again scanned Marie's body. "Guess it's just you and me now. And since it's my camp, it's my rules." He reached for the oil bottle. "I think you'll enjoy some of this oil, and I'll be pleased to do the honors. Then I'll enjoy the pleasure of initiating you into the membership of Sunnyglow Slopes. He nodded toward the large air mattress and began to pour from the bottle.

Show time, Marie decided, winking at Simpson. "If we're going to do what I think you're suggesting, I'll need some protection. It's right here in my purse."

Simpson nodded eagerly, his anticipation visibly rising as he watched her open her purse.

"Here it is," Marie announced drawing her Glock and leveling it at the startled man. "All a girl needs. And I respectfully decline membership in Sunnyglow Slopes."

Simpson's ego and protuberance deflated simultaneously.

Chapter Twenty-two

Kerry's torrent of tears gradually subsided after several minutes of body-wracking expiation. Del felt dampness on his bare shoulder where Kerry's face rested, as she clung to him like a frightened child. Occasional sobs now emerged, and her body periodically shifted in cocoon-like adjustment to his reassuring embrace. When she squirmed again and sighed contentedly, he realized he was sweating. He pondered the relative merits of the cover that separated them.

Finally, raising her head from his warm shoulder, she drilled red-ringed, dark brown eyes into his. "You're so kind and gentle," she breathed, before attaching her moist lips in a lingering kiss.

His response was no less spirited, with a prolonged encore that seemed to him like the natural thing to do.

"Whew," she finally sighed. "You sure know how to comfort a girl."

Flush-faced, Del managed a slight grin. "Truly my pleasure, even if I should probably feel ashamed of taking advantage of you at a vulnerable time."

She stretched with feline grace and settled back in his welcoming grasp, tracing her fingers lightly over his face. "You didn't take advantage of me. I crawled onto the bed with you, if you recall, and you've been just wonderful." She hugged him tightly and kissed him again before standing up. "I think I'm cured, sort of."

He smiled at his disheveled hostess. "It may sound very self-serving, but I'm more than happy to help you work out your problems. You're a kind and lovely lady, and, for the record, one hell of a kisser."

Kerry's drying eyes simmered. "Takes two to tango, and I return the compliment." She looked at her reclining patient. "Hope I didn't mess up the splint. I'd better check."

"I think it's okay," Del began to assure as Kerry lifted the blanket.

"Oh my," Kerry blinked, quickly dropping the blanket that settled unevenly over his body. "The splint looks fine," she stammered.

Del blushed. "Sorry, couldn't help it. It just happens sometimes. I'm only human, you know."

Kerry gulped. "Yes, I know. <u>Very</u> human. I'd better make us some lunch."

Del nodded. "Good idea, give us energy to tackle your problems."

"Some of them, anyway," Kerry murmured.

***

Malloy was slowly traversing the paved narrow country road that his wife was known to have followed. He had turned off on several side trails that led to small, unoccupied cabins, with no sight of her car. He had also passed by one washed-out side road, and one that had a chain crossing it. He continued his search, growing increasingly apprehensive as the hours passed and he fell steadily behind in his promise to meet his associates at the mountain store where the phone call had originated. Marie and I will join you shortly was the phrase racing through his mind with accelerating grimness. I should have been with her, he ruminated, again passing the chained entranceway.

***

"He wasn't much help," the acting search coordinator addressed his colleagues as they gathered in the gloomy atmosphere outside Ben's General Store in a tiny mountain community near Echo Lake, California.

"I'm amazed he even remembered seeing a good looking young woman about the time of the call," another agent observed, "the way he had his eyes glued to that TV screen."

"He did mention an old couple also in the store about the same time," the coordinator reminded.

"Right, but Ginny in the office said the caller's voice sounded young, and she's rarely off the mark," his associate observed. "She's had special training in voice identification."

"In any event," the coordinator pursued, "this is our starting point, so we spread out from here. Mike should be along shortly, as soon as he locates Marie. Meanwhile, let's start looking. We have limited descriptions of the young gal and the old couple, plus damned little info on the vehicles—an old tan pickup and a maroon Jeep. Guess we should be happy old Ben tore himself away from his soap long enough to glance out the window briefly."

"Yeah," one of the searchers laughed. "I damned near choked when he said old Ben would never become a slave to TV."

Chapter Twenty-three

Charlie Simpson's mouth gaped open. "You said you weren't a cop! What are you doing with that gun?"

"I'm not a cop, Charlie, but I am an FBI Agent, and you came dangerously close to assaulting a Federal officer. That's 20 years in the slammer, as the old pros like to say."

"I didn't do anything."

She tilted the gun barrel downward. "I do believe you were planning to."

"It would have been sequential."

"I believe you mean consensual, and it sure as hell wouldn't have been. I declined the 'honor,' remember?"

"Well, whatever the word is, you don't know what ya missed," he snickered with returning bravado.

"I think I can live happily without the knowledge. Now, let's cut the crap. I'm here to talk to Julie as soon as she wakes up and then I'm on my way. No further trouble from you and I might forget checking out what your lovely guests were smoking. Do I make myself clear?"

Simpson looked again at Marie's pistol. "Yeah, it's clear, but I still think we could have had fun."

"Guess it's my loss then, eh Charlie?" She shifted her gaze briefly at the surrounding cabins. "How long are your guests engaged in their, ah, 'private contemplation'?"

Simpson smirked. "Varies. Five minutes for some, an hour or more for others. I hold all the records. Sure you don't want to change your mind?" he asked, taking a step toward her.

"Hold it!" Marie ordered in an authoritative voice, aiming the gun meaningfully. "One more step and the only record you'll hold is being the only prick around here without one."

Simpson stopped. "Geez, take it easy. Those things are dangerous."

"My point, exactly, Charlie. Are any of those cabins vacant?"

"Yeah, mine."

"How about Julie's?"

"She's rooming with me."

"Cozy. Okay, pick her up and carry her into your cabin. And no funny stuff."

As they passed some of the cabins a variety of muffled moans, yelps and giggles could be heard. "Enlightenment exercises," Simpson grinned, pushing open a heavy plank door with Julie's dangling feet. "Where do you want her?"

Marie's eyes scanned the rustically furnished cabin, settling on a large waterbed dominating the center of the room. "Right there," she ordered, watching as Simpson flopped Julie face down on the undulating mattress. She was about to remonstrate against the rough treatment when Simpson suddenly pivoted on his feet and leaped from his crouch, slamming his right forearm against the side of Marie's head. Caught unaware, she dropped her gun and toppled to the wooden floor.

"Ha! You should have paid more attention to my conditioning exercises," he gloated, seizing the automatic and pointing it at the stunned woman. "Who's in charge of things now, Ms. FBI?"

Still groggy from the blow, Marie looked up from the floor. "Don't make things worse for yourself. You're now obstructing justice, in addition to assault."

"You're a laugh, girlie. I've got the gun and you haven't begun to feel the assault I'm going to provide." His eyes glowed. "This is going to be a double-header afternoon. You now, and Julie when she wakes up. Hop up on the bed."

Marie began to slowly comply while assessing her options when voices were heard from outside. "Charlie," a female voice called, "it's time for the exchange."

He grinned at Marie. "See, we share things here. Our members are very democratic." His urgings for democracy were becoming evident.

When the voice called his name again, Simpson moved toward the door. "Wait here," he ordered. "Maybe you'll both be ready when I finish ministering to the flock."

As he exited, Marie heard the loud thud of a dead-bolt sliding home. She looked around at the windowless room, lighted from above by a small skylight, then at the unconscious woman sprawled on the waterbed. She tested the door and found it immovable. Resting dejected on one of the two cabin chairs, Marie tried to recall when she had experienced a worse day. Her spirits brightened when she remembered the small cell phone she had stuffed in her purse that morning.

Extracting the instrument and punching in a number, she smiled broadly. Better days ahead, Charlie.

***

"I still don't know why you wanted to come through the middle of the damn city," Sulfur Sal groused as they inched along in heavy downtown traffic in Salt Lake City.

"Cause I wanted to see the Temple," Loose Louie replied. "I'm thinking of becoming a Mormon."

"Shit," Sulfur Sal sneered, "why the fuck you want to be a Mormon?"

Loose Louie replied, "I hear you can have all the wives you want. Keep giving 'em kids and they do all the work. It's a great deal. That's why."

"You sure about that?"

"Hell yeah, I heard Dom talking about it in the restaurant one night. Look at all those good looking broads out there. Just waiting for a man."

"They do look pretty good," Sulfur Sal agreed, surveying the crowded sidewalks. "Do ya need an application or something?"

"Don't know. Thought I'd ask at the Temple. They probably keep a supply of broads waiting there to try out. That's it right ahead. Let's pull over."

"There's no place to park."

"Right there," Loose Louie pointed.

"There's a fire plug there," Sulfur Sal noted.

"Do you see a cop around, Sal?"

"Well, no."

"They don't have 'em out here. No crime. It's like a giant commune. No rules, just a lot of screwing. A huge supply of women." He opened the door.

"Wait a minute," Sulfur Sal said, turning off the engine. "I'm coming with you."

***

Sulfur Sal appeared ready to practice his specialty on his brooding cohort as they left the auto impound lot of the Salt Lake City Police Department. "You stupid fuck! You almost got us arrested! We were lucky to get the fuckin car back!"

"They ain't very friendly to visitors," Loose Louie muttered. "Three hundred bucks, and the tow truck put a scrape on Nicky's front bumper."

"Nicky's going to put a major scrape on you if he finds out, you dumb shit. 'Oh, don't bother about the fire plug. No cops around.' I gotta be a idiot to listen to you."

"Guess I got some bad info back East, Sal. Ya won't tell Nicky, will ya?"

Sulfur Sal looked with contempt at his partner. "He'd have me whacked for going along with you. I never shoulda listened."

"You already said that, Sal. Okay, I made one mistake. I'm sorry."

"One mistake!" Sulfur Sal exploded, almost swerving into a parked police car as they exited the fenced yard on the outskirts of town. "What about your great Temple idea? 'Full of waiting broads' and all that shit? We find one old guy in a black suit at the entrance who laughs like hell when you ask him for an application for a bunch of wives."

"Maybe they keep them in the back for themselves," Loose Louie proposed weakly.

"You don't listen, do ya? The guy said that poly stuff was outlawed years ago."

Loose Louie continued to pout. "Guess Dom had some bad info."

Sulfur Sal snorted. "Dom ain't had good info since his mother dropped him on his head when he was a baby. I didn't know you were talking about <u>that</u> Dom. Geez, you're almost as bad as he is."

Loose Louie decided to pursue a less touchy subject. "What we going to do now, Sal?"

"Now we do what we were sent to do. Find the broad, get the book, and whack her. One, two, three."

"Yeah, we can do that, and we're getting close."

"We also lost four hours screwing around on your great idea. We should be in Nevada by now."

"We go through Reno, don't we, Sal?"

"Yeah, why?"

"Don't they have all them casinos with the big payoffs there?"

"They're just like Atlantic City."

"No, Sal, I heard it for a fact. They pay off big to attract all the rich fags from California."

Sulfur Sal shot his partner a look of disdain. "Hear that from Dom too?"

"No, I got it from a real good source, a dealer at Trump's place in Atlantic City. He's worked in Nevada, too, and swears it's true."

"And what are we going to use for money, smartass?"

Loose Louie released a knowing look. "How much we got left from Nicky's stake?"

Sulfur Sal almost lost control of the speeding Lincoln again. "You crazy? Nicky would kill us if we lost it."

"I tell ya, Sal, we can't lose. The guy I told ya about gave me a fool-proof system only the dealers know. It's for roulette, and I got it written down. We make up the money you spent on that hooker, the traffic fine, and the tow-away charges, and make a little extra to finance a good night in Reno. Don't you think we need a night off?"

"But what if we lose?"

"Can't," Loose Louie said, extracting a small folded note from his pocket and reading from it: "Start with $50, alternate red and black and change numbers every other spin. Double the bet every time you win. Match the bet when you occasionally lose to make it look legit. Subtract two numbers from each win for your next bet number and stop when you win $50,000 or they'll get suspicious. That's it. Guaranteed to work every time," Loose Louie concluded with a satisfied smile. "All our problems solved, and we got extra money to play around with, like entertain some of them long-legged showgirls with the bare tits."

Sulfur Sal narrowed his eyes in deep thought. "You say this system is guaranteed to work?"

"Absolutely. We'll have more money than we can count."

"I don't know, sounds kinda risky, Louie."

"Guy told me about it drives a big Mercedes, Sal, and has so many broads chasing him he had to get an unlisted number."

"Lots of broads, huh?"

"Yeah, like those long-legged showgirls in Reno. The ones with the big, bare, tits. They love winners."

Sulfur Sal nodded. "We do have to go through Reno, I guess."

"Yeah, and we've made good time. We keep rolling like this and we can be there early in the morning. We check into a fancy hotel, get cleaned up, make a bundle in the casino, select our playmates and celebrate with champagne and a good lay and be on our way."

"Does sound kinda good, Louie. Sure it'll work?"

"Can't lose, Sal."

Chapter Twenty-four

"Your cooking is better than ever, if that's possible," Del congratulated as he finished the veal piccata and took another sip of wine.

Kerry smiled. "You must be hungry, or you haven't been very well taken care of." She paused, "You married or something? I didn't see a ring."

Del looked at his left hand. "No, never been married, but I . . ."

"Me neither," Kerry broke in, a look of sadness replacing her smile. "I was about to be married when Jeff was killed, along with my dad, by the bastards who are looking for the book. By the way, where is it? Isn't it time to get that settled?"

Del leaned back on the plumped-up pillows. "I agree, but first tell me about Jeff, and what happened to him and your dad. It'll help clarify the significance of the book."

Del listened quietly while Kerry tearfully recounted the events of the murderous night and her flight from New York.

"Jeff was a gentle, fun-loving guy who had just finished college. I was taking art classes at the Pratt Institute when we met. I love to paint. That's what I was doing when you jumped into my life. Jeff helped pay his way through school drumming with our band. He was good. Very good. Old timers said he sounded like Gene Krupa. We fell in love, and were about to be married. It was serious, and we began living together." She paused. "People in love often do that these days." A smile of memory surfaced. "He was a great lover, too."

A wistful look reappeared. "We had just returned home from our nightly gig when my father unexpectedly knocked on our door. He looked nervous, and almost frantic—kept looking around behind him. He said he had something he needed to hide in a safe place, and handed me a small briefcase. I was wondering what was going on when two husky men appeared. They must have been following him. They shouted something and shot him. I'll never forget the sounds. I felt paralyzed with shock and fear. Jeff pushed me into the bedroom and told me to run. He went back to confront the hoods. While I was fleeing down the rear fire escape, I heard more gunshots. The bastards shot and killed my Jeff. Terrified, I escaped in a cab to my Aunt Agnes' apartment, where she gave me refuge and money to hide out here in her cabin."

"You're a brave woman," Del said when she finished. "And I'd like to meet your Aunt Agnes. She sounds like a real trooper." He looked around. "She also had good taste in mountain cabins, and favorite nieces."

Kerry looked pleased. "Only niece."

"A special person to whom I owe a lot."

Kerry shook her head. "No, nothing special, just a girl trying to survive. But that brings us to the book now, doesn't it? Where is it?"

Del grinned. "Closer than you think. You were right on top of it a little while ago. It's under the mattress. Take this plate, I'll roll on my side and you can pull it out."

Kerry jumped up eagerly from her bedside chair.

Del wondered why he hadn't mentioned Anna. *Maybe I'll get the chance later.*

✱✱✱

Marie waited impatiently while the number of the command center rang several times before the answering machine clicked in. Damn, was her reaction when the message beep sounded about the same time Julie started to stir on the waterbed. "It's Marie," she whispered into her cell phone. "I'm being held captive at a nudist camp called Sunnyglow Slopes off the main road in my search zone. Chain across drive-way. My car is around the corner. Hurry," she concluded, watching Julie turn face up just as Marie disconnected and thrust the phone back in her purse.

"Who you talking to?" Julie slurred, her glazed eyes blinking open.

"You," Marie replied. "I've been talking to you, trying to wake you up."

"Who in hell are you? I don't remember seeing you before."

"We kind of met before you passed out. I think you were on a flight."

Julie tried to focus her eyes. "Christ, I got a headache. What did you say your name is?"

"Marie. Marie Stanley. I'm an FBI Agent looking for a friend you may have seen parachuting out of a plane."

Julie looked at Marie intently. "FBI Agent? Didn't know they had such good looking ones. You've got a great body, too. You straight?"

Marie nodded. "Straight as they come, with a great husband."

"What ya doing here then? All they have here is a bunch of pee wees."

"I noticed, but like I said, I'm looking for a lost friend. Here's his picture."

Julie's eyes widened when she studied the photograph. "I'd of re-membered him if I'd seen him. He looks like a real stud. No wonder you're looking for him. Is he good?"

"Yes, he's a good man."

"That's not what I meant."

"Yeah, I know what you meant. The answer is that he's a friend – just a friend. Charlie said you saw something falling out of the sky. Could it have been him?"

"Sure wish it was," Julie said with a laugh. "I sure as hell wouldn't be here talking to you." She scanned Marie's body again. "Sure you're straight? Not AC-DC?"

"Straight DC, Julie. Do you remember what you saw fall from the sky?"

Julie's eyes closed momentarily. "I see all kinds of things when I'm smoking. Horses, dragons, pianos, race cars, cash registers – you name it, I've seen everything."

Marie's spirits plunged. "Just hallucinations then?"

"Guess so. That's what my shrink thinks. Says I should stop smoking." Her melancholy look became puzzled. "Is that all you wanted to know? And why are you and I alone here? Where's Charlie?"

"Some woman called him out for 'the exchange'."

Julie grinned. "He'll be back after he pops a pill. He initiate you yet?"

"I declined the invitation, and he's in big trouble for holding me against my will. We're locked in this place."

"No shit? He must want you bad." She moved closer. "I can see why. Sure you don't want to get it on while we're waiting?" She reached out to touch Marie.

Marie stepped back. "One hand on me and you get charged with assaulting a Federal Officer. You can see a lot of stuff falling out of the sky in a Federal pen. So back off."

"Okay, you don't need to get bitchy. I was just asking. You might enjoy it."

"I'll enjoy getting out of this loony bin, dearie. The sooner, the better."

The sound of a sliding dead bolt turned their heads toward the cabin door.

Chapter Twenty-five

Assistant Special Agent in Charge Phil Whitman was shaking his head in disbelief as he peered out of the fog-shrouded fifteenth-floor window of his FBI San Francisco office. "That area sounds like the Bermuda Triangle, Mike. Two agents disappearing without a trace. What in hell is going on?"

Malloy's voice on the speaker-phone sounded worried. "Del's disappearance is somewhat understandable, but Marie's doesn't make sense. I've got to go to the command post and meet Del's fiancée, Anna, and then I'm going back to the area where Marie was supposed to be. I need to double-check the maps, too, to see if I missed something. The rest of the troops have relocated to Echo Summit." Malloy's voice conveyed his concern.

"She'll be okay," Whitman said encouragingly. "You know how resourceful she is."

"That's what I keep telling myself, Phil."

"Keep me posted, Mike, and yell if you need more help."

"I'll find her," Malloy vowed, terminating the call.

***

Kerry's chair abutted Del's mattress, and their heads almost touched as they jointly scanned the ledger book of the late Carlo Vita. The bedside lamp blinked periodically as thunder rumbled in the distance, and occasional shafts of lightning flashed outside the bedroom window. "One of those mountain storms," Kerry observed. "Loud and kind of scary. I'm glad you're here."

"Me too," Del replied, gently stroking Kerry's smooth cheek with the back of his hand before redirecting attention to the brown leather book. They spoke little as Del slowly turned the pages, waiting for Kerry's nod before proceeding. When they reached the last completed page, bearing a date just before the murders, their questioning eyes met. "What does it all mean, Del?"

"It's pretty clear. Mob payoff records to politicians, and debts owed by a variety of prominent people, probably for gambling losses or drug purchases. Heavy duty, to say the least, and something they'll do anything to get back. You're correct to be worried about your safety."

"Now you can understand why I feared you might have been sent by the mob."

Del smiled gently. "They're dangerous and merciless, but they're not that smart. As far as I know, they don't have a parachute hit squad. But I don't underestimate their persistence. I'm sure they're looking like hell for you and the book."

"So what do we do?"

"Get ready for the worst, and get word to my office. We need to get the book into the Bureau's hands."

"That's what my Aunt Agnes recommended."

"She's a smart woman," Del agreed.

The storm outside seemed to move closer, the cabin lights blinking with more frequency.

Del looked serious. "I need you to call my office again and let them know where I am. We can also turn over the book. It's really important, and not possessing it will provide more safety for you."

"I feel safe with you, but I know what you mean."

A downpour of rain suddenly hammered on the roof, prompting Del to look up. "Hope it misses the bullet hole."

Wind gusts were now buffeting the cabin, wailing sounds whistling through the nearby trees whose limbs brushed the cabin's roof and sides. A nearby lightning strike momentarily blacked out the lights, which fluttered back on after a few seconds.

"Rough out there, Kerry. Hope it clears tomorrow so you can go and make the call."

Kerry looked guilty. "I have a confession. My phone isn't broken."

"What!?"

"I didn't want the mob to trace any calls here. But now that I know you can be trusted, and that the FBI will come to help, you can call your office yourself. I'll go get the phone."

Del's look of surprise faded into a bemused smile. "Kerry, I don't know whether to spank you or kiss you."

Kerry smiled back. "Since there's a choice, how about a kiss? That might help me find the phone faster."

"You make that decision easy," Del said, spreading his arms.

The kiss was long and tender. Del decided that there was really not that much of a hurry to place the call. Kerry's reaction was so stimulating that she hardly noticed the loud clap of thunder that accompanied the nearby bolt of lightning, the one that extinguished the lights.

Chapter Twenty-six

Anna Chen was waiting at the command post when Malloy returned from his futile search. The slender Amerasian beauty, with long, glistening black hair, rushed into his embrace. "It's so good to be here," she said, hugging him. "Any news? The nice men who flew me in from San Francisco said they hadn't heard anything."

Malloy sighed. "They were partly right, Anna, but we're checking out a lead just across the state line in California that looks good. I don't want to raise false hopes, but a woman called the office and said he is okay. Unfortunately she didn't reveal his location, but the search party is concentrating on the area where the call originated. It looks promising, but we still haven't found him."

Anna squealed joyously. "I'm so excited. Just to know he's alive."

"We still haven't found him," Malloy reiterated.

"Is that why you look so grim, Mike? I thought you'd be thrilled too."

"Oh, I am, but another problem has popped up—Marie is missing now too."

"Oh my Lord, what happened?"

"She was out looking for Del this morning. We decided to split up to cover more ground, and she just seemed to disappear. No radio message or anything. I just came back from the sector she was supposed to be in – nothing."

"Oh, Mike, I feel terrible, and if something happened to her while she was searching for Del, I don't know what I'd do."

"Hope and pray right now, Anna. They are both survivors, you know."

"What can I do to help? There must be something. Marie is such a special person. She helped me when I needed it—gave me shelter at Virginia Beach when those atomic bomb smugglers were trying to have me killed. I owe her a lot."

"She'll be all right," Malloy said with little conviction in his voice before noticing the blinking red light of the answering machine. "Damn," he muttered, pressing the message button. "I should have checked that as soon as I came in." Both held their breaths as they listened to Marie's whispered message.

"You're a good luck charm, Anna," Malloy proclaimed as he replayed the message and jotted down notes. "Chain across the driveway," he repeated, suddenly remembering seeing such a side road. "Hell, I think I went right by it. It could be the place. 'Sunnyglow Slopes?' Don't recall seeing any such sign," he mumbled. "Probably going too fast."

Anna looked on with a broad smile, watching Malloy's surge of spirits. "Well, what are we waiting for?" she asked. "Let's get going!"

Malloy hesitated only a few seconds as he considered the Bureau prohibition against involving non-FBI personnel in an official operation. "Anna, you are hereby deputized as a special FBI operative and invited to accompany me to a nudist camp."

"Best offer I've had all day," she giggled, following his fast-moving form toward the Bureau car.

✷✷✷

Mary Agnes O'Brien nervously paced the oriental carpet in her Queens' apartment, looking again at the phone she had just put down on the coffee table after her second, futile try. The silent line elevated the feeling of concern that had been bothering her all day. *She hasn't called me, and now I can't get an answer. Something must be wrong.*

Could those monsters have found her? She looked at the mantle clock. Nine PM. *I've got to do something.*

With business-like proficiency, the former nun telephoned her school administrator and secured an emergency leave of absence, while simultaneously packing a suitcase. Minutes later she was talking with an airline reservations clerk who was happy to fill a last-minute over-priced coach seat on an early morning flight. Her next step was to notify the building superintendent that she would be gone indefinitely. She paused. *He is such a nice man, maybe I should tell him in person.*

***

Henry Wilhelm was tuned into his favorite sports channel when he heard a knock on his apartment door. Formerly a source of irritation, late-night tenant requests were now almost welcome since the death of his wife the previous year. When he opened the door the sense of welcome surged. "Well hello, Ms. O'Brien. Do you have a problem of some kind? All you had to do was call and I would have taken care of it immediately."

"Well I may have a problem, but it has nothing to do with the building. Ah, may I come in? I'd rather not talk about it in the hall."

"Oh, certainly, Ms. O'Brien. Excuse my poor manners," he apologized, stepping out of the doorway. "I'm not used to being visited by such a special lady."

Mary Agnes blushed. "You are such a gentleman, Henry, and my name is Mary, or Mary Agnes, as you prefer."

He smiled. "Mary was my mother's name, God rest her soul. A beautiful name. Won't you sit down," he invited, clicking off the TV and pointing to an upholstered side chair. "Excuse the clutter. I guess it's a classic bachelor's pad now, since Nora passed on."

"That was a great loss, Henry. I know how much she meant to you."

"She thought you were pretty classy too, and would have been happy to know that you attended the funeral. Thank you."

"Remember the good times, Henry. You'll see her again."

Wilhelm brightened. "That's what she promised near the end. But tell me what the problem is, and how I can help."

"Well, to make a long story short, I need to take an emergency trip out west, and I wanted you to know I would be away."

Wilhelm's instincts as a twenty-year precinct sergeant with the New York City Police Department surfaced like a ballistic sub. "Why don't you tell me the long story? I sense trouble."

She nodded. "Remember those two men who visited me last week?"

Wilhelm frowned. "Mafiosa. They bothering you again?"

"Well, I'm not sure. Let me tell you about my niece."

Wilhelm listened attentively while his tenant related the story of the murders, the book, and Kerry's flight. "Now I haven't heard from her, and her phone is dead. I'm afraid they may have somehow found where she is. I'm very worried."

Wilhelm nodded agreement. "You have a right to be. Those people aren't nice, but no offense, I'm not sure what a genteel lady can do against them. The Feds should be notified."

"That's what I've been telling Kerry, but she's kind of stubborn – part Irish, you know."

"I don't think you should go out there by yourself."

"Oh, I'm going all right. I'm full Irish, you know. Talk about stubborn."

Wilhelm smiled. "You're not going alone. I'm going with you."

"But Henry, you have to run the building here and everything. I couldn't ask you to do that."

"I've got vacation time built up, my nephew can handle things here till I get back, and I've always wanted to visit California. I'm going."

"But, Henry."

"Shush please, Mary Agnes. I'm full German, by the way. You want to talk stubborn!"

A few minutes later the airline reservation clerk was delighted to sell the last available seat on flight 629.

Chapter Twenty-seven

Charlie Simpson displayed a satisfied grin on his gaunt face as he reentered the cabin. "I see you're both awake—couldn't wait, could you?" He waved Marie's gun ominously. "Who's first?"

Julie spoke up. "She says she's a G-girl, or something, and will put us in jail if anyone touches her."

"Ha, who's got the gun? She can't do a damned thing except what we tell her to do. We do what we want, and then we let her go. She's trespassing anyway."

Marie interrupted. "I'm not trespassing. You invited me onto the property and that's when things started to go downhill for you. Guess you're too stupid to know how much trouble you're in. Kidnapping's a capital offense, you know."

Julie blinked. "What's a capital offense?"

"Death," Marie enunciated in as emphatic a voice as she could muster. "Lethal injection, electric chair, even hanging in some jurisdictions."

"Jesus!" Julie shouted. "Hanging?"

Marie nodded solemnly. "By the neck. You won't be smoking, dangling at the end of a rope."

"Kee – ryst, Charlie, what have you gotten us into?"

"Calm down, Julie, she's just bluffing. It's all bullshit. She probably ain't even an FBI'er. Just a nosy reporter or something come to spy on us."

Marie was about to suggest they check the credentials in her purse when she remembered her cell phone.

"You got some identification?" Simpson demanded.

Marie remained silent, staring back at the two bronzed bodies that hovered like hungry vultures.

Simpson snorted, "See, I told you she's bluffing. Too good looking to be a cop anyway. I guessed that right from the start. I think she's really looking for some action, and is just too bashful to admit it."

"She does look pretty good," Julie agreed. "I already told her that."

"Well, maybe we should just welcome her properly to Sunnyglow Slopes. She ain't been initiated yet."

Marie felt like she was on an auction block. Her level of apprehension increased when she couldn't avoid noticing Simpson's growing state of arousal.

Julie's face was also becoming flush. "Don't the camp rules require that she be initiated in front of everyone?"

He winked at the natural redhead, who had begun to slowly run her hands over her body. "We make the rules, and there are always exceptions. Besides, with just the two of us here, it's her word against ours. We can have some real fun."

Julie was now stroking herself. "Then I can have a smoke, Charlie?"

His gleaming eyes ravished the stunning body of his nude captive. "Help me, and you can have some of the good stuff."

They both advanced on the alarmed woman agent.

✴✴✴

"Pretty nifty, huh?" Loose Louie queried his partner as they strolled through the crowded gaming rooms of one of Reno's newest casinos. "Look at all the broads."

Sulfur Sal squinted. "All's I see is a lot of blue-haired grandmothers swarming around the slot machines."

"You're looking in the wrong direction," Loose Louie countered. "Look at the babes in tight blouses and short skirts serving drinks."

Sulfur Sal squinted harder. "They look kinda old to me. Where's the young long-legged, bare-titted show girls?"

"They don't mingle out here, dummy. They save themselves for big rollers like us, in what they call 'the privacy of our room.' Soon's we get our tokens, we start playing. Did ya see the size of the beds in our rooms? It won't be long we'll be bouncing off 'em like beach balls."

"I don't know, Louie. I'm wondering if this is a good idea after all."

"Oh, for Christ's sake, Sal, we already agreed we'd get rich and have some fun. Why ya getting chicken now?"

"Well, I'm worried we might lose. Nicky will whack us for sure."

"Jesus, Sal, I told you the system is foolproof. We can't lose. Come on, let's get a grand in chips. That's all we'll need to get the flow going, and then we're on our way."

"Well, if you're sure, Louie. I'd sure like to see some action with them show girls."

"Hey, Sal, in thirty minutes you'll be calling me a genius."

Chapter Twenty-eight

"What happened to the lights?" Kerry asked in a worried tone when the bedside lamp didn't blink back on after a minute or two.

"Well, you either didn't pay the bill, or that last lightning bolt knocked out the power," Del replied lightheartedly.

"You don't sound very concerned."

"Guess I realize there's not a heck of a lot we can do about it. Imagine it happens frequently up here. And that's quite a storm out there. Do you have candles?"

"Yes, I saw lots of them scattered about the place. You're probably right about the frequent outages. They even happen in New York City occasionally."

"Now that's a chilling thought, New York City without power. Wonder what the crime surge would be."

Kerry grinned. "I think you've finally convinced me that you're in law enforcement. Who else would think of something like that?"

Del chuckled, "A crook."

"Oh, Lord, just when I was feeling more secure with you."

Del tried to sound reassuring. "I'm sorry. Just a smart-aleck Connecticut Yankee pulling your chain."

"Connecticut? You didn't mention that before."

"There's a lot of things we don't know about each other. Kind of nice to find out, though."

"So, what would you like to know about me?

"I'm curious about people's first names. Yours is vibrant, and a perfect fit."

"Kerry?" she said with a laugh. "That's easy. My Irish mother, Kathleen O'Brien, wanted to contribute a touch of the old country-where her ancestors originated—County Kerry. When I was old enough to understand, she explained that County Kerry means the land of the descendants of Ciar, who was the love-child of the High King Fergus Mac Roth and legendary Queen Meabh. Pretty regal, huh? And, she told me, Ciar means dark, implying dark hair and brown eyes. That's probably more than you expected."

"No, it's intriguing, and describes you elegantly—black hair, brown eyes, and a queenly appearance."

"There goes that blarney again. You must have some Irish too."

"About a quarter, I'm told."

"Del doesn't sound Irish. Delmar? Delmont?"

"No, Delbert. Old family name. I was named after my grandfather, who was quite a legend."

"Did he parachute into trees too?"

Del grinned. "No, his fame came from being a Texas Ranger."

"Wow. That's impressive. A Texas Ranger. Why didn't they call you Tex?"

"Maybe because he moved to Connecticut. Glad my folks didn't name me Con."

"Texas to Connecticut is quite a distance."

"There was a reason, but I must be boring you."

"Oh, no. You tell a great story, and I like to hear your voice. Please, go on."

"Well, granddad was an excellent shot, and back when J. Edgar Hoover and his small group of agents were shooting it out with guys like John Dillinger and Pretty Boy Floyd, they needed some additional sharpshooters, and hired a number of Rangers as Special Agents, including Delbert Houston Dickerson. When the gang wars ended in the

Midwest, he was transferred to New Haven with his family, and that's how I happened to be born in Connecticut.

"That's really fascinating. You seem to have inherited some of your grandfather's traits."

"Guess so. From what I've heard, he was always at the scene of action. He whetted my appetite for law enforcement with his stories about the FBI. Granddad led a vigorous life for 93 years. One of a kind."

"Sounds more like you're two peas in a pod."

"Could be," Del said with a smile. "He also had a keen appreciation for lovely women."

"There you go again," Kerry said. "Can you ever turn it off?"

"What?"

"Your damned charm! Don't you realize what effect you have on women?"

"What do you mean?"

"That's it! You don't have a clue. Let's get back to reality."

"Whatever you say, Kerry, the Queen."

"Ohh, you are too much. What are we going to do now? You were getting ready to call your office. Tell them to send PG&E while you're at it."

"No power means no phone either. We're back to square one."

"Damn," Kerry sighed. "Just you and me against the world, eh?"

He reached out to her hand, finding it in the dark. "I have confidence in us. Let's get organized. Before you light some candles, tell me what our heat and cooking sources are."

Standing up, Kerry stumbled against the bed and was kept from falling by Del's muscular arms. "Cripes, can't see a damned thing. Thanks for the catch. Do you always have women falling into your arms?"

Del continued to hold her. "Not like you," he replied, squeezing her arms gently before releasing her. "Okay now?"

"Sort of," she replied slowly. "I'll see if we can shed some light on our plight. Hey that's good, light on our plight, I'm a poet."

"You're more than that. I heard you sing. How about a little cheery music while we survive this ordeal?"

"Really? You heard me singing?"

"Yes, when I was first waking up. You sounded beautiful."

"You really think so?"

"Really, even if I'm a captive audience. I'd appreciate anything you'd like to sing."

"Well, guess a little music wouldn't hurt. At least you can't bolt for the door."

"I'm listening, Kerry."

As Del heard Kerry moving cautiously around the darkened room he listened raptly to her pure, lilting voice presenting the words and melody of one of his favorites. *You Don't Bring Me Flowers Anymore* softly filled the air. Neil Diamond would approve, was his sincere assessment.

***

"How much further?" Anna asked, as Malloy piloted the beige Ford around tight curves at breathtaking speed.

"We're about to the place where I saw the chained entrance. It fits the area Marie described. Look closely."

Malloy slowed to permit closer inspection, and hadn't gone a mile when Anna exclaimed, "There! A chain across that trail."

Malloy stopped and backed up, pulling into the entranceway before seeing the small sign, 'Sunnyglow Slopes.' "This is it, Anna. Good eyes. Let's go exploring."

Carrying the 12-gauge Remington shotgun extracted from the car trunk, Malloy led them past the tree-mounted phone. "Surprise visit," he muttered, ignoring the phone.

Turning the first curve of the winding trail, they almost bumped into Marie's car. "No question, now," Malloy said, peering inside the locked vehicle. His eyes widened with alarm. "Her clothes," he said grimly. "Let's go."

∗∗∗

"Thanks," Wilhelm said to the flight attendant who had just engineered a seat exchange that put him next to Mary Agnes.

"Thank that older gentleman up there," the attractive blonde replied. "He said he likes to see husband and wife sit together."

"But we're not married," Wilhelm blurted, his face reddening.

The attendant smiled understandingly. "Well you're certainly a lovely couple," she said, before moving away.

Wilhelm was still blushing when he turned to his seatmate. "I'm sorry. I didn't mean to embarrass you."

She patted his arm and released a reassuring smile. "You needn't apologize. I feel complimented. And I meant to tell you how handsome you look in that blue blazer."

Wilhelm continued to blush, looking intently at the fair-complexioned woman wearing a slightly tailored beige wool dress that complimented her slim figure. "You are a kind lady, Mary Agnes. I'm honored to be with you."

"You sure you aren't part Irish, Henry? I detect traces of blarney."

"No, I'm serious, and I'm glad you agreed to let me accompany you."

"You make me feel very secure, Henry. It's a good feeling. Now let's get some rest. We'll need all our energy when we get there."

Wilhelm nodded and pressed the seat recliner button. Closing his eyes, a hopeful smile emerged as he visualized a variety of experiences with Mary Agnes O'Brien.

Chapter Twenty-nine

"Okay genius, what the fuck we going to do now?" Sulfur Sal screamed. "You've blown almost all the money we got from Nicky. What happened to that fool-proof system?"

"The table had to be rigged," Loose Louie muttered.

"Why didn't you figure that out before you kept buying more chips? Shit, we're in the toilet now."

"Well you have to prime the pump sometimes. I don't know what went wrong."

"What went wrong, you shithead, is that I listened to you in the first place."

"We still got a few hundred, Sal."

"You shouldn't have paid cash for the room—shoulda used one of those phony credit cards."

"Nicky said he didn't want any records," Loose Louie reminded.

"He didn't want a lot of things you did, you dimwit."

"We did, Sal. Ain't we in this together?"

Sulfur Sal slumped on the edge of the bed. "And we ain't got enough for one of them showgirls. What a disaster! What we gonna do?"

Loose Louie continued to look dumbstruck. "Guess all we can do now is make the hit. That'll make Nicky happy. He'll forget about everything else."

"Let's hope so, Louie, and let's get moving. The sooner we finish the job, the sooner we get rid of your shitty ideas. Why did I listen to you? Coulda had one of them long-legged, big-titted showgirls right now with the money you blew."

"That's the breaks, Sal, win some, lose some."

Sulfur Sal's glare was murderous.

Loose Louie grabbed his suitcase and darted for the door.

∗∗∗

"It looks cozy," Del complimented, surveying the array of flickering candles Kerry had placed around the room.

"I also found a couple of small propane lamps in the main room and kitchen," she said. "Guess they lose power a lot up here. We should have plenty of light."

"Good, how about heat?"

"There's a wood-pellet stove in the main room. It's what's been heating us all along. And there's a big supply of pellets," Kerry added. "We're also lucky to have a propane stove."

"Looks like Lady Luck is smiling on us, Kerry. All the comforts of home, plus a great singer. Thanks for the melodies. You do *The Power of Love* better than Celine Dion."

"Knock it off, or I'll start suspecting that you are a con man after all. But thanks anyway. It does a girl good to be flattered."

"It's not flattery when you recognize a special talent."

"I sing from the heart, Del. Gets me into trouble sometimes. But while we're speaking of trouble, I'll leave as soon as it gets light in the morning and call your office. I'll give them your location this time."

"That's a good idea, Kerry. I don't mean to be an alarmist, but after seeing the book I do worry for your welfare. We can use some help."

"Funny, but I don't feel frightened with you here. Maybe I'm too dumb to be worried."

"No, far from dumb. You were smart enough to get out of town fast."

Kerry smiled. "Maybe. Anyway, I was smart enough to pull you out of a tree."

"And drag me here. That took brains and guts. Thanks again."

Kerry studied her chipped, crimson-red fingernails. "You're not bad company, when you're conscious. You talk English. I really wondered when you mumbled in that foreign language when you were out of it."

Del chuckled. "Korean. I can imagine what you were thinking. Did I do anything else strange in my coma?"

Kerry's face flushed, remembering her amazement when detecting his surprising erections. "No," she finally replied, "I guess you were pretty normal." Sensing a growing feeling of stimulation, Kerry changed the subject. "Ready for another one of my kitchen creations?"

"Can't wait. You're superb there, too. A lady with many talents."

"More than you know," she murmured, heading out of the room.

Chapter Thirty

When Simpson tried to push Marie onto the waterbed, she decided it was past time for action. Her sharp kick to his crotch with her sturdy Reeboks was a solid hit that doubled him over and elicited a howl of pain.

"Bitch!" he roared, staggering upright with blazing eyes. Marie's gun remained firmly gripped in his right hand, and he instinctively used it as a club, slamming it against the side of her head.

A stream of blood flowed from the edge of Marie's left eye, as the room went dark and she sagged to the floor.

"Should have shot her," Simpson moaned, hobbling around in pain. "Damn that hurts."

Julie smirked. "I can imagine. Hope there's no permanent damage."

"I'll damage her permanently if there is," he groaned, clutching the traumatized area while glaring at the collapsed body that was beginning to twitch. "Let's tie her up till we decide what to do with her."

"Why don't we let her go? What if she is a cop of some kind? We could be in big trouble."

Simpson shook his head emphatically. "I told you she's bluffing about that. Hell, I should charge her with assault. Look at what she did to me."

Julie ventured a quick glance. "Yeah, bet it does hurt. What do you want me to do?"

"Give me that belt over there and I'll tie her hands behind her back."

As she began to revive, Marie felt her hands being bound, and from her peripheral vision saw the edges of the body behind her. Slamming her head back sharply, she caught Simpson's mouth squarely, prompting another shout of pained rage, and drawing a spurt of blood from his smashed upper lip.

"Shit!" he yelled again, raring back and feeling the blood. "She's a wildcat!" He slapped her viciously across the face and stood up. "I'm going to fix you good, lady," he vowed, kicking her right thigh. "You didn't know when you were well off."

Marie could feel drops of Simpson's blood dampening her shoulder, and felt a stickiness by her injured eye.

Julie stood helplessly. "Geez, Charlie, this is getting bloody."

"Get me a wet cloth," he ordered, pointing to the corner sink. "And bring me that jump rope on the table. I'm going to hog-tie this whore."

"You're adding years to your jail time," Marie warned. "Both of you."

"One more fucking word, and I'll use this goddamned gun," Simpson roared. His outraged tone was convincing. Marie remained silent as she felt her ankles being tied together.

"What now?" Julie asked, holding a damp washcloth over Simpson's mouth.

"She's going to get the full initiation ceremony on the 'Platform of Joy' in front of the entire group," he mumbled. "Me first, then the rest of you. It'll be a day she'll never forget."

Julie's eyes glistened with perverted anticipation. "Let me be second, Charlie."

Lord, Marie prayed, let someone have received my message.

* * *

"Christ!" Sulfur Sal shouted, looking at the black Lincoln propped up on cement blocks and absent its four chrome-plated wheels. "What the fucks gonna happen next?"

"Sonofabitch," Loose Louie agreed, studying the startling sight in the shadows of a dimly lit side street.

"I told ya to park in the hotel garage," Sulfur Sal moaned. "But no, ya said it was safer on a side street."

"Didn't want any more scratches on Nicky's car. He would be pissed."

"Whatcha think he's gonna be when he learns that ya let someone swipe four of his fancy wheels."

Loose Louie gulped again. "He don't hafta know does he?"

"How's he not gonna know, Louie? The fuckin wheels are gone."

"We get some more, Sal. They sell them all over."

"What with, dumbass? You just lost our stash. They're fuckin expensive."

Loose Louie looked morose. "Guess we gotta use one of them credit cards."

"Nicky said to only use cash, shit-for-brains. Doncha remember?"

"Yeah, but this is an emergency. He don't gotta know."

"Godalmighty," Sulfur Sal exploded. "You keep digging a deeper hole. Why in hell I ever hooked up with you I'll never know."

"We grew up together, Sal. Did time together. Our mothers are cousins. We're blood."

Sulfur Sal kept staring at the wheel-less car and shaking his head. "A disaster. Just another fuckin disaster. Hate to think I'm related to you."

"Hey, Sal," Loose Louie brightened, "I was just thinking. Maybe we oughta report this to the cops."

Sulfur Sal froze, dropping his head. "Jesus H Christ," he moaned. "Please stop thinking, Louie. Whatta we going to report? That some bad people stole the wheels off two wise guys from New York on their way to whack a broad?"

Loose Louie's brow wrinkled. "That don't sound so good, does it?"

"No, Louie, it don't," Sulfur Sal muttered with resignation. "Let's go find some damned wheels."

Chapter Thirty-one

Nicky "The Nose" Vincente blinked nervously through the thick lenses of his black-rimmed glasses at the neatly dressed man sitting across his grimy desk in the Bossa Ristorante Italiano office. "You don't think we should give my boys more time, Tony?"

The family consigliere crossed his tennis-trim legs, careful not to inflict a wrinkle on his well-tailored charcoal-gray trousers. "No, Nicky," Anthony Conn replied coldly. "The boss thinks we may have already waited too long. He wants the book back <u>now</u>. Thinks we probably should have gotten help out west right away."

"But we didn't want the family out there to know what happened."

"Well, they know, Nicky. You know how the word gets out. Makes the boss very unhappy. He wants action. Told me to arrange for local help."

Vincente squirmed. "What about my boys?'

"What about them? You said you hadn't heard from them since they left."

"We agreed not to talk until the job was done, Tony. Never know who's listening." He signaled his message by cupping his hand over his ear. "Maybe the mission's already been accomplished."

"Then why haven't you heard?

"Good question, Tony. They shoulda called."

Conn nodded. "That's the way I see it. Hope they get there first. The boss will be especially unhappy if they don't."

Vincente was visibly sweating, well aware of what 'boss unhappiness' meant to him, to say nothing of his subordinates. "Can't we hold off a couple of days?"

The consigliere shook his head. "Too late. They're on the way."

"Who's going, Tony?"

"The cowboy crew."

"Jesus! I've heard of them. They don't leave anything to find. The boss really must be serious."

Conn stood up and straightened his trouser crease. "Believe me, he is. He even asked me how big a family you have."

Vincente wiped the perspiration from his forehead with the back of his hand. "I'm betting on Sal and Louie," he croaked weakly, sensing a sudden urge to empty his bowels.

***

"This candlelight and wine atmosphere is spoiling me," Del confessed, raising his glass of chardonnay. "And the chicken parmigiana was superb."

Kerry, dressed in a snug white turtleneck and black slacks, sipped from her glass and smiled. "They say the way to a man's heart is through his stomach. Maybe I have designs on you."

"I'd be flattered," Del replied, again questioning himself why he hadn't mentioned he was engaged. Deciding to do just that, he added, "but there are some more things you don't know about me."

Kerry nodded, "Probably a lot. You're not gay, are you?"

Del laughed, "No, that's not one of my mysteries."

"I didn't think so. You look pretty normal to me. Pretty manly," she added, feeling slightly flushed as she recalled her various observations of his body. She refilled their glasses from the bottle on the small tray table separating them. "The dim light reminds me of a confessional. Makes me feel like telling secrets."

"It's been said that confession is good for the soul."

"Makes me feel like talking. It's probably the wine."

"Truth serum," he chuckled.

"Makes me want to ask questions."

"Go ahead, Kerry, ask away. I'll be your answer man. A good way to pass a stormy night."

She glanced at the window. "I think it's letting up a little. The rain isn't as hard. Okay, Mr. Answerman, here goes. Do you think I'm pretty?"

"That's easy. You're not only pretty, you're beautiful."

"Really think so?"

"Yes, really think so. Next question."

"You have to answer honestly, Del."

"I am. Nothing but the truth."

"All right. Do you get urges?"

"Well, yeah, guess everyone gets urges. What kind do you mean?"

"Sexual urges."

Del hesitated. "Yes. We agreed I was normal, didn't we?"

"I thought so. Remember, you promised to answer honestly."

"I remember," Del replied with growing apprehension.

"Okay, next question. Do you have sexual urges involving me?"

Del paused, feeling suddenly warm. "Yes," he finally said.

"Good," Kerry said, standing up. "That's what I thought. Guess I'll do the dishes now."

Del couldn't ignore the elevated blanket.

Despite the dimness, neither could Kerry.

"I'll be back," she promised.

***

"Don't look so guilty, Henry," the attractive matron mildly admonished as they stood at the Holiday Inn registration desk. "It's the only room left, but it has two beds and I trust you."

"Oh I wouldn't try . . ." the blushing man began before the woman whispered "shush, I know I'm with an honorable man. It will be alright."

A crooked smile filled Wilhelm's rugged face. "I'll protect you, Mary Agnes."

"I know, and I'll be able to sleep soundly, and be ready for our drive to the cabin in the morning. It'll take us a couple of hours, unless it's raining as hard there as it is here."

"Good thing I rented a four-wheel-drive SUV, Mary Agnes. It should get us through the worst roads."

"You're a resourceful man, Henry. Now let's go to our room and get our beauty sleep."

"You don't need any," Wilhelm stammered. "You're beautiful enough already."

"Oh, you are too kind," she said, pecking his cheek with an impromptu kiss.

Wilhelm's crimson cheeks matched his red tie as he followed his unexpected roommate into the elevator.

Chapter Thirty-two

Despite the stimulation, Del drifted off to sleep during Kerry's absence. He stirred when he heard her returning. "Wish I could be of help with the dishes. I feel like a useless lump."

"Don't feel guilty. Isn't a woman's place in the kitchen?"

"I don't believe that, Kerry."

"Glad to hear it. Neither do I."

"I'd have guessed that, but I wish I could contribute something."

"You have. You're good for my morale."

"Well, glad I'm good for something."

Kerry chuckled. "Oh, I'm convinced of that. Now if you will kindly avert your eyes, I'm going to get ready to take a shower before all the hot water is gone. I discovered we have an electric hot water heater. Without electricity, it'll be cold soon."

"Good thinking. Wish I could take one, too."

"I'll bring you a wash cloth and a pan of water."

"That would be nice. After you finish your shower. I'll just rest here in the meantime and listen to you sing."

"Who said I was going to sing?"

"Doesn't everybody with a golden voice sing in the shower?"

"There's that blarney again," Kerry laughed.

Eyes closed, Del could hear the faint sounds of clothing being removed, and fought the temptation to raise at least one eyelid. "I'm serious. You lift my spirits. Please?"

"I'll see. Any requests?"

"Whatever moves you. I know it will be good."

Five minutes later, the sounds of running water echoed in the cabin, overpowered by the stirring refrain *Kiss, Kiss, Kiss, Kiss*. He almost rolled out of bed when he heard her lusty follow up, *Great Balls Of Fire*.

***

Her scent announced her return. "Can I open my eyes now, Kerry?"

Her chirp of laughter sounded musical.

"Water, Gunga Din," he gasped.

"It's right here. Should I pour it on you?"

"I think a wet washcloth will do," he said, taking the basin from her and placing it on the bed. "Shower feel good?"

"Fabulous, I feel like a new woman."

"The old one is pretty neat," Del said, watching Kerry dab lingering beads of water from her short, wavy hair, movements that emphasized the hourglass figure straining against her tightly-belted white terrycloth robe.

"Watch the flattery, mister. A girl can only stand so much."

"I like your perfume. Obsession?"

"Why yes. You an expert on women's perfume too?"

"I saw it in the bathroom," he confessed, not adding it was also Anna's favorite. "I enjoyed your singing. Thanks."

"My pleasure, and you better use that water before it gets cold. Can you manage it, or do you want your nurse to help?"

His gaze lingered on the striking woman. "That's two questions, Kerry, and the answers are yes, and yes, but I think I'd better do it myself."

Kerry thoughtfully studied her patient, "Yes, I guess that would be a good idea. I'll go put the dishes away."

***

Del had completed his sponge bath when Kerry returned, humming *Wind Beneath My Wings*. "You get me started, and I can't stop."

"Don't. I feel like a VIP with such royal treatment."

"Do you feel better?" she asked, removing the basin from the bed.

"Much, only one more essential and I'm ready for the land of nod. Would you hand me the broom?"

"Oh sure, almost forgot. You did point out that you're only human. And how's the leg? You never asked for more Advil."

"It's felt better, and the wine has had an effect, but maybe another pill will help me sleep."

"You've been so pleasant; I forgot you must be in pain. Sorry about that. Here's your magic broom. Let me help you get started."

"You're strong," Del complimented as Kerry assisted him in moving from the bed to his primitive crutch, the close contact and intriguing fragrance stimulating.

"You too," she murmured, tingling from the feel of his muscular body. She listened to the fading thump of his broom crutch, and felt the intensified beating of her own heart. When he returned a few minutes later, her pulse raced again as she helped him back into bed. She gently repositioned his splinted leg on a pillow, and covered him. "I'll get your pill," she breathed.

"Thank you again, Ms. Nightingale," he said, when she handed him an Advil and a glass of water.

"You're a good patient," she said, lightly kissing his cheek before retreating to her own bed. "Good night."

"Good night to you, Kerry. You've been wonderful. I don't know how I can ever repay you for your kindness."

Quiet reigned for several minutes before he heard Kerry's soft voice. "You asleep?"

"No," he replied, "but why aren't you? You must be exhausted."

"Too wired, I guess, and thinking that I'll be losing my star patient as soon as I call your office."

"I was thinking the same thing. It's been quite special being here with you."

"Yes. I'm glad you dropped in," she quipped. "I'll miss you."

"Likewise, Kerry."

"Guess we should get some sleep," Kerry murmured after a prolonged pause.

"Guess so," Del echoed. "Sounds like the rain has stopped."

"Yes. That should make it easier for me to go call for help. Then you can kiss me goodbye."

Del strained to see her reclining form in the flickering light of the solitary burning candle. "Speaking of that, your goodnight kiss was rather perfunctory, if I may make a selfish observation."

"I know."

"Why?"

He was wondering if she had dozed off when she finally answered. "I was afraid."

"Afraid of me?"

Her response was low. "No, I'm afraid of myself. I have a hard time controlling my emotions sometimes. Must be the Irish and Italian blood."

The simmering sensuality swirling around in the perfume-scented air, caused Del to hesitate before responding. "I'd say it's a delightful combination. And, if I had my broom handy, I'd hop over and deliver a proper goodnight kiss on those beautifully blended lips."

Her voice was husky when she replied. "Maybe I should save you the trip. I'd hate to have you fall. Might lose my nursing license."

"We wouldn't want that," he concurred, watching her turn back her blanket. Despite the semidarkness, his eyes didn't miss seeing the red silk shorty nightgown that had inched up toward her waist.

She slipped quickly into his arms, lips meshing together, tongues eagerly seeking. Pausing momentarily for air, she squirmed closer and breathlessly gasped, "Hold me close."

He enthusiastically embraced the exciting woman, pondering the proper role of a grateful guest.

"Closer!" she urged.

Chapter Thirty-three

Their brisk ten-minute walk had been silent at Mike's caution that "sounds carry." He was dressed in a forest-camouflage jacket with matching cap. Anna wore a dark green cotton pantsuit with white piping that provided an oriental touch. Her long black hair was piled inside Mike's dark blue cap bearing the initials FBI.

"We blend well with the surroundings," he whispered, shifting his shotgun to his left hand. "Let's slow down and approach cautiously. I think I hear voices ahead." He extracted a small pair of high-powered field glasses from a jacket pocket and handed the shotgun to Anna. "Please don't drop it or pull the trigger," he said quietly with a quick grin, "and keep it pointed forward." As they inched ahead, the voices grew louder.

✶✶✶

"Bring her up here," Simpson ordered the two men firmly grasping Marie's arms. "She's going to find out the joys of Sunnyglow Slopes living."

"You're making a big mistake, Charlie," Marie declared defiantly. "You're leading this whole sorry collection of misfits straight into jail cells."

"What's she mean?" one of her escorts asked.

"Claims she's an FBI Agent," Julie chimed in.

"And I say that's bullshit," Simpson scoffed. "She's trespassing, and she attacked me. She's going to learn a lesson. Put her on the throne of delight, boys."

Bound hand and foot, Marie found herself lying sideways on a large blanket-covered air mattress dominating the elevated platform.

Circling the log stage, the totally nude guests of Sunnyglow Slopes looked through glazed eyes at the unfolding drama with lecherous fascination.

***

"God Almighty," Mike mumbled, peering intently through his binoculars at the lurid scene from the edge of the tree line surrounding the clearing. "Hand me the shotgun."

***

"You've got to hold her arms and legs when I untie her," Simpson directed his hovering followers. "She wants to make it exciting."

"You will all be sorry," Marie yelled, struggling ineffectively against the pinning hands as her aroused assailant maneuvered to position himself above her.

"Relax and enjoy," Simpson was panting when the booming shotgun blast shattered the surrounding quiet.

Stunned eyes shifted to the pair rushing forward from the woods, the taller, camouflaged individual waving a shotgun and shouting, "FBI! Everyone stay in place!"

Marie took the opportunity to break free from the restraining grips and leaped up, toppling her deflating attacker to the floor. She reclaimed her Glock from its position by the mattress and leveled it at Simpson. "Give me an excuse to pull the trigger," she addressed the astounded man with deadly emphasis.

"What took you so long?" she quipped to her rescuers who quickly reached her side.

"Weren't sure you wanted us to break up your party," Malloy replied, breathing a sigh of relief while keeping his shotgun trained on the now cowering nudists. He surveyed his naked bride and cracked a grin. "Is there something about your recreational interests you forgot to tell me?"

Marie smiled back. "You two are badly overdressed if you want to join the club. Hi, Anna," she added. "Glad to see you too."

"Seriously, Marie, what the hell is going on?" Malloy asked, handing her his jacket and inspecting the congealed blood near her eye. "Who did this?" he demanded.

"King Kong, there," Marie said, pointing at Simpson, whose bravado had faded as swiftly as his erection. She quickly recounted her attempt to locate the woman who may have seen Del fall from the sky, and her subsequent detention by Simpson. "Turns out she sees all kinds of things," Marie added, pointing to the glassy-eyed redhead. She then nodded to Simpson. "I told this yahoo I was an FBI Agent, but all his brains are below his waist. I think he needs a vacation in a nice Federal pen, somewhere with lots of sun, like Alaska maybe."

Malloy looked grim. "What about the rest of these oddballs? What charges are in order?"

Marie surveyed the group. "They could all be charged as accessories, I suppose, but I doubt it's worth the trouble. Without this jackass I imagine they'll drift to some other whacko movement. The local sheriff might be interested in the field crop they're growing, though. Let's just concentrate on Charlie."

Malloy nodded. "Makes sense. It would waste a lot of time transporting this whole weird gang, and we need to catch up with the rest of the search party. They received a good lead on Del, not far over the state line in California."

"Great news, Mike. Let's get going. Charlie can wear the blanket. Get him used to being dressed."

Malloy produced a set of handcuffs, and not too gently secured Simpson's hands behind his back. "For the record," he addressed the sullen nudist, "I'm Special Agent Mike Malloy, and you're under arrest." He recited the Miranda warnings. "You've already met Special Agent Marie Stanley."

Simpson stared glumly. "She really is an FBI Agent then?"

"Really. Let's go."

Chapter Thirty-four

"I'm glad the skies cleared," Wilhelm said, steering the Chevy Suburban 4x4 south on Highway 395 below Reno, Nevada. It was a few minutes after eight.

"It's a glorious morning," Mary Agnes agreed, studying the road map in her lap, and the typed directions to her cabin. "It's been some time since I was up at the cabin," she continued, "but I remember it as a beautiful place, even though it's quite remote, and the last mile or so of road is rather challenging."

"I like challenges," Wilhelm replied, pulling back into the right lane after passing a slow-moving truck.

"I hope you enjoy the area, Henry, and I thank you again for accompanying me. I feel very safe with you."

Wilhelm glanced in her direction. "It's a pleasure being with you, Mary Agnes. I won't let anything happen to you."

She touched his arm affectionately. "You're a fine man, Henry. I just hope we don't find any trouble there. I'm still worried that I haven't heard from Kerry."

"It'll be all right," Wilhelm promised, increasing their speed, still tingling from her touch.

★★★

The dark blue van with the tinted windows moved out of the razor-wire-topped fenced lot on the edge of Reno at precisely nine AM. At the wheel was a tawny-complexioned man in his early forties, dressed in western-style jeans. Relaxing in the passenger seat was a similarly dressed man whose features closely resembled the driver's. "Let's make this quick, Ramon," the passenger urged his brother. "I've got tickets for the Ricky Martin concert the night after next."

The driver laughed. "You and your music, Pedro. Maybe you should have stayed with that band."

"I preferred to eat," the younger Morales replied. "This pays better."

"Much better," his brother affirmed. "And you still have a lot of time to play your guitar. I imagine you brought it with you."

Pedro's bright teeth flashed. "Wouldn't leave home without it. It's resting in the back with the supplies."

"So if we hit a bad bump," Ramon teased, "the music at the pearly gates will be guitar."

Pedro looked serious. "Don't hit a bump. How much did you bring?"

"More than enough to blow off the top of the damned mountain. You know our reputation. Nothing left. Good advertising."

"They're paying well. It must be important, Ramon."

"And it should be easy, except I wish we didn't have to find some damn ledger book. Means we'll have to eliminate the girl first."

"Yeah, it's always more fun when they go flying without warning. Easier on them, you know."

The driver snickered. "You're a real bleeding heart, Pedro. Next you'll want to let her say her final prayers."

"I'll say them for her," the younger man said, "but what if those guys from New York get there first? What did the boss say their names were?"

"Sal Rinalti and Louie Milano. Ever heard of them?"

"No, Ramon, and the boss said he hadn't either. Just that they must of gotten lost or something."

"Well, let's hope they stay lost. Don't want a couple of east coast guineas screwing up our job."

Pedro read their directions aloud. "Not too detailed," he said. "We'll have to ask people around there where 'Lofty Pines' is. Fancy name."

Ramon snorted. "Probably dreamed up by one of those eastern fairies. When we finish the job they can rename it 'Shredded Pines'." Both mustachioed men laughed.

"Watch for bumps," Pedro reminded.

✦✦✦

"Well, I better be off," Kerry said with a slight tone of regret as she removed Del's breakfast tray from the bedside table. "Did you have enough?"

Del paused, before concluding she was referring to his breakfast. "It was just right, Kerry. You really know how to cook. I'm spoiled."

She blinked her dark eyes. "I've enjoyed spoiling you. Pretty soon someone else can do the job."

Del smiled at the glowing woman dressed warmly in grey exercise sweats. "You look rosy cheeked this morning, Kerry. You slept well?"

"Yes. I was totally relaxed."

"It's a good feeling, isn't it? About last night," he began.

"Don't, please," Kerry interrupted. "It doesn't need discussion. It was wonderful."

"You're an extraordinary woman. Will you kiss me again before you leave?"

Kerry slowly moved closer. "You like to play with dynamite, don't you?"

Del could almost hear the timer ticking.

✦✦✦

"You shoulda turned right back there at the light," Loose Louie complained as the big Lincoln came to a dead-end stop in a new town-house development in Carson City.

"You was reading the fuckin map," Sulfur Sal retorted. "Why didn't ya tell me?"

"I did. You ain't listening. Maybe you can't drive and listen at the same time."

"Oh, so you can, smartass? So why don't you drive, and make sure we don't end up in someone's yard."

"Sounds good to me, Sal. At least I know a highway from a alley."

"It's yours, shithead!" Sulfur Sal yelled, slamming on the brakes and jumping out of the driver's seat. "Show me your stuff."

"Ya don't gotta get all huffy, Sal. You're probably just tired."

"Well I sure ain't tired from screwing all them broads in Salt Lake City, and those long-legged, bit-titted show girls in Reno."

Loose Louie remained silent as he slid behind the wheel. "Where's that adjustment thingy? I gotta move the seat up."

"Right there," Sulfur Sal said, reaching across Loose Louie's lap, just as the car lurched backward and collided with a bright yellow, cement-filled metal stanchion.

"Jesus Christ!" Sulfur Sal yelled as his neck snapped backward to the headrest. "What the shit ya doing?"

"Must of shifted into reverse," Loose Louie mumbled, shaking his head and trying to clear his vision. "What hit us?"

"What hit us you nitwit? You backed into that fuckin post. Didn't ya see it?"

"Guess the mirrors were out of adjustment," Loose Louie muttered, leaving the car to inspect the damage. "Just a tail light," he noted, looking at the shattered red lens sprinkling the pavement.

Sulfur Sal stood unsteadily, rotating his neck while he examined the damage. "And a big dent in the bumper, plus a lot of yellow paint."

"Paint'l come off," Loose Louie said, watching an approaching crowd of curious residents from nearby units. "Let's get outta here."

Sulfur Sal saw the same thing and moved quickly into the car. "Yeah, and step on it. We don't need any more trouble."

The Lincoln's new tires squealed as Loose Louie roared out of the cul-de-sac, but not before one of the residents jotted down the New York license number of the disappearing car.

"Slow down!" Sulfur Sal shouted, as the Lincoln careened around a corner. "You're drawing attention to us."

"You said to step on it," Loose Louie shouted, looking at his partner with confusion, instead of at the red dumpster parked at the corner.

"Look out!" Sulfur Sal screamed, quick enough for Loose Louie to twist the wheel from a head-on collision with the dumpster, but too late to avoid scraping the length of the car's right side.

"God Almighty!" Sulfur Sal moaned, slumping in his seat. "I'm teamed up with a genuine, 100 percent, fuckin idiot."

Silence reigned for several minutes, as the slowed Lincoln found its way back onto Highway 395. "Here we are," Loose Louie finally said, glancing at his brooding seatmate who continued to twist his head. "You okay, Sal?"

"I gotta headache."

Loose Louie nodded sympathetically. "And I gotta go to the crapper."

Chapter Thirty-five

After an hour's drive, Wilhelm and Mary Agnes were approaching South Lake Tahoe and searching for a fast-food restaurant with clean restrooms and good coffee. They took a chance on a new-looking McDonald's, and figured luck was running in their favor. They soon sat sipping from steaming cups. "It's not much further," the former nun commented with a hint of nervousness.

The retired policeman caught her concern. "It'll be all right, Mary Agnes, but I wish I could have brought my gun."

She looked uncomfortable. "I never liked the idea of violence."

"Believe it or not, neither do I. Most cops don't. It's a last resort, but a question of life or death sometimes." He stared thoughtfully into his coffee cup. "I've lost a lot of close buddies who let their reluctance to pull the trigger become a fatal hesitation that left their wives widows, and their children fatherless."

The attractive middle-aged woman studied the sturdy figure across the small table. "I've always honored the sacrifices of 'New York's Finest.' You've been unsung heroes to me. My uncle, Michael O'Brien, was a Captain, in the Thirteenth Precinct I believe."

Wilhelm nodded. "I've heard of Mike O'Brien. They called him 'Iron Mike.' He had a good reputation as an honest cop."

"That's him. Ruled his family with an iron fist, too, but they all turned out well. One's a priest, another a doctor, the third a busy housewife with a passel of kids. But I digress from the discussion of guns. Guess I'm just a little afraid of them."

"Well, you don't have to worry about me going on a shooting binge, since I had to leave my old partner behind, airline regulations and all."

She squeezed his hand spontaneously. "My 'Blue Knight' will protect me, bare handed, if necessary."

A rush of color flooded Wilhelm's fair complexion. "You can bet on that," he assured, adding with a wry grin, "but knights had swords and lances, didn't they?"

"Touché," she laughed. "I just don't want anything to happen to you for being so helpful. The people involved are not very nice, as you could tell by those two hoodlums who visited me. And when I told you about the book and murders, I realized even more that the FBI should have been notified."

"I agree," Wilhelm said. "It's a case for those guys. We've always had our rivalries, but there's been a lot more cooperation than is publicized. In fact, a lot of our top officers sent their sons and daughters into the Bureau. 'Go with the best,' one of my old Captains said he told his son, who is now an Agent in Charge somewhere. Yeah, it's a case for them alright. Should we call them now?"

Mary Agnes looked thoughtful. "Let's check the cabin first."

✳✳✳

"What the hell is that?" Sulfur Sal exclaimed as he stared at the blinking yellow lights on the road ahead.

"Looks like a road-block or something," Loose Louie replied, obeying the reduced- speed signs.

"What's that sign say, Sal? Inspection Station? What the fuck's that?"

"I don't know, but all the cars are stopping, and a guy in uniform is asking questions."

"Shit. You got the guns well hidden?"

"Yeah, unless they tear the car apart."

Third in line, the Lincoln moved slowly forward, its two occupants perspiring nervously. "Maybe we should turn around, Louie."

"Too late now, there's a big fuckin truck behind us."

"Shit. Guess we just gotta play it smart," Sal was commenting when the uniformed man approached Loose Louie's window.

"Good morning gentlemen," the affable produce inspector greeted. "Anything to declare?"

"We ain't done nothing wrong," Loose Louie blurted.

The inspector laughed. "No, I'm sure you haven't. I was just inquiring if you are transporting any prohibited fruits or plants?"

Loose Louie giggled. "Oh, that's what you meant," he replied, sighing with relief. "No, we ain't got nothing like that."

"That's right Officer," Sulfur Sal joined in. "We're just two businessmen on vacation."

"Go ahead," the inspector waved. "Enjoy your stay in California."

Hinky, the inspector mumbled to himself, watching the car disappear, and jotting down the license number. He also noted the dented rear bumper and smeared yellow paint, as well as the shattered taillight lens. Merits an NCIC check.

"Guess we outsmarted that hick cop," Sulfur Sal said, rubbing his aching neck.

"Yeah," Loose Louie agreed, "but I gotta go to the can again."

"Jesus," Sulfur Sal moaned. "I'm gonna get you a box of diapers."

Chapter Thirty-six

The Assistant Special Agent in Charge was smiling as he addressed Mike Malloy on the speaker phone from his San Francisco FBI office. "It's a nice change to hear good news from the boondocks," Whitman said. One found, one to go. Must be something to that 'Luck of the Irish' baloney."

"Mutton," Malloy responded.

"What?"

"The Irish eat a lot of mutton. The baloney is for Krauts, like you."

Whitman snorted, "Kraut? Have your powers of observation completely evaporated? I'm black, you know."

"Oh, I never noticed. Okay, chitlins."

Whitman guffawed. "Think I'll send you back to sensitivity class, Malloy. And now that we've had our fun, I've got a bundle of additional news."

"Shoot, Phil."

"First, we received data from a New York informant that two hit men are headed for the same area that you're searching. Supposed to have a contract on Kerry Vita, daughter of a family bookkeeper who got whacked recently."

"That's the good news, Phil? What's it mean?"

"It might mean something when we connect it to a certain New York license number of a vehicle we know is registered to a rising Brooklyn mob guy named Nicky Vincente. It seems that license number just showed up twice on the National Crime Information Center, once on a property damage report in Carson City, Nevada, and a short time later at a California state-line inspection station. We just talked with the inspector, who described the car's occupants as two swarthy men with New York accents acting very nervous."

"A possible connection, Phil?"

"It might be a stretch, but stranger things have happened. And we did get that anonymous call from a woman telling us that Del was okay. Who knows?"

"Don't these coincidences only happen in the movies, Phil?"

"I said it was a stretch, but it's a lead, and you keep telling me that your buddy, Del, has more lives than a cat. Also, I have a bonus for you. An agent who just transferred in from New York worked organized crime there, and is familiar with Vincente's operation. He was undercover quite a while, and the Bureau feared he was getting close to burnout. He's supposed to be pretty sharp, so I'm loaning him to you for the search. He's on his way."

"Damn, Phil, maybe I should be an ASAC. You guys just sit in the office and solve everything."

Whitman uttered a drawn out "sheet," and continued. "It's a little after noon and we've already had four bank robbery alarms, a terrorist threat against the water supply, a possible kidnapping, and we're being picketed again by the Gay-Lesbian Task Force. Want to swap places?"

"No thanks," Malloy hastened to say. "They have the right man for the job."

"Seriously, Mike, let me recommend you again for administrative advancement. We need seasoned investigators like you in the upper echelon. You were on a fast track once."

Malloy was suddenly reminded of his earlier assignment to Washington Headquarters where his first wife had died during childbirth, along with the loss of their baby, a sorrow the Bureau helped assuage by honoring his request to return to field assignments. "Thanks anyway, Phil," he replied quietly. "I really like it where I am."

"Don't blame you, Mike. Just let me know if you change your mind."

"Will do, and thanks for all the good stuff. I like the possibilities, even if they seem too good to be true. I'll be joining the rest of the search party near that country store shortly, and then it will be an all-out push. We'll find our boy."

***

The wail of the approaching siren almost caused Loose Louie to lose control of the Town Car. "Shit! I ain't speeding," he complained to his equally startled partner who interrupted his sore neck rotation to look back at the pulsating blue and red lights.

"Maybe they're on to us," Loose Louie nervously proclaimed, slowing to stop on the highway shoulder, and watching the approaching uniformed officer through the rear-view mirror. "What should we do?"

"Play it cool," Sulfur Sal instructed, fondling the Colt automatic he had retrieved from under the seat and concealed beneath a jacket next to him.

"Good afternoon," the tall Hispanic California Highway Patrol officer greeted. His nameplate identified him as A. Martinez. "Could I see your registration and operator's license please?"

"It's my cousin's car," Loose Louie explained, producing the registration certificate and his New York driver's license. "What were we doing wrong, Officer?"

The officer perused the documents and studied both men before replying. "Nothing serious, Mr. Milano, just a defective tail light. What happened?"

"Oh," Loose Louie replied, breathing easier, "someone backed into me in a parking lot. Drove off without even leaving a note. Pretty lousy behavior."

The officer nodded. "Must have been a yellow truck. How'd you get the red racing stripe on the right side?"

"Another bad break," Loose Louie muttered, "a hit and run in the same parking lot. Don't wanta go back there."

"No, I wouldn't," the officer responded. "Did you make a police report?"

Loose Louie looked increasingly uncomfortable while Sulfur Sal spoke up. "We didn't want to bother the police with such minor things. You have your hands full taking care of serious crimes."

"Yeah, like looking for murderers," Loose Louie interjected.

"We have insurance," Sulfur Sal added.

"It's always a good idea to report such offenses," Martinez suggested. "Your insurance company probably expects it. And I'd get your tail light lens replaced as soon as possible. It's a technical violation the way it is, but I won't cite you. Looks like you've had enough trouble already."

Loose Louie eagerly agreed. "We'll do that right away, Officer, and thanks for your courtesy. You're a credit to your uniform, sir."

"Drive safely," the officer said, handing Loose Louie his documents and returning to his patrol car where an emergency message was emanating from his radio.

"Lucky bastard," Sulfur Sal said, concealing his gun again under the seat. "Doesn't know how close he came to ruining that pretty uniform."

"I think I'm getting an ulcer," Loose Louie moaned. "Never seen so many fuckin guys in uniforms asking questions."

Sulfur Sal snickered. "'A credit to your uniform, sir.' I thought you was gonna kiss him."

"Ya gotta con these guys, Sal. Don't act suspicious, ya know."

Back in his cruiser, California Highway Patrol Officer Anthony Martinez listened to an urgent request for immediate assistance at a multiple-car accident a few miles back. Swiftly turning around, he roared off with siren blaring and emergency lights flashing, deciding to temporarily postpone his planned NCIC check on the suspicious vehicle.

"He's one lucky stiff," Sulfur Sal again proclaimed, looking at his watch and shaking his head in disgust. "Christ! We keep losing time with all this farting around. We shoulda been there by now. Better not have any more fuckin delays."

Loose Louie looked uneasily at his partner. "I gotta go to the bathroom again, Sal."

Chapter Thirty-seven

Del had hobbled to the bathroom in Kerry's absence, and had just finished laboriously washing his jockey shorts when he heard the rumble of her returning Jeep. He was struggling to secure a bath towel around his waist when he heard her footsteps in the main room. "That was quick," he called out.

"The damn road is washed out about a half mile down the hill," she said from the hall outside the bathroom. "I tried to cross, but it's just too deep. I backed up when my feet started getting wet. What are you doing?"

"My undies. After three days, they were getting rather ripe. I'm glad you're okay. We don't want to lose our 'Mountain Mama' in the creek."

Kerry chuckled. "You don't worry about things, do you? I wasn't able to make the call," she apologized, watching him emerge from the bathroom on his improvised crutch.

"Like a good friend often says, 'better days ahead'."

"You look cute in that Pendleton shirt and skirt," she said, watching him thump his way back to bed. "I'm going to put on my hiking boots and head back down the mountain. Shouldn't have worn sneakers in the first place. I'll get your message out."

He paused, maneuvering to climb back into bed. "<u>Our</u> message, Kerry. You're the one to be concerned about. My welfare is secondary."

She moved to help him. "Damn, why aren't you an ornery old goat, or someone I don't care about losing?"

He looked into her misting eyes. "It's been special, Kerry, whatever happens."

"Yes," she said, supporting his shoulders as he swung back into bed. "How's the leg?"

"Still hurts," he admitted, watching as she gently placed it on the pillow and noticing how she avoided looking at the skimpy towel that minimally covered him.

"How about another pill?" she asked.

"I think that would be nice, and maybe one of your patented kisses to comfort your lucky patient."

A few minutes later she delivered both.

***

The elderly clerk in the tiny mountain post office stroked her chin, striving to place "Lofty Pines." The two Hispanic men dressed similarly in western garb provided no occupant names. "I've heard of it," Eva Summers said, "but it's not in our delivery zone and I can't find it in my directory. I think it might be near Echo Summit – that's about thirty minutes from here. Closer as the crow flies," she smiled, "but the crow doesn't have to climb some of these narrow and slippery roads. Be careful. A lot of cars and trucks have tumbled off."

"Thanks for the help and the advice," Ramon Morales politely responded, leading his brother back to their van.

"You heard her," Pedro Morales reminded, "narrow and slippery."

"Yes, I heard her. Maybe you should start playing church music on your banjo."

"Guitar," Pedro corrected, "and please be careful. I really want to go to that Ricky Martin concert."

"No problem," Ramon assured, slapping his younger brother on the shoulder. "We vaqueros don't make mistakes."

***

Wilhelm slammed on the brakes of the Suburban 4X4 just after completing one of the countless 'S' curves they had encountered during the past fifteen minutes, The SUV came to an abrupt stop just a few feet from the raging stream.

"I suspected it was going too easy," Mary Agnes sighed, gazing at the watery gorge separating them from the narrow road on the other side. "And we're probably within a mile of the cabin."

"Are there any other ways up there?" Wilhelm asked.

"Nothing wide enough for a vehicle. Possibly some foot paths if we could find a narrower place to cross the stream. How are you at hiking?"

"It's been a while since I walked a beat, but I've stayed in shape."

"I can see," she smiled. "So how about a stroll in the woods?"

"I'm game if you are. Guess we can just leave the SUV here. It's sure not blocking traffic."

"No one around to give out a parking ticket, Henry, and it's stopped raining, so we'll just be two city slickers enjoying the great outdoors. Isn't it beautiful?"

Wilhelm's eyes remained locked on hers. "Beautiful," he murmured. "By the way, what kind of animals do they have around here? The four legged variety, I mean."

Absorbed by the lingering fear that Kerry's pursuers had somehow found her, the former nun looked serious. "That's right, we have to be concerned about all kinds of wild life. I recall my brother mentioning that there were occasional bears, along with the usual less dangerous small animals. Lord, protect us."

"Still want to go ahead?" he asked. "I don't want to place you in danger."

Her look conveyed grim determination. "I have my 'Blue Knight' to protect me. Let's go."

He nodded. "I figured you would. I don't think much frightens you."

"I place myself in God's protective hands," she said simply. "And yours."

"Wish I had my gun now, or at least my sword and lance. God helps those who help themselves, I've heard said."

Her eyes danced. "Sound theology, I'd say. I'm ready when you are."

"Excuse me a minute," he said, returning to the car and reappearing shortly with a tire iron and the cellular phone that had come with the vehicle. "Insurance," he grinned, "and I suggest we both select a sturdy walking stick from these fallen limbs to help with the uphill climb."

She grabbed his arm and impetuously kissed his cheek. "I told you you were resourceful. I'm a lucky lady."

The retired policeman felt ten feet tall as he led the way along the stream's bank in search of a crossing spot.

Chapter Thirty-eight

Malloy maintained a firm grip on the steering wheel of the Ford Taurus as it rolled briskly along Nevada Highway 395 south of Carson City. Marie was at his side, and Anna Chen was in the back seat, still wearing Malloy's FBI cap. "I feel like a part of the Bureau," she enthused, "being involved in your exciting work. Do you raid nudist camps often?"

Malloy chuckled. "It's a first for me, but you never know from day to day. I don't recall ever hearing of an agent rescuing his exhibitionist wife from such a place." He turned to Marie. "Those clothes feel confining? Anna and I would probably understand if you wanted to return to nature."

Marie jabbed his arm playfully. "Only if you two join the festivity," she teased.

He shook his head. "Wouldn't that be a headline? *FBI Car Full Of Nudists Nabbed In Nevada.*"

"I'm sure the Director would be thrilled," Marie laughed. "There'd be a new rule in the Agent's Handbook the next day."

"And two Agent job openings the same day," Malloy amended.

"That sure was a weird group," Anna said. "They weren't very appealing, except for you, Marie," she hastily added.

"You're not pulling a 'Julie' on me are you?" Marie laughed. "Now that was one screwed-up woman. I hoped for a while that she had actually seen Del."

"Well, I admire your effort to check out the possibility. Sorry you had to deal with that horrid Charlie. What will happen to him?" Anna asked.

"The U.S. Attorney and local agents are handling the paperwork," Malloy explained. "He'll be held until they decide final charges, and we'll have to come back to testify, but I guarantee he won't be 'initiating' anyone for a while. He did cause us to lose a lot of time processing him, however, so his ugly shadow continues to hover. By the way, Whitman is sending us a recent arrival from New York. An Agent who worked undercover against the mob, and just got pulled out. Whitman thought he might be valuable to us. The guy volunteered his services."

"Every little bit helps," Marie commented. "And I imagine he's relieved to get out in the fresh air. Undercover work is a real ulcer-builder."

Malloy turned toward Anna. "You know that Marie has had some hair-raising undercover assignments. It can really take a toll on a person's psyche. It takes a special person, like Marie, to survive with all their values."

"It's fun at times, though," Marie noted, "if you don't pick up any bad habits."

"Like nudist camps?" Malloy teased. "Maybe Marie is still having flashbacks or suppressed urges."

"I'll flashback you," Marie threatened, playfully punching her husband's arm again.

"Let's hope so," Malloy said, returning his concentration to the fast-moving traffic. "It won't be long now," Malloy said to Anna.

"I'm so grateful," she replied. "I can just visualize Del suffering in some miserable hovel."

✷✷✷

"Wish there was some fuckin street signs around here," Loose Louie complained as the mud-splattered black Lincoln came to a stop before the small building displaying a fluttering United States flag.

"This ain't Brooklyn," Sulfur Sal reminded, unlatching his seat belt. "But these post office people are supposed to know everything. Wish the directions were better."

"Afternoon gents," a gray-haired senior citizen warmly greeted as he left the post office, holding the door open for the two burly men with thick beard stubble.

"Afternoon," Loose Louie stammered back, caught off balance by the unaccustomed courtesy as he watched the man climb into his pickup.

Inside, the postal clerk asked pleasantly, "How can I help you?"

"We're lookin for a friend's cabin," Sulfur Sal said. "He didn't give us very good instructions. It's named 'Lofty Pines'."

Eva Summers smiled broadly. "Your friend must be having quite a party. You're the second people today asking for directions there."

Loose Louie looked at Sulfur Sal with raised eyebrows.

"What's your friend's name?" asked the clerk.

Loose Louie's mouth gaped open.

"Smith," Sulfur Sal finally replied. "John Smith."

"Yeah, John Smith," Loose Louie repeated. "We call him Johnny."

"That's a common name," the clerk remarked, thumbing through a series of printed directories. "No, can't find a John Smith, believe it or not," the clerk finally said. "Have a Sam and a Ralph, though, but they're a long way from Echo Summit, which might be near the 'Lofty Pines' cabin the other men mentioned. It's about a half-hour from here."

"These other guys," Sulfur Sal inquired cautiously, "what did they look like? Maybe we know them."

"There were two. Hispanic. Mustaches. Thin. Blue jeans. Around forty. Looked like they could be related. Drove a dark blue van with Nevada plates."

"You got a good memory," Sulfur Sal complimented.

The clerk nodded her head. "Not too many strangers come through here. You notice them."

"Well thanks for the help," Sulfur Sal said.

"Happy to be of service," the woman answered. "And like I told the other gents, drive carefully. The roads are narrow and slippery, especially when wet. And tell John Smith to drop by sometime. I'd like to meet him."

"We'll do that," Sulfur Sal promised.

Loose Louie looked worried as they drove off. "Who do ya think the two guys are, cops?"

"Don't have any idea," Sulfur Sal replied with a frown. "Could be cops. They don't sound like anyone I know. But the cops around here wouldn't need directions."

"They did mention 'Lofty Pines.' It don't sound good, Sal."

"You ain't gettin cold feet are ya?"

"Oh, hell no. You know better than that. Just thinking we gotta be careful. I'll sure be glad when we finish the job. Too many things have gone wrong. Think we should call Nicky?"

Sulfur Sal scowled. "And tell him what? That we wrecked his car and blew all the dough and haven't even got to the fuckin cabin yet?"

"No, I guess that don't sound too good," Loose Louie conceded.

"We'll call him after we get the book and whack the broad, Louie. We're due some good luck for a change."

"Yeah," Loose Louie was agreeing, when he saw a furry animal scurry out in front of the car from the thick roadside underbrush. The Lincoln swerved sharply left but a loud thump signaled impact with the animal as the brakes screeched, bringing the car to a stop, but not before its left front fender crashed into a sturdy pine tree bordering the narrow road.

"Jesus Christ!" Sulfur Sal screamed, rubbing his forehead, which had just collided with the windshield. "What did you hit besides the tree?"

"Dunno," Loose Louie mumbled, staggering out of the car and around to its front.

"Smells like shit," Sulfur Sal cried, as he held onto the hood and studied the splattered black and white remains. "Ya hit a fuckin skunk, you idiot," Sulfur Sal yelled, holding his nose.

"It jumped right out in front of the car," Loose Louie defended, pinching his own nose. "Couldn't help it."

"God Almighty!" Sulfur Sal moaned. "Let's get outta here. I can't stand the stink. How bad is the front end?"

"Kinda bent up, and the headlight's busted, but the fender's not touching the tire. We can still drive it."

"Phew!" Sulfur Sal exclaimed. "Hurry up. Our luck's gotta change."

Chapter Thirty-nine

Mary Agnes and her protector had gone less than a thousand feet when they encountered a fallen fir tree straddling the stream that had narrowed drastically.

"Here we are," Wilhelm announced, taking the woman's hand and guiding her carefully over the rushing water. "I suggest we go back on this side to the road, and follow it up to the cabin. Less chance of encountering an animal."

She huddled closer. "Anything you say, Henry. I'm in your strong hands."

Warmed by her choice of words, Wilhelm led the way, cautioning her to remain quiet and listen carefully.

"I'm a good listener," she whispered, following closely behind his broad back that she guessed would be quite muscular under his red plaid shirt.

They reached the road and found the grade gradual, so they were barely winded after a quarter mile or so when Wilhelm raised his hand and held a finger to his lips. "I think I hear someone coming down the road," he whispered. "Let's take cover in the underbrush."

The sounds of footsteps grew louder as they huddled closely together. Wilhelm wondered if he was invigorated by the scent of the surrounding woods, or the stimulating woman next to him. Whatever it's origin, he liked it. He gripped the tire iron firmly. They waited silently, straining to see through small breaks in the heavy foliage as a solitary figure gradually came into view. Suddenly, Mary Agnes grabbed Wilhelm's arm. "The saints be praised, it's Kerry!" Jumping up, she raced forward. "Kerry! It's you!"

The unexpected reunion was tearfully exuberant, professions of disbelief and gratitude between the women profuse. Wilhelm was eventually introduced. "My protector," the aunt proudly acknowledged.

Henry saluted with his tire iron. "It's a pleasure to meet you, Kerry. You live up to your aunt's glowing description. She says you're her favorite niece."

"Only one," Kerry laughed. "I have so many questions, and a lot to tell you. A storm knocked out the electricity and phone line. I was on my way to the country store to use their telephone and call the FBI."

"That's why I couldn't reach you," her aunt said. "I was so worried about you when I got no answer to my calls. We think you are in great danger."

"Del thinks so, too," Kerry said. "That's why I'm going to call his office."

Their looks were questioning.

"Del's the man I pulled out of the tree. Turns out, he's an FBI Agent! His leg is broken, and I need to let his office know where he is and that he is okay. He says I have something valuable the mob wants back."

"The ledger book," Mary Agnes said. "Henry knows all about it. He's a former policeman, and I trust him with my life. We can talk freely in front of him."

Wilhelm blushed and shuffled his feet, remaining silent.

"Right now I have to go and make that call. Do you want to come with me, or go to the cabin?" Kerry asked.

Wilhelm coughed, gaining their attention. "I believe we should all stay together and go to the cabin. There's safety in numbers."

"But the call?" Kerry interrupted.

Wilhelm smiled. "I think we can do that from here," he said, extracting the cell phone from his shirt pocket. "Never had such gadgets when I was on the force, but I'm a firm believer in progress. Let's see if it lives up to it's billing."

"He's so clever, Kerry. My 'Blue Knight'."

Wilhelm beamed. "What's the number?"

***

When the call reached the San Francisco FBI office, Whitman was preparing to present a minority face to the picketing Gay-Lesbian Task Force in an effort to convince them of the Bureau's regard for diversity. He welcomed the reprieve, and dispatched a female Hispanic agent to represent him, before picking up the call from a man who claimed to know the whereabouts of Special Agent Del Dickerson.

Whitman pressed the record button and signaled his secretary to start a trace as he listened to the firm voice of "retired New York City Police Sergeant Henry Wilhelm, badge number 4768."

"I'm convinced of your authenticity, Sergeant," Whitman said, "and thanks for calling. If you don't object, I'm listening to this call on my speaker phone so my associates can also hear you. Love this toy."

"No objection," Wilhelm said, proceeding to summarize the situation, and their fears of mob violence. When he mentioned that Del was safe in the hands of a lady named Kerry Vita he was almost deafened by Whitman's shout of glee, "Our million in one dream come true!"

Wilhelm provided the precise location of the cabin, and directions to it, emphasizing the washed out road.

"Damn," Whitman interjected, "that area is close to where they've been searching, but one they hadn't reached yet. You can believe they will be along pronto. What's the condition of Del?"

"Haven't seen him yet, Mr. Whitman, but the young lady who rescued him thinks he has a broken leg. Otherwise, he's supposedly okay."

"Sergeant," Whitman began, "I don't want to unduly alarm you or the ladies, but you're all currently in great danger until our folks get there." He recounted the informant's information from New York, and the sightings of two hit men in the Lincoln they might be driving. "What weapons do you have?"

Wilhelm laughed. "I've got a tire iron, and the rescue lady, Kerry, she's the one that called earlier, says that Del has a small revolver with four rounds left."

"Four rounds?"

"Yeah, seems one went through the roof early in their relationship."

Whitman couldn't suppress a small laugh. "Sounds like our boy. He's one of a kind."

"That's what Kerry says."

"Not to burden you further, Sergeant, and the dots are not all connected yet, but we just received an informant tip from our Las Vegas office that two high-powered Nevada 'exterminators' have been dispatched to do an expedite job near Lake Tahoe. They're known as 'The Cowboys' and their specialty is obliteration by dynamite. The contract reportedly originated in New York, so we have to assume the possibility of a connection."

Wilhelm paused, digesting the information. "Is that why they call this the Wild West?"

"Sorry to pass on such heavy stuff, Sergeant, but you deserve to know. I'll leave it up to you if you want to tell the ladies, but tell Del as soon as you see him. Despite his eccentricities, he has a good head on his shoulders. And on a brighter note, he's lucky as hell, as you can tell."

"Sounds like we could use some luck, Mr. Whitman."

"Our troops are on the way, Sergeant. Hold the fort."

"No problem. Hell, we have four bullets and a tire iron. No sweat."

"I like your style, Sergeant. I'd like to buy you a cold one when this is over."

Wilhelm was quick to accept. "Sam Adams. That's what I drink back east. Make it a case."

Chapter Forty

"Phew, it still stinks like crap," Sulfur Sal complained as the battered Lincoln lurched to a halt on the washed out trail. "Sure this is the right road?"

"That's what the sign down there said, Sal. 'Lofty Pines.' The arrow pointed this way. Guess that rig couldn't make it across." He pointed at the green SUV parked several feet short of the fast-moving stream.

"Don't look that deep to me," Loose Louie said. "Bet we can make it."

"So why didn't that guy do it then?" Sulfur Sal asked.

"Probably got no balls. Lots of pansies out here. Coulda been a scared broad. We can do it."

"I dunno, Louie. What if we get stuck?"

"With all the power we got? We'll breeze right through. No problem."

"Ya sure?"

"Yeah, we rev it up and go like hell. We're half way cross before we even touch water. Seen a guy do it on TV."

"Maybe we oughta walk."

Loose Louie snickered. "Ya know how to walk on water? We gotta get to the other side, dummy. The car's the only way."

Sulfur Sal looked confused. "Ya really think it'll work?"

"Piece of cake," Loose Louie assured.

***

Del heard the voices of people entering the cabin, surprised again by Kerry's quick return. He tensed when he heard a deep masculine voice, and gripped the butt of his snub-nose revolver concealed under his blanket. He relaxed when he saw Kerry's beaming face as she rushed through the doorway.

"Wonderful news," she shouted, leading the middle-aged couple into the bedroom. "Meet my Aunt Agnes and her friend, Henry."

"He's also my protector," Mary Agnes said proudly, before grasping Del's hand. "So nice to meet you, Del. Henry's the scout for the reinforcements that are on the way."

"Hank Wilhelm, N.Y.P.D. Retired," the ex-officer declared, pumping Del's hand. "I talked to your office. Told them where you are. They're sending a bunch of your buddies right away. They're worried about how you're doing, among other things."

Del grinned. "Well, I'm getting better by the minute, and I'm glad to know you reached my office, but I must give a lot of credit to Kerry for being such a lifesaver. She's tops."

"My favorite niece," Mary Agnes asserted.

"Your only niece," everyone said with a laugh.

"Whatever," Kerry's aunt conceded. "So what do we do while we wait for the rescuers?"

"How about some lunch?" Kerry suggested. "Everyone must be hungry."

Wilhelm glanced at his watch. "It has been a while since breakfast."

"Sounds fine to me," Del agreed.

"Good, this group seems easy to get along with," Mary Agnes declared, heading for the door with Kerry. "We have a lot to catch up on while we're fooling around in the kitchen. We'll leave you two to get acquainted, and Henry, I think it's okay to put down the tire iron."

As soon as they were alone, Wilhelm moved closer to Del's bed. "I hear you have a gun with four rounds left," he said quietly.

Del nodded. "It's in my right hand."

"Hope you're a good shot. Your office said there's heavy-duty trouble on the way – a hit team from New York, and possibly another one from Nevada. I didn't want to frighten the ladies, but I hope your buddies get here first."

"Double trouble," Del muttered. "We sort of expected the New York delegation, but the second one confirms how important that book is."

"You have it well hidden?" Wilhelm asked, adding hastily, "don't tell me where it is – the fewer people who know, the better."

Del nodded. "Kerry and I reviewed it the other night. It's dynamite all right – to kill for, as the saying goes."

"Well," Wilhelm said through tight lips," I hope the Bureau responds as swiftly as they do on TV. And, oh yeah, Mr. Whitman said to tell you that Anna is with the search party."

"Anna?" Del exclaimed with astonishment, just as Kerry walked into the room carrying a tray loaded with sandwiches.

"Who's Anna?" Kerry asked, examining the startled look on Del's face.

✷✷✷

"You crazy bastard!" Sulfur Sal screamed as cold mountain water surged around his ankles. "I thought you said we'd fly across," he shouted at Loose Louie who was frantically trying to restart the flooded engine of the black hulk that rested immobile in the middle of the fast-moving stream.

"It dint go as far as I thought it would," Loose Louie confessed, trying again to crank the engine while his right leg immersed to the knee repeatedly pressed the accelerator pedal.

"Thought you saw it done on TV?" Sulfur Sal challenged.

"Well it was a motorcycle," Loose Louie admitted, "and there was this great big ramp. That's it! We dint have a ramp."

"Why the fuck didn't you think about that before, you stupid shit? Now we're stuck in the creek."

"Without a paddle," Loose Louie joked with a cockeyed grin.

"It ain't funny, you moron. Why the hell I keep listening to you I don't know. You belong in a nut house. Now what the fuck we gonna do?"

"Guess we gotta walk, Sal. I don't think it's gonna start."

Sulfur Sal looked at the water line that almost covered the hood and shook his head forlornly. "What'd I do to deserve being hooked up with a loony-tune who thinks he's in a submarine?"

Loose Louie brightened. "Can't smell the skunk anymore."

The murderous look in Sulfur Sal's eyes hastened Loose Louie's attempt to open his door. "Shit!" he shouted. "It won't open."

Near panic, Sulfur Sal tried his door with the same lack of success. "Christ! We're trapped. Open the windows."

With growing hysteria, they looked at each other as the submerged electrical system failed to respond.

"How the hell we gonna get outta here?" Sulfur Sal shouted.

"We gotta think," Loose Louie declared, scratching his head.

Minutes passed as the cold water settled around their waists, and both tried futilely to open the doors. The shorted-out electric window switches still failed to respond. Suddenly, Loose Louie shouted, "I got it! We shoot our way out."

Sulfur Sal stared at his partner.

"Shoot out a window," Loose Louie elaborated. "Crawl out and walk to the shore. We're on our way."

Sulfur Sal nodded. "Ya know, that's just what I was thinking."

"Which window, Sal?"

"What difference does it make?"

"Well I don't want Nicky to get upset."

Sulfur Sal's look was one of disbelief. "You fuckin ruin his car and get it stuck in the middle of a creek and you're worried about which window to break?"

"Well, I was just thinking."

"Stop thinking, Louie. Give me your gun."

"Why not use your gun?"

"What? And have Nicky think it was my gun that shot out his window? You gotta be logical Louie."

"Oh," Loose Louie grunted, leaning back as Sulfur Sal blasted the glass out of Loose Louie's window.

Chapter Forty-one

"What was that?" Del asked, calling attention to the three sharp distant cracks, and delaying a response to Kerry's question.

"Could be gun shots," Wilhelm said, his conditioned ear more convinced than he was willing to acknowledge to the women. "Hunter's probably," he added, looking at Del for reinforcement.

"That's probably what it is," Del said, privately scoffing at the idea of hunters using pistols in the surrounding woods. His eyes met Wilhelm's, a barely perceptible nod communicating their concern.

"The sandwiches look wonderful," Wilhelm said, redirecting the conversation.

"They sure do," Del affirmed. "Kerry is a wonderful cook." He looked at her with admiration.

Kerry's cool dark eyes fixed penetratively on Del's. "Who's Anna?"

Del swallowed a large portion of corned beef on rye, and coughed several times before replying. "My fiancée," he managed to squeak, before choking up again.

***

"Christ, I'm cold," Sulfur Sal grumbled, shivering uncontrollably on the far shore of the stream as he drained water out of his shoes.

"But we made it," Loose Louie gloated, wringing water out of his soggy jacket.

Sulfur Sal looked back at the half submerged car and shook even more. "Do ya realize that we're out in the fuckin woods, soaking wet with no car and no money?"

"You worry too much," Loose Louie replied, checking the extra clips for the Beretta that he gripped in his dripping right hand. "This'll solve all our problems. Do the job. Get the book. Dry out. Give the good news to Nicky and everyone's happy."

"What about the car and the money?" Sulfur Sal persisted.

"I tell ya, ya worry too much. I'll think of something."

"That's what I'm afraid of," Sulfur Sal groaned as he sloshed up the hill behind Loose Louie.

✷✷✷

Her tone was frigid. "You didn't tell me you were engaged."

"I tried to," Del protested, "but something always seemed to come up just when I was going to mention it."

She continued to glare. "Yeah, I noticed."

Wilhelm intervened. "We need to prepare for unwelcome visitors, in case they show up before your Bureau people."

"I agree," Mary Agnes seconded. "It's always good to be prepared. Do we have any weapons besides Henry's tire iron and Del's gun?"

"He's also got his broom, and a lot of brass," Kerry sniffed, staring grimly at Del.

"Now, Kerry," Mary Agnes counseled, "we need to work together through this problem."

"Let's start with locking the doors and windows," Wilhelm directed, "and see what we have in the kitchen."

"There's lots of knives," Kerry volunteered, glowering at Del.

"And I saw a big fireplace in the main room," Wilhelm noted. "Has to be a poker and such. Let's get to it," he urged, moving out of the bedroom, closely followed by Mary Agnes.

"Please let me explain," Del pleaded to Kerry who was trailing behind the others.

"Bastard!" she hissed on her way out.

***

"What do we have here, Pedro?" the elder Morales asked as they rounded a narrow bend and saw two vehicles.

"More witnesses than we want, Ramon, but where are the people, and who are they?"

"The driver of the SUV is obviously smarter than the other one, Pedro. Looks like a Lincoln in the water. Wasn't that what those eastern hot shots were driving?"

"That's what I remember. Can you see the license plate?"

Ramon strained to see. "It's barely visible, but when the water level drops once in a while I can make out the top. Why don't you get out and get a closer look?"

Pedro's white teeth flashed a smile as he hopped out of the van. "Little brothers do the leg work, right?"

Ramon laughed good naturedly. "Little brothers and guitar players. They're equally annoying."

The younger Morales was back in a minute. "New York. I could just make it out. They're ahead of us."

"Then we must hurry, my brother. The prize is a worthy one. Too bad they didn't get lost like we did. They may live to see their subways again."

"What about the SUV, Ramon? Does it belong to someone living around here?"

"Or the law?" Ramon finished for him. "Our minds work alike. We must assume the worst, and proceed accordingly. Our first task is to cross the water. Upstream or downstream?"

Pedro studied the terrain and listened quietly to the rushing water. "Upstream," he said.

"Why?" his brother questioned.

"The sound. It is louder upstream, indicating a blockage of some type, like rocks or fallen trees. A place to cross."

The older brother smiled benevolently. "You have learned well the messages of the land, Pedro. Give up that silly guitar. You are a son of nature."

Pedro smiled indulgently. "My guitar sings songs of the earth, Ramon. It will entertain us as we watch our adversaries drift in the wind."

"Then let us be off. Everything we need is in the backpacks. Except your guitar, of course."

"It's light," Pedro said, shouldering his load. "Mayhem and music. Think I'll compose a song with that title."

Chapter Forty-two

It was late afternoon when the wheezing and soggy hit men rounded a curve in the narrow dirt road and sighted the tree-shrouded cabin. "There it is," Loose Louie whispered.

"Looks quiet. Hope she's got heat," Sulfur Sal muttered through chattering teeth.

Loose Louie pointed at the chimney. "Look at the smoke. We'll be warm as toast soon. Wonder how many people are inside?"

"There's only one car there, Louie."

"Yeah, but what about the SUV by the creek? We gotta figure whoever was driving it might be inside. I dint see any other cabins on the way up."

Sulfur Sal nodded and fondled his automatic. "We got enough fire power to wipe out a whole fuckin house full. Place sure is dark and quiet though."

"We gotta get a closer look, Sal. See how many people are in there. Let's circle around to the left. There's lots of cover, and there's a bunch of bushes near that side window. We gotta be quiet though," he said just when Sulfur Sal sneezed.

"Jesus Christ! I said we gotta be quiet," Loose Louie admonished, jerking his head to look at the house and see if there was any discernible reaction. "Ya gotta control yourself."

"Easy to say," Sulfur Sal grunted. "You ain't getting pneumonia."

"I was in the same water."

"Yeah, but you ain't as skeptical. That's why they call you numb-nuts."

"Is that why?" Loose Louie asked with a surprised look. "I always thought it was a insult. You sure?"

Sulfur Sal smothered a smile. "Trust me. You go first."

"Why don't you go first?"

"Cause you got better eyes."

Loose Louie brightened. "Oh yeah, you're right. I'll go first."

"I'm right behind you," Sulfur Sal said, squelching another sneeze.

Dark shadows were quickly engulfing the area as the pair crept through underbrush toward the cabin. Muted oaths were periodically uttered as the points of small fallen branches and pine cones penetrated their skin. They were within ten feet of the windows when a burst of blinding light flashed, illuminating the surrounding ground.

Reactively diving into the nearest large thicket, they looked at each other. "What the fuck?" Sulfur Sal exclaimed.

A broader look at the cabin revealed light emanating from the windows. The hum of an electrical compressor starting up could be heard.

"Someone just turned on all the lights," Loose Louie whispered.

"Yeah, I noticed, shithead. Ya think I'm blind?"

"You don't use very nice language sometimes, Sal."

"Keyriste," Sulfur Sal growled. "Ya gonna lecture me about my language at a time like this? Do you think they saw us?"

"Dunno. Watch the front door."

"We can't see the front door from here, genius. Or the back door either."

"Then stay still and listen," Loose Louie directed, sensing a sudden increased dampness in his trousers.

"What the fuck's that smell?" Sulfur Sal demanded minutes later. "We near another skunk?"

Lose Louie remained silent.

"Smells like shit," Sulfur Sal continued, moving away from his partner. "What is it?"

Loose Louie finally responded. "You know my problem, Sal. When that damn light went on, it just happened."

"God Almighty!" Sulfur Sal moaned, pinching his nose. "Tell me this ain't happening."

Minutes passed with no sounds of doors opening. Occasional faint shadows could be seen through the two visible windows. "I'm gonna take a look," Sulfur Sal announced.

"I thought I had better eyes?"

Sulfur Sal sneered. "They'd probably smell you coming. You stay here and try to clean yourself up. I'll go," he said, slithering away.

Loose Louie managed to discard his soiled shorts by the time Sulfur Sal wiggled back ten minutes later. "I seen one guy lying in bed, and two or three other people moving around in another room. Couldn't see them too clearly, but two of them looked like women. It oughta be easy enough."

"How we going in, Sal? They might have the doors locked."

"Yeah, I saw the front one when I was out scouting. It looks pretty solid. We surprise 'em. There's another window on the same side the guy's on. Had a small light on. Looks like a bedroom. No one in there. That's how we go in. Now here's the plan."

Loose Louie listened closely, asking only, "Why do I knock on the front door?"

"Cause ya look like a lost soul. They'll feel sorry for ya. They'll think you got attacked by a skunk."

"Oh," Loose Louie replied, "Okay."

Sulfur Sal raised his left wrist. "Let's synthesize our watches like commandos do."

"What?" Loose Louie queried.

"Check our watches. We gotta go in at the same time."

"Oh yeah, Sal, I seen that on TV. Neat."

"What time ya got, Louie?"

"Four twenty. How about you?"

"I got five of five. Sure yours is running?"

Loose Louie brought the wristwatch closer to his face, and then held it to his left ear. "Ain't ticking and the little hand ain't moving."

"That means it ain't working, dummy."

"Yeah. Musta stopped when we was in the water. Whatta we do to synthesize ourselves now?"

Sulfur Sal closed his eyes and furrowed his brow momentarily. "We count like they do on a football play. Ya know how to count, don't ya?"

Loose Louie looked wounded. "You're really insulting today. Sure I know how to count."

"I'm not so sure after Reno," Sulfur Sal reminded. "How high?"

"All the way, Mr. Smartass. One, two, buckle my shoe, three, four, shut the door, five, six . . ."

"Okay wise guy. Don't get cute. We hit the place on the count of one thousand. After we leave here, we count to one thousand, you knock on the front door and I go in the window thirty seconds later. When they hear the window break, the doors open, they get distracted, you draw on them and we're both inside and in control. Got it?"

"One thousand sounds kinda high, Sal."

Sulfur Sal shook his head and stared at his partner. "Unbelievable, just fuckin unbelievable. Okay, let's do five hundred twice. Think you can handle that?"

Loose Louie beamed. "Piece of cake, Sal. Let's go."

Chapter Forty-three

The sudden illumination inside the cabin startled the occupants, already tense from an awareness of their peril.

"Close the blinds and curtains," Wilhelm immediately directed. "Let's not make it easy for any unfriendlies out there."

Mary Agnes elected to take care of the bedroom, nodding amiably to Del as she briskly moved to the windows. "Things are brightening up," she quipped as she closed the heavy drapes.

"I wish you could brighten Kerry's outlook," Del entreated. "She acts like I'm Dracula."

"I believe her feelings are deeply hurt, Del. She is a very loving and emotional girl."

"I know," he mumbled, "and the last thing I want to do is hurt her."

The former nun smiled benignly. "I don't know what transpired between you two, but she is part of my family, my only niece," she laughed lightly, "and I'm ready to protect her like a mother bear safeguards her cubs. If I thought you had intentionally harmed her, I might revert to New York ways. How'd you like two broken legs?"

Del jerked back with shock, trying to gauge the seriousness of the ex-nun who studied him with bemusement.

"You surprise me," he finally stammered with a wry grin. "I hereby certify that I did not, and would not, intentionally harm her in any manner." He raised his right hand. "So help me God."

The comely matron chuckled. "I'm glad you're a religious man. Prayers appear to be prudent for us all, especially right now. Rest easy," she said with whimsical eyes as she headed out of the room.

***

"How's Bozo?" Kerry grunted when her aunt rejoined the group in the main room.

"Reflecting on the errors of his ways, Kerry. I think there is hope for him."

'Hmph," Kerry muttered. "You always see the good in people."

"Benefit of the doubt, my dear," her aunt counseled, beginning to segue into one of her favorite discourses on forgiveness. She was interrupted by the jarring ring of the telephone.

All eyes focused on Kerry as she cautiously picked up the handset. "Hello," she said. Visible relief flooded her face as she momentarily covered the mouthpiece and whispered, "It's the FBI."

"Yes, he's in the bedroom, Mr. Malloy," Kerry answered coldly. "I'll rehook the bedroom phone so you can talk with him. And please hurry," she added earnestly. "Everyone here is pretty nervous."

***

"You have a call," Kerry addressed Del brusquely a minute later, as she handed him the reinstalled bedside phone and stood nearby with Wilhelm and her aunt who had followed her into the bedroom. The trio watched as Del listened and nodded, saying little. The grimness of his face conveyed his concern as he hung up. "Help is close," Del relayed, "but it'll probably be a half hour before they get here. They wanted to come in by helicopter, but the woods are so thick there is no place to land. They could drop a Hostage Rescue Team, but it would take longer to bring them on site than it will for the ground forces to arrive." Del studied the apprehensive faces looking at him and forced a grin. "Only thirty more minutes and you'll meet normal FBI agents, including the legendary Mike Malloy, agent extraordinaire."

"And Anna," Kerry added, in a provocative tone.

"And others," Del parried, turning his head to look directly at Wilhelm. "He reiterated the message Phil Whitman gave you."

Wilhelm nodded almost imperceptibly, announcing that he would go and double check the security of the doors. "Be alert," he reminded everyone, a caution no sooner issued than a loud knock reverberated from the heavy oak front door. "Stay here," he ordered, grasping his new weapon of choice, a sturdy fireplace poker. He began moving swiftly toward the door.

"I'm coming with you," Mary Agnes declared, waving the rolling pin she had found in the kitchen. "You guard Kerry," she ordered Del, "Or I'll do what I mentioned."

The knock sounded again.

✶✶✶

Ramon and Pedro Morales had found the predicted upstream crossing point, a series of large, semi-submerged boulders that provided a slippery but workable passage. Acutely aware of the fragility of their cargo, they proceeded slowly, with extreme caution.

"Mistakes are for others," Ramon reminded his younger brother, burdened with his heavy backpack and cherished guitar case. "Our load will be much lighter on the return trip," he assured.

"It's gotten rather dark," Pedro murmured, moving carefully behind his sibling.

Ramon replied softly. "All the better for our mission. It won't be long before you're strumming a requiem."

Chapter Forty-four

The recognition was instantaneous as soon as the door cracked open. Wilhelm tried to slam the barrier in the face of one of the thugs he remembered visiting his tenant, but the simultaneous crashing sound of a window breaking at the side of the cabin momentarily distracted him. It provided just enough time to permit the burly hoodlum to force his way through the opening and seize Mary Agnes, who was hovering behind Wilhelm. Using her as a shield, with his Beretta automatic pressed against her temple, he roared at Wilhelm, "Drop that thing! Now! Or the bitch dies!"

Overwhelmed by the sudden onslaught, Wilhelm looked helplessly at the frightened woman, muttering with guilt-filled eyes, "I'm sorry."

"I said drop it!" Loose Louie repeated sharply. "And fast!"

"Don't hurt her," Wilhelm entreated, dropping the fireplace iron loudly on the plank floor.

"Where's Kerry?" the gunman demanded. "She's the one we want."

"I'm right here," Kerry answered, walking tight-lipped into the room at the point of a Colt automatic wielded by Sulfur Sal who had captured her as she rushed to the site of the breaking glass. "These are the monsters who murdered Jeff and my father," she announced bitterly, glowering at the two gunmen. "It's nice to see you Neanderthals again."

"I'm Italian," Loose Louie protested.

"Me too," Sulfur Sal quickly agreed.

"It's a small province in Italy," Kerry said. "I'm sure you have relatives there."

"Yeah, you're probably right," Loose Louie said. "We got relatives everywhere."

"Who else is here?" Sulfur Sal barked.

"Just a guy in the big bedroom with a broken leg," Kerry volunteered. "He's a sad case," she added in a loud voice.

"You know why we're here," Sulfur Sal said, moving to exchange places with Loose Louie. "Check the bedroom," he instructed his partner, "and blast the bastard if he gives you any trouble." He returned his attention to the captives. "Where's the fuckin book?"

Everyone stood mute, turning to watch Loose Louie returning. "Just a young guy in bed. Looks unconscious. He won't give us no trouble."

Brownie points for Del, Kerry thought.

Sulfur Sal commanded attention again. "Okay, we don't got time to fuck around. I want the Goddamned book right now or I start firing the bullets in this fuckin gun!"

Mary Agnes tilted her head toward her captor. "That's not very nice language, Salvatore. I don't think your mother would approve."

Sulfur Sal paused. "Okay, may my sainted mother rest in peace, please give me the nice little book and maybe you'll be around for another sunrise."

"Now that's much better," the former nun congratulated, "and would you kindly stop pressing that horrid weapon against my skull. You're giving me a headache."

"Well, all right, but don't try nothin. Louie, tie 'em to the chairs. Start with the big guy. Use the cords from them drapes. Now, back to the book, where's the fuckin thing?"

"Tsk, tsk," Mary Agnes said.

"It's not here," Kerry spoke up.

"What!" Sulfur Sal exploded. "Where the fuck is it?"

"Tsk, tsk," Mary Agnes repeated.

Sulfur Sal glared and waved his pistol. "One more 'tsk, tsk' and there won't be any more, sister."

The certitude of the threat was convincing, and silence ensued as Kerry and her aunt were bound to the wooden chairs. "I told ya she wasn't scrawny," Loose Louie declared as he completed the protracted process of binding the curvaceous younger woman with hands that wandered licentiously. "Look at them jugs," he rasped, breathing heavily. "Built for comfort. I think we need to get something straight between us," he snickered.

"Keep it in your pants," Sulfur Sal ordered. "We got business to take care of."

"But you said . . ."

"Later," Sulfur Sal replied, looking at the captives whose countenances masked the helpless rage they felt. "So where is it?" Sulfur Sal again demanded with deadly emphasis.

Kerry stared back defiantly. "I mailed it to the FBI."

"What!" Loose Louie yelled, a worried frown clouding his broken features. "That ain't good."

"She's lying," Sulfur Sal snorted. "They'd be here by now if she was telling the truth."

"They're on the way," Kerry retorted.

Wilhelm's anxious eyes pleaded for her to shut up.

"She's bluffing," Sulfur Sal said.

"But what if she ain't?" Loose Louie sounded nervous.

"Means we gotta move fast, Louie. I'm thinkin maybe you should have your heart to heart conversation with the broad. Convince her we mean business."

"Yeah," Loose Louie agreed, eyes ablaze. "I'll inject a little truth serum," he leered, moving to untie her.

"Wait!" her aunt spoke up. "You don't have to do that. The book is here."

"Just what I figured," Sulfur Sal snickered, ignoring Loose Louie's look of disappointment.

"Where?" Sulfur Sal demanded, his agitation rising. "My trigger finger is getting impatient. Maybe it's time to send Sister Tsk, Tsk to the pearly gates. Or maybe this big brave janitor who couldn't protect a sick canary."

Wilhelm's muscles contracted fiercely against his tight bonds as he clenched his jaw shut.

Sulfur Sal approached the captives, moving his automatic's point of aim back and forth between the women. "Okay, times running out. Where's the fuckin book?" he shouted at Mary Agnes.

"I don't know," she quietly admitted.

Furious, Sulfur Sal slammed the tip of the gun's barrel against the side of her head, drawing a spurt of blood above her right eye.

"You miserable animal!" Wilhelm yelled. "You rotten, miserable coward."

Sulfur Sal turned and struck Wilhelm viciously on the side of the neck, then chopped down on the top of his head, almost upsetting his chair. Blood poured from a gash on Wilhelm's crown as his eyes blinked shut.

"Stop!" Kerry yelled. "I'll tell you where it is. Just don't hurt them any more."

"Now that's more like it, girlie," Sulfur Sal grunted, turning suddenly at a sound from the rear of the cabin. "What's that?" he asked Loose Louie, who was also looking that way.

"Dunno," Loose Louie replied, cocking his ear.

Thump. The sound repeated.

Chapter Forty-five

"Move swiftly, hermanito," Ramon encouraged. "We need our bargaining chips in place before we confront those bungling New York dagos."

Moving with practiced stealth in the outside darkness, they had seized advantage of the slightly ajar front door, hearing the ongoing dialogue, and catching brief glimpses of the cabin's occupants. "They have done much of our work for us," Ramon whispered with delight as they expertly placed bags packed with dynamite in a covered wood bin near the front door and in a flower box below the living room side window. They carefully inspected the positioning of the electric blasting caps attached to the dynamite before quietly retreating to safety behind sturdy trees a hundred yards away. Ramon fondled the garage door opener remote and smiled triumphantly at his brother. "Ready?"

"Ready," Pedro beamed, his flashing white teeth bright in the enveloping darkness.

***

The thump-thump grew louder as all heads and two automatic pistols were directed at the figure of the towel-clad, sandy-haired man hobbling into the main room. Kerry couldn't restrain her initial reaction. *That's a man, the bastard.*

"Who the fuck are you?" Sulfur Sal shouted.

"It's the guy in the bed," Loose Louie explained. "Thought he was unconscious."

"You're fuckin unconscious," Sulfur Sal sneered.

"What's he gonna do to us with a broom?" Loose Louie laughed.

"What I am going to do," Del spoke distinctly, "is place you two under arrest."

Sulfur Sal burst out laughing. "You're placing us under arrest? We got two guns and three hostages and you got a broom. Ya gotta be loony."

The hostages stared at Del with unbridled amazement, including Wilhelm who had regained consciousness, the flow of blood slowing from his head wound. His bleary eyes signaled his understanding of the plan, but conveyed a degree of doubt.

"The guy's a nut case," Loose Louie agreed, ridiculing the man teetering precariously on one leg.

"I am FBI Special Agent Del Dickerson and I repeat, you two gentlemen are under arrest. Untie these people immediately and surrender your weapons. Prepare to take custody of these prisoners, Sergeant Wilhelm."

Sulfur Sal was laughing so hard, he had to sit on a chair. "An escape from fuckin Bellevue," he chortled, almost rolling off his perch.

"It's not a laughing matter," Del firmly declared, "and your refusal to comply with my orders just aggravates your offenses."

"I'll aggravate your orders with a slug right through your silly little head," Sulfur Sal snarled, abruptly curtailing his laughter.

"That would guarantee your execution," Del announced. "Murder of a Federal Officer means the death penalty."

Loose Louie stopped laughing. "Is he right, Sal?"

"He's crazy. He don't look like any FBI agent I ever seen."

"He's sure different," Kerry volunteered.

"You stay outta this," Sulfur Sal ordered. "Where's your badge? Or that thing with your picture on it?"

"They were lost," Del answered, sensing that his attempt at delaying tactics was running it's course.

Sulfur Sal glared. "See, just another fuckin lie."

"Yeah," Loose Louie concurred, shaking his head with disgust. "Can't anybody be honest anymore?"

"Okay," Sulfur Sal said with steely firmness, looking at his watch and brandishing his Colt. "Sixty seconds and this little pony starts barking. We start with the old broad. One, two, three . . ."

"I'll get the book," Del said in a conciliatory tone.

***

"Hold it!" Ramon Morales quietly cautioned, watching the small group of figures silently emerging from the thick woods behind the cabin. "We have company."

The brothers watched intently from their place of concealment in thick underbrush at the outer edge of the cabin clearing. They counted four camouflaged figures, and observed them taking positions around the cabin, two near the front door and the others separating to locations outside the two bedroom windows.

"Our education progresses," Ramon whispered. "It's good we concealed our presents."

Suddenly, the sound of a ringing telephone shattered the nighttime stillness.

***

"Christ!" Sulfur Sal swore at the unexpected noise, which erupted as he was slowly following Del's tedious progress toward the bedroom. "Get it, Louie," he directed.

"This is getting complicated," Loose Louie groused, shifting the gun to his left hand as he picked up the handset with his right. "Hello," he said tenuously.

Loose Louie's heavily hooded eyes bulged as he listened and repeated the message to Sulfur Sal. "It's the FBI!"

"Fuck!" Sulfur Sal responded, just as a shrill whistle sounded outside and the unsecured front door burst open. Two nimble figures darted through opposite sides of the opening with serious-looking handguns spanning the room. Del dropped suddenly to the floor, leaving a clear line of fire for the dark-haired agent who had rushed in from the small bedroom.

"Drop it!" the intruder ordered, at the same time Del swung his broom at Sulfur Sal's gun-wielding hand, knocking the weapon loose.

Loose Louie fared no better, as Henry Wilhelm seized the moment to kick his unrestrained feet violently upward, catching the startled gunman squarely in the crotch. Before he was able to straighten up from the heart-stopping crunch, Loose Louie was staring down the barrel of Malloy's menacing 40-caliber Glock. "You're under arrest," Malloy announced.

Surrendering his gun and gasping for breath, Loose Louie squeaked, "Second time I heard that tonight."

"Better believe it," Malloy replied, beginning the Miranda warnings as Marie Stanley began untying the hostages, and Anna Chen rushed to aid her sprawled fiancé.

Handcuffed and listening to Special Agent Chris Scannelli's version of the Miranda warnings, Sulfur Sal's dark scowl seemed more directed at Loose Louie than his captors. "Never should have tied up with that dumb fuck," he moaned. "It's been one fuckin disaster after another."

"Tsk, tsk," the former nun clucked.

Chapter Forty-six

Exclamations of thanks for their rescue were heartily voiced by the freed hostages. Malloy introduced the rescuers, concluding with Chris Scannelli, who was identified as having recently served in the New York office, investigating people like the two handcuffed hoodlums who glared at their captors from uncomfortable positions on the floor. Kerry covertly appraised the trim, dark-haired agent with sparkling near-black eyes and classic features. Unusually attractive, she thought, releasing a smile of greeting as their eyes met.

"What kept you?" Del jibed from his reclining position on the floor, his head resting comfortably on Anna's lap. "We were running out of delaying tactics."

"You didn't leave a forwarding address, for one thing," Marie chuckled, "and there was a washed out road, plus a long walk from the creek. And also some odds and ends, like the nudist camp."

"Nudist camp?"

"It's a long story," Marie answered.

"It was fun," Anna chimed in, gently stroking Del's cheek, a gesture observed by Kerry who had been furtively assessing the striking Amerasian beauty.

Malloy broke the celebratory mood. "We're not out of the woods yet, no pun intended. These goons were just one wave. 'The Cowboys' are still out there."

Kerry and her aunt looked quizzical. "The Cowboys?" Kerry inquired.

Del and Wilhelm exchanged knowing glances.

"Another pair of bad-asses out of Nevada, true names Ramon and Pedro Morales," Malloy informed. "Brothers. Their specialty is dynamite destruction, and I do mean destruction. They believe in total elimination of evidence. We have good reason to believe they've been dispatched to complete the job that Milano and Rinalti were assigned. A little mob insurance, you might say."

"Then we are still in danger," Mary Agnes remarked. "And we need to get this brave young man to a hospital." She pointed at Del. "He risked a lot for us and my favorite niece."

"Your only niece," Del, Kerry and Wilhelm reminded her in chorus.

The ex-nun smiled. "Sort of a private joke," she explained. "From what you've said, Mr. Malloy, shouldn't we get out of here right now?"

"Ordinarily, I'd agree, Ms. O'Brien, but we have an injured man and two prisoners to transport, and it's pitch-black outside. We have two agents covering the vehicles in the 'parking lot' by the creek, in case someone shows up there, and we have a squad following fast with an all-terrain vehicle that can run right up to the cabin. They could be here within the hour. I believe it would be prudent to wait."

"Sounds logical," Mary Agnes reasoned, "so why don't we help make Del comfortable in the meantime."

"Yeah, how's the leg?" Malloy asked. "That's a pretty fancy splint."

"Kerry did it," Del said brightly. "She's been wonderful. She also rescued me from the tree. An exceptional lady."

Kerry flushed slightly. "Do it every time I find a guy in a tree."

Anna sensed a look in Kerry's eyes that betrayed her lighthearted words.

Malloy and Scannelli moved to help Del struggle to his feet. "Oops," Del said, feeling his towel work loose and fall to the floor.

Blushing, Anna rushed to restore the covering. "Where are your clothes?" she exclaimed.

"Kerry cut most of them off," Del acknowledged with a reddening face. "My shorts are drying in the bathroom."

Kerry's placid expression contradicted her internal turbulence.

"Oh," Anna said, directing unspoken questions in the direction of Del's stunning rescuer.

"Let's get nature boy back to bed," Malloy intervened, helping Scannelli lead Del out of the room.

"This has certainly been an interesting experience," Kerry's aunt was dryly commenting when the telephone rang.

Picking up the handset, Kerry's face turned somber as she listened. "It's a man asking for the head FBI man. I guess that's you," she said, handing the phone to Malloy who had just returned to the room. "Say's he's one of the cowboys."

"This is Special Agent Mike Malloy, FBI," the imposing man said into the mouthpiece. "To whom am I speaking?"

Complete silence filled the cabin as all ears were tuned to the G-man's end of the conversation.

"Just a cowboy. All right, what can I do for you?" Malloy's face remained professionally impassive as he listened. "How do I know what you are saying is true?" he finally interjected before listening again.

"In fifteen seconds," Malloy confirmed, looking at his watch and gesturing for the others to cover their ears, an action no sooner complete than there was a tremendous explosion in the nearby woods, rattling the cabin doors and windows.

Malloy shook his head and listened. "Yes, I'm convinced of what you say, but I can't do that."

The grimness of Malloy's jaw signaled his seriousness. "Yes, I'll think it over, and I realize there's not much time to decide."

A short period intervened. "You will do what while we are thinking?"

Another brief interlude ensued before Malloy concluded, "Yes, that should be very entertaining."

Malloy disconnected and took a deep breath, gazing into the questioning eyes of his companions. "It's one of 'The Cowboys,' without question, even if he refused to acknowledge his name. I would guess it's Ramon, the older brother. The explosion was one stick of dynamite set off by remote control a quarter mile away from the cabin."

"Powerful," Wilhelm observed.

Malloy nodded. "He wanted us to know they are serious."

"I'm convinced," Kerry commented before Malloy continued, his somber expression deepening.

"He claims that he has the perimeter of the cabin stacked with dynamite – that all it will take is a tap on his remote control and we are all dust particles, if we don't give them what they want."

"What do they want?" Del questioned, hobbling back into the room on his broom crutch, large towel secured, and settling into a chair positioned between Anna and Kerry.

Malloy nodded his head slowly up and down. "The book, of course."

The dispirited crew looked at each other. "Then maybe we should let them have it," Mary Agnes suggested.

"Let them have the fuckin thing," Sulfur Sal shouted from his corner.

"Shut up!" Wilhelm shouted back.

"Will they let us go then?" Kerry's aunt pursued.

Malloy shook his head. "Not completely. They want Kerry to deliver it."

"We was told to whack her," Loose Louie blurted.

"Thanks and shut up," Wilhelm ordered, waving Loose Louie's Beretta in his direction.

"I told him we couldn't do that," Malloy declared.

Kerry looked solemn. "I'll take my chances they'll have a change of heart. I can't let all of you die because of me."

"No way," Del asserted, a declaration totally supported by all except the prisoners.

"Certainly not," Mary Agnes confirmed. "I'll take her place."

"That's our job," Marie interjected. "If it's anyone, it's me."

Malloy looked at his beauteous wife. "I said we couldn't do it. They want us to think it over, so let's get thinking."

"Give 'em the fuckin book and the broad," Sulfur Sal yelled.

"Yeah, the scrawny broad," Loose Louie quickly agreed.

"One more naughty word from you, Salvatore, and I'll put you in one of my dresses and shove you out the door," Mary Agnes promised with iron-willed authority.

Silence followed until Anna asked, "What's that?" cocking her ear towards the outside wall.

"Sounds like guitar music," Chris Scannelli volunteered, picking up the refrain of the *Streets of Laredo*.

"Oh yeah," Malloy remembered. "The guy said we would be entertained by his brother while we thought things over. He said he wanted an answer by the time the music stops." Keep playing, Pedro, Malloy silently prayed.

Chapter Forty-seven

"Where is it?" Kerry demanded of Del. "I know you hid it again."

"Where you won't find it," he replied. "I'm not going to let you sacrifice yourself."

"None of us will let you do it," Scannelli concurred. "We'll find a way."

She looked at him thoughtfully. "I say what's on my mind. You're too young and too good looking to get blown apart."

Scannelli grinned at her. "You're a 'Big Apple' girl all right, and to return the compliment, you're too lovely to be atomized."

"I like this guy," she said, looking directly at Del. "He speaks straight. I'm going to look," she announced, stomping off defiantly.

"She won't find it," Del assured, "but let me go and try to calm her down. Anyone have a bright idea yet?"

Everyone's head registered negatively, including Malloy's as he put down the cell phone. "The Hummer is still almost an hour away, and bringing up the guys from the creek could stampede 'The Cowboys' into premature action. A simultaneous speedy breakout seems like the only possibility of getting at least some of us out, but that could backfire, pardon the expression. It takes only a second to touch the remote button. As long as we have the book, we have a bargaining chip."

"Until the music stops playing," Wilhelm reminded, standing protectively next to Kerry's aunt, as Del thumped out of the room.

"Keep praying and thinking," the ex-nun encouraged.

***

"Tell me where it is, you snake," Kerry hissed as she proceeded to explore every conceivable hiding place in the big bedroom. Del's mattress had already been pushed off the bed.

"Why are you so angry with me, Kerry? I never lied to you."

"But you didn't tell me you had a fiancée either, did you?"

"I tried to, but something always came up."

She looked up and down his sparsely covered torso. "We've had this conversation before."

"Kerry, I swear I never meant to hurt you. You're one of the finest people I've ever known, and you're beautiful."

"But you're in love with someone else."

"Yes, but that doesn't mean I don't feel great affection for you."

"Like a good friend, right?"

"Yeah, I guess so, but more than just a friend. I'd like you to be a special friend."

"Well maybe you can explain that to St. Peter, who we might be visiting soon." Tears filled her eyes. "I fell in love with you, damn it."

Del tilted her chin up, gazing into her watery eyes. "You'll always have a place in my heart, Kerry." He lightly kissed her pouting lips, mildly surprised by her fervent return kiss. She stood back and looked at him with a teasing grin. "Maybe I got the last one."

"Last what?" Anna asked, striding through the doorway and placing a warm kiss on Del's cheek.

"Second last," Kerry muttered.

"What?"

"Last place to look," Del quickly answered.

"Well, whatever," Anna conceded. "I sometimes have difficulty understanding some American sayings."

"You're actually from China?" Kerry asked.

"Taiwan," Anna replied.

"You're a good looking broad. You'd wow them in New York's Chinatown."

"Thank you," Anna blushed, "but I wish to be as American as you. And, to borrow from your vocabulary, I think you're a good looking broad, too."

They both laughed as Del stood sedately by.

"May I help you search?" Anna offered.

"Why not?" Kerry said, "I was about to push these box springs off the bed and gimpy here isn't too nimble."

"I thank you for taking such good care of him for me, Kerry. I can tell that you are a very compassionate person."

"I've been told that, Anna, but I don't always believe what I'm told. I've been burned too many times." Her glance at Del was brief but meaningful.

"Push on that end," Anna directed, moving in rhythm as the box spring slid to the floor.

"What's that?" Kerry asked, gazing at the faint lines in the wooden floor almost obscured by a coating of dust.

"Looks like a door of some type," Anna remarked, looking down. "Perhaps a trap door. Many buildings in the Orient have them."

"A trap door," Del repeated, his face brightening. "You two beauties may have solved our problem. Get Mike, quickly."

When Anna rushed into the main room, Malloy was on his cell phone listening grimly.

"The Cowboys ," Marie whispered.

"Yes, we can hear the music and we enjoy it," Malloy was saying as his eyes read the excitement on Anna's face. He winked at the others and spoke into the mouthpiece. "No, we still have to convince one of our party, but expect to have full agreement shortly."

He paused to listen. "Yes, we realize you are growing impatient and that your brother is getting tired, but just give us a little more time. We understand how important the book is to you and wish to comply with your requests."

Malloy listened again. "Okay, demands," he grimaced. "Soon, and tell your brother he sounds great."

"What is it?" he asked Anna after disconnecting.

"Come and look. Our prayers may have been answered." The group followed Anna enthusiastically.

"Damn!" Malloy declared, looking at the faint outline of a two-foot by three-foot flush trap door that had been covered by Del's bed. It had blended in so uniformly with the plank floor that it was barely discernible unless observed from an angle. The bed was pushed aside and everyone was searching along the seams for an opening latch of some type.

Malloy scratched his head. "Must be a secret lever someplace."

"Did you know about a hidden room or area, Aunt Agnes?" Kerry asked.

The former nun shook her head. "No, your Uncle Ed never mentioned it to me."

"Wonderful man, bad drinking problem," Kerry informed the others. "Loved whisky, wine and women, in that order I understand."

"Whisky and wine," Del repeated. "I don't recall seeing a bar or wine rack in the place. Did you make many alterations when you inherited the cabin, Ms. O'Brien?"

"No, it's almost the same as it was, except for some pictures and curtains. Never even moved the beds."

"Wine," Del muttered again. "Was he a connoisseur?"

"He claimed to be," the former nun replied. "He had quite a wine cellar in his Manhattan brownstone."

"Wine cellar," Del said, snapping his fingers. "Bet that's what's down there."

"Could be," Malloy agreed, "now we have to find a way into it – and time is running out."

"Has to be a way," Del mumbled, thumping around on his broom and stepping onto the outlined area as his broom handle came down on one corner of the cutout. Suddenly the section tilted upward on one side, throwing him abruptly to the floor and flipping his towel up.

"Eureka!" Malloy shouted as he and Scannelli lifted the trap door to reveal an angled wooden stairway.

"I wish you would stop exposing yourself to the others," Anna suggested, covering Del again. Kerry shot him a knowing look.

"Who has a flashlight?" Malloy queried, a question no sooner asked when Wilhelm thrust one into his hand. "From the kitchen."

Kerry swiftly returned with another one, plus a handful of candles and matches that she distributed to the exhilarated group. Malloy was starting down the stairway when his cell phone rang again. "Damn," he cursed, "if it's them, I have to keep stalling."

Without discussion, Marie took his flashlight and headed into the darkness.

Malloy moved to a distant corner of the bedroom, breathing deeply to compose himself for a calm response. The voice he heard conveyed a tone of anger as he listened to the latest message before responding.

"No, I'm not trying for a 'Mexican Standoff', Ramon. The woman is ready to come out. She is bidding farewell to friends and relatives."

Malloy's visage was one of restrained exuberance as he watched Marie's head bobbing up through the floor opening, with the others huddling around it expectantly.

"Yes, she's bringing the book and no, I'm not being sentimental. I do expect you to keep your word that the rest will be spared."

Malloy rolled his eyes at the others in the room. "Yes, a word of honor is important," he agreed, ending the call. "Lying sonofabitch," he told the others, rushing to the opening.

"It's a deep excavation," Marie reported, "almost as large as the cabin. Stone walls and thick overhead beams. Dirt floor and some thick roots or vines on one wall. Cool and a little damp. Some free standing wine racks, and a number of wooden cases stacked on the floor." She read his questioning eyes. "And yes, I think it can withstand a blast of the degree we expect."

"Good enough for me," he said, kissing his wife's glowing cheek. "How can a guy be so lucky?"

"Ask me that later, after the blast." Her eyes glowed. "We'll have our own blast."

"Can't wait," Malloy grinned. "Let's get everyone down under."

"They're all there already, except you, me, Del, and the prisoners."

Their eyes met, minds meshing.

"They're murderous bastards," Marie commented, glancing at Loose Louie and Sulfur Sal. "What would they do for us?"

"Nothing," Malloy admitted, "but we are not like them. That's the difference. We have to bring them along."

Marie nodded. "I didn't figure otherwise, but we have to get Del down first. He doesn't bend too easily."

Scannelli rushed up a minute later. "Everyone's down there but Brooklyn's finest. We had Del halfway down when he demanded to go back up. Ever get assaulted with a broom? Anyway, he hobbled to the corner of the bedroom and pulled a snubby and this out of the pile of trash."

"The ledger," Malloy rejoiced. "The kid is one of a kind."

Scannelli nodded. "And lucky, I hear. Let's hope it holds. We finally got him back down."

"Is everyone else secure down there?" Malloy asked, watching Sulfur Sal and Loose Louie bump roughly down the stairway.

"Except you and me," Scannelli replied, taking the proffered ledger book from Malloy's hands.

Malloy pointed at the wine cellar stairs. "Your turn to get down there." Watching Scannelli disappear, he pulled out his cell phone and punched in the number "The Cowboys" had provided. Poised on the steps with just his head visible above the floor Malloy heard the phone answered.

"Yes?"

"This is a collect call for 'The Cowboys.' Fuck you!" he shouted, dropping down and pulling the thick trap door shut.

Ten seconds later, with everyone hugging the outside walls and grabbing the hard packed floor, a sonic-like boom sounded above, knocking dust and debris from the overhead rafters that bulged and cracked. The concussion lifted the sprawled survivors several inches off the earth and the sound of falling debris rocked the covering above. Bottles fell from some of the shelves, accompanied by the sounds of breaking glass and the powerful aroma of alcohol. Flashes of brilliant light snaked through the edges of the trap door's opening, but it appeared to hold secure as the sounds of airborne debris continued to echo from the ruins above.

"We made it!" Wilhelm finally declared. "Hip, hip, hooray!"

"Looks like it," Malloy cautiously replied. "Is everyone ok?"

"Yes and yeah" were the responses as Malloy called each person's name.

"Good, now we have to find our way out. We may have a ton of junk on top of us, and I would imagine some rather irate Cowboys topside."

"I have full confidence in you working it out," Mary Agnes addressed Malloy. "And I liked you closing salute. That's what we used to say on bad days in the convent."

Chapter Forty-eight

Erie quiet permeated the wine cellar, flickering candle-light revealing random glimpses of the concerned faces of the survivors who sat on the floor or atop whisky cases.

Malloy resumed his leadership role, keeping his voice low and confident. "It is only a matter of time," he comforted. "Our backup crew is only minutes away. Move around only as necessary, and be careful of broken glass. The place smells like a distillery."

"But what if they don't know we're here?" Sulfur Sal cried. "They might think we got blown up and go home."

"Pipe down," Wilhelm ordered. "They don't dump their buddies like you bastards."

"Now, Henry," Mary Agnes admonished. "Don't lower yourself to the level of these miscreants."

"What she call us?" Loose Louie wondered.

"Assholes," Scannelli clarified.

"Oh, why dint she say so?"

Sulfur Sal tried to see his partner through the darkness. "Cuz she's a nun, numbnuts. She can't say things like that."

"I don't like the dark," Loose Louie complained. "Can't someone turn on some lights?"

"We're underground," Sulfur Sal informed. "There ain't no lights. Gotta be a mole to see."

"I don't like moles either," Loose Louie continued.

"Okay, knock it off," Malloy interjected. "No conversation unless it's essential. We need to conserve the available air."

"It's essential. I gotta go to the bathroom," Loose Louie persisted.

"Jesus Christ," Sulfur Sal swore. "Shoulda left ya upstairs."

"Anymore out of you two and you'll be gagged," Malloy decreed. "You," Malloy directed Loose Louie, "use that far corner on the right. Everyone else vacate that area but keep your movements to a minimum."

While the Brooklyn hoodlum melodrama progressed, Anna was holding Del possessively, alarmed by how heavily he was perspiring. She held the back of her hand to his feverish forehead. "Does it hurt much, honey?"

He replied through clenched teeth. "I was doing pretty well until we tumbled into the cellar."

"And now?"

"Hurts like hell," he confided.

Sitting nearby with Chris Scannelli, Kerry overheard the exchange. "Must of knocked the bone out of alignment again, she said. "Let me take a look." With Scannelli holding her flashlight, Kerry hovered over Del and manipulated the leg into the proper alignment. The relief was immediate, and Del emitted a heavy sigh of relief.

"Thanks, nurse, you're the best."

"And don't forget it," she said, before turning toward Scannelli. "Let's go explore."

Anna watched the pair move away. "She's very nice, Del. You were fortunate to fall into her hands."

"Yes, I've had a lot of good luck. Like you," he said kissing her with affection.

"She's in love with you," Anna said.

"Why do you say that? She's kind to all sorts of strays."

"I can tell," Anna replied, "but I got you first."

"And last," Del affirmed, marveling at the wondrous prescience of womankind.

∗∗∗

Kerry and Scannelli were painstakingly examining the perimeter walls when he stopped and inhaled a deep breath. "Smell that," he said, moving back so she could move closer to a root-encrusted section of the wall.

"Fresh air," she declared, inhaling deeply again. They began to claw at the entangled growth that extended from ceiling to floor.

Scannelli unsheathed a five-inch hunting knife from a belt scabbard and attacked with vigor, watching with anticipation as the intertwined roots fell away. "There's a door of some sort behind all this stuff," he said. "Go get Malloy, but don't excite the others. We don't want to raise false hopes."

"You're a pretty neat guy, Scannelli. Why didn't I know you in New York?"

"Guess we moved in different circles, Kerry."

"I'm not like my father," she said defensively.

"I didn't mean anything by what I said, please believe me. I think you're pretty damned nice, and if we get out of here I'd like to treat you to some first-class manicotti."

"I make it better than the restaurants."

"I accept," he said, patting her playfully on the shoulder. "Now go get Malloy."

She smiled. "Hmm. Keep touching me and I'm not going anywhere."

"Be gone vixen," he laughed, returning to his task with renewed enthusiasm.

By the time Kerry huddled back next to him, Scannelli had cleared an area approximately two feet high and two feet wide. He moved aside for Malloy to take a look. "There's a metal door with an interior latch, Mike. Looks like an escape hatch of some type, but I can't reach the latch from here."

"I can," Kerry said. "I'm not held back by those broad shoulders. Boost me up." Mike and Scannelli shrugged their shoulders and lifted her into the opening, watching her wiggle forward. "There's a rusted gizmo stuck into a thingamajig, but I can't move it," was her muffled report. "But I can feel air around the edges. I need a hammer or something."

"How about a rock?" Scannelli asked, picking a baseball size one up from the ground and pushing it forward alongside her body.

"Having fun?" she teased, taking the rock from his hand alongside her ribcage and moving it ahead of her to where she could attack the closure. A series of clanging sounds were interspersed with some earthy declarations before she yelled, "It's moving. Give me a flashlight," she said, moving backward until her rounded hips were provocatively outlined by the opening in the cut-away roots. She grunted and pulled the door inward. "It's a metal lined chute," she said flashing the beam of her flashlight back and forth. "Goes up on an angle – about thirty degrees, I'd guess."

"Is it big enough for people?" Malloy wanted to know.

"Big enough for me," Kerry estimated, "and probably enough for you guys in your underwear. Doubt if those Brooklyn clowns could make it through, and it might be tight for Henry."

"Go get Marie," Malloy directed Scannelli. "Quietly."

Kerry looked at Malloy, guessing his intentions. "Why can't I go?"

"You can follow, Kerry, but we need someone skilled with firearms to go first. It has to be an agent. We don't know what's waiting for us at the other end. I hope you understand."

Kerry nodded acquiescence. "Guess I see your point."

"We have possibilities," Malloy told his wife a few minutes later, flashing the light into the opening. "Could be our way out. It's kind of narrow, though."

"Let me take a look," Marie said, preparing to climb into the chute.

"Slow down," Mike interjected. "Let's think this through. I'm responsible for everyone here. I should go."

Marie looked at her broad-shouldered husband. "And get stuck? It might narrow down. That would really help us all."

"But I don't want to put you at risk."

"Thanks, macho man, but aren't we trained to use the most qualified agent for the job?"

Malloy didn't argue. "Yes," he conceded.

"So why are we waiting?" Marie asked.

"Okay," Malloy reluctantly agreed, "but we're going to take some precautions."

"Sounds like you're getting ready for sex," she laughed. "Okay, what?"

Malloy summed up her needs. "You take your gun and flashlight, your gun tied to one ankle. We fashion a rope and secure it to your other ankle in case we have to pull you back. We don't know if it narrows or turns, or what is at the other end. If we feel three tugs on the rope, we start pulling you back."

"Got it. What do we do for rope?"

"We fashion one out of our clothes, like my jacket," he said removing his camouflage jacket. "Start cutting strips about an inch wide with your knife, and knot them together," he directed Scannelli.

"And I have too many things that could get me snagged," Marie noted, proceeding to remove her cotton-twill pantsuit.

Scannelli almost sliced his finger when momentarily distracted by the stunning five-foot-eight figure of the former dancer now clad in beige panty hose and a small overflowing bra.

"Just can't keep your clothes on, can you?" Malloy kidded, watching some of their cellar mates moving toward the site of activity. He quickly briefed them on the situation, cautioning them not to be overly optimistic.

"How we doing?" he asked Scannelli, who was being industriously aided by Kerry.

"Probably need more material to be on the safe side," Scannelli replied.

"That's easily solved," Kerry announced, stopping her knotting and proceeding to remove her heavy cotton sweats.

Scannelli's eyes widened as he stared through the flickering light at Kerry's hourglass figure, now minimally covered by lace-trimmed black bikini panties and a miniscule matching bra. "Wow," he muttered, refocusing his eyes before his sharp knife almost sliced off his left thumb. "Me next," he said minutes later, removing his camouflage jacket and trousers and slicing away.

"Wow, wow," Kerry said with glistening eyes. "Even better than I thought."

"That should do it," Scannelli said after testing the security of the knots.

Marie tied her Glock to her left ankle with a short section of the improvised rope and Mike secured the lengthy section to her right one, squeezing her calf firmly. "Please be careful," he whispered.

Marie smiled. "Load me into the cannon, boys."

Chapter Forty-nine

"**S**top ticklin me," Loose Louie complained.

"I ain't touchin ya," Sulfur Sal retorted. "My fuckin hands are cuffed behind my back."

"Well, something's ticklin my neck. Can you see what it is?"

Sulfur Sal leaned over and examined his partner's upper body. "Looks like a spider."

"A spider!" Loose Louie screamed. "I hate spiders. Kill it!"

"It's just a little fucker."

"I don't care how little it is, do something."

Sulfur Sal began blowing, causing the spider to retreat a few inches, and then return between puffs.

"It's running all over me," Loose Louie shouted. "Probably a black widow. Get rid of it!"

Sulfur Sal began to butt at the insect with his forehead, missing the spider but connecting squarely with Loose Louie's nose.

"Shit, hit the spider, not my nose. I think you busted it."

Attracted by the commotion, Wilhelm wandered over. "What are you idiots doing now? This some kind of a mob sex ritual?"

"I'm being attacked by a giant spider," Loose Louie screamed. "It's gotta be a black widow or something. Help me out."

Wilhelm moved his candle closer. "Not a black widow," he said. "Could be a scorpion."

"A scorpion!" loose Louie yelled, appearing close to fainting. "Kill it!"

"I heard that could be bad luck," Sulfur Sal interjected.

"Bad luck's dying from a spider bite, ya dumb shit. Someone do something!"

"Splat!" was the resonating sound heard around the small world of the confining cellar as the palm of Wilhelm's hand squarely connected with Loose Louie's neck, sending him sprawling on his side.

"A pleasure to be of service," Wilhelm said, moving away.

"You okay?" Sulfur Sal asked a minute later, watching his partner sit back up.

"My nose hurts and I gotta headache, but nothin's crawling on me no more."

A short distance away, Mary Agnes welcomed Henry's return. "What was that all about?"

"Just rendering a public service," he laughed. "A baby spider was panicking one of our brave hit men. You might say I struck a blow for justice."

"You're nice to have around," she said, linking her arm with his.

✷✷✷

"How is she doing?" Kerry asked, watching the supply of home-made rope slowly disappear into the chute.

"I'd say she's gone about fifty feet," Malloy replied, carefully feeding the remaining line and maintaining light tension to detect any signals for help. "No tugs," he said tersely as he fed in more rope.

Inside the closure, Marie was inching forward in what she discovered became a round pipe a few inches from the entrance. She estimated it to have a two-foot diameter and be composed of metal, probably steel. Cold steel. She could hear her pistol clanging against the metal as she progressed. Relieved to find it had no curves and appeared to be of uniform circumference, periodic gusts of cool air encouraged her to keep moving. Soon, in the distant reaches of the flashlight's beam she saw a blockage of some type. She guessed she had advanced at least a hundred feet by then. She squirmed ahead.

Back in the cellar, Malloy was growing worried. Little of the rope remained unfurled. The concern in his eyes was conveyed to Scannelli and Kerry, who hovered close. "No luck so far," he began to say when he felt three distinct tugs on the cord. "She signaled," he said, as lengths of the impromptu line returned with little effort on his part. It was piling up fast at their feet when the clang of her pistol against the pipe signaled her proximity, and her feet suddenly appeared. Seconds later, Marie stood shuddering in Malloy's arms, trembling from the cold, but exhilarated with her discovery.

"I found a door that must be at ground level. It has to be over a hundred feet from the cabin. It's metal, and too heavy for me to budge, but I could feel air all around its edges. The chute is a round pipe, about two feet across. I need something like a pipe or pole to push the thing open. It'll take a lot of strength."

"Let's see what we can find down here," Malloy replied.

"The stairway," Scannelli said. "How about a two by four?"

"Sounds good, Chris. A piece about five to six feet should do it, without nails. I don't need puncture wounds," Malloy said.

"You?" Marie inquired.

Malloy replied, "I'm going up next. You said it's big enough for me."

"But I've already been there."

"And you blazed the trail, but you admitted it was too heavy for you to move."

"But with the two by four . . ."

"Didn't we already agree we pick the most qualified agent for the job, Marie? Fair or not, I have more upper body strength."

"You pulling rank, Mike?"

"If I have to. You know it's the right thing to do. You'll be the second one up."

"You're the boss," she said with a tone of resignation that Malloy suspected would exact a future penalty.

"Here it is," Scannelli declared a minute later. "Wilhelm pulled that stairway apart like it was cardboard. A few whacks by him with some rocks and you're also nail free. Watch for splinters, though. It's old wood."

Malloy stood poised in his underwear, gun tied to his left ankle, signal line secured to his right, length of lumber in his right hand, and flashlight in the other.

Marie giggled. "Wish I had a camera. Today's well-equipped G-man on the job."

"That's my girl," he grinned, kissing her smiling lips. "Keep that great sense of humor. You're in charge here now."

She hugged him impulsively. "Yes, sir. I love you, sir."

"Don't stop," he whispered, crawling into the opening.

As he inched forward, Malloy thought of the extraordinary woman he had met and married in Jackson, Mississippi. Both widowed, they fell extravagantly in love, unleashing a world of wonder neither had envisioned would ever replace their first loves. Their shared moments of professional challenge and private exultation crowded his memory as he aggressively moved forward to the barrier. I'll get us out some-how, was his vow as he reached the barrier and futilely tried to elevate the heavy metal door with his hands. He then dragged the two by four section forward and moved back for maximum leverage, grasping it firmly as he repeatedly propelled it against the door's edges. There was no initial discernible movement, as the board kept bouncing back, al-most causing it to escape his grasp. He continued to explore for weak-nesses in the covering, and shouted for joy when he detected minor movement on one side of the cover. Concentrating his attention on that area, he expended his last reserves of energy as he hammered away. Finally, the snap of breaking metal elicited a muted "hallelujah," as the cover flipped back, exposing a wondrously starry sky.

Malloy cautiously raised himself to peer through the opening, uncertain of what attention his pounding may have generated. He saw he was surrounded by heavy underbrush, and was situated about a hundred feet across the parking area from the smoldering remains of the cabin. An ethereal silence reigned in the cool night as he retrieved his pistol and continued to gulp lungfulls of the rejuvenating air. He untied his ankle tether and gave two sharp pulls on the line the agreed signal for others to come ahead. Crouching down while scanning the horizon, he could detect no sound or movement, a silence soon invaded by the sudden appearance of Marie, quickly followed by Kerry, and then Scannelli.

"Anna insisted on staying with Del, and Ms. O'Brien with Wilhelm," Marie whispered. "I assured them we would have them out post-haste. Louie and Sal are worried about being abandoned."

"Let them sweat for awhile," Malloy remarked, a sentiment no one challenged.

"Now what, Chief?" Marie inquired. "You've got a half-naked squad of demented followers, three guns and lots of goose bumps."

"Should have brought my cell phone," Malloy said, "so we could tell our buddies what's going on."

Marie's eyes sparkled. "How about mine?" she asked, reaching into the center of her bra and extracting the small device. "These things come in handy," she said, amidst the light snapping of retracting elastic.

"Wonder woman," Malloy said, taking the device from her outstretched hand. "Any more goodies in there?"

"You should know," she said with a provocative smile.

Grinning, he took the phone and called the agents at the creek. "Yeah, we're okay, Sam. We found a wine cellar below the cabin and survived the blast you heard. Some of us got out in an escape tunnel. You're right, the explosion was a big one. The little one before was a warning shot. But we still have six people under the debris, and two ticked off Cowboys on the loose. Be alert. Where's the Hummer?"

Malloy suddenly pulled the phone from his ear, and the surrounding trio could hear the staccato sound of gunfire bursts belching out of the instrument. "Ohh, I'm hit!" Malloy heard next, "and Larry's down. No warning," the weakened voice gasped, "Noooo . . ."

"Sam! Sam!" Malloy beseeched, "Come in, Sam!" There was no response, and Malloy looked at the others with despairing eyes. "Sounds like the bastards ambushed Sam and Larry at the creek."

"Good Lord," Scannelli said in a mournful tone, shaking his head. "That shouldn't have happened. What did he say about the reinforcements?"

"He didn't have time to answer," Mike said. "Damn, sounds like 'The Cowboys' took out two of ours and got away. Where the hell is that Hummer? I have to go down there."

"Let's go," Marie said, heading for the creek.

"Watch things here, Chris," Malloy said, rushing to catch up with his wife.

Chapter Fifty

The Hummer borrowed from the U.S. Forest Service was roaring along the two-lane blacktop of California's Route 50, Special Agent Craig Black at the wheel. "How far?" he yelled at his front seat passenger with the map.

"Two or three minutes to the cabin road," Rob Saunders replied. "Funny, I can't get through on the radio to Sam. Had a good signal a little while ago."

"Keep trying," Black directed. "Wish we had radio contact directly with Mike."

"Sam was relaying fine until just a few minutes ago. Hope nothing happened."

"Me too," Black responded grimly, increasing their already substantial speed and straining to see the edge of the road with the vehicle's brilliant headlights.

The two agents in the rear seat hung on tighter. "Watch that sharp curve ahead," one cautioned, seeing the reflective caution sign.

Black slowed to navigate the hairpin turn, glancing briefly at the sheer drop to his left. "Hate to slip over that," he remarked, picking up speed again. "We'd still be airborne."

"Can't help our friends if we don't get there, Craig," the other rear seat occupant soberly noted.

Black speeded up.

***

"Can't trust the fucking gringos," Ramon Morales bitterly complained from behind the wheel of the speeding van. "But, at least we taught them not to cross 'The Cowboys'."

"And we gave them a bonus reminder," Pedro added, "with those two peons near our van."

"Yes," the older brother agreed with a satisfied smile. "Fish in a barrel."

"Speaking of bonuses, Ramon, will we be paid in full? We don't have the book."

"Neither does anyone else, Pedro. We can guarantee it has gone up in smoke."

"Did we use enough?" Pedro wondered. "We have quite a bit left – almost a case. And lots of blasting caps."

"You saw the ruins, Pedro. I'd say we used more than enough. We can use the leftovers for another job and charge both employers," he added with a sly wink.

"You are a business genius, big brother. I learn much from you."

"Stick with me and you'll go far, Pedro. And be sure to keep the caps well separated from the sticks." He began humming a Latin tune. "I like your banjo playing."

"Guitar," Pedro corrected.

"I tease you, hermanito. Why don't you entertain us as we go to collect our prize?"

Pedro was soon soulfully strumming his guitar. "Be careful on these narrow roads," he warned. "There's a lot of boom-boom in the back."

Ramon laughed. "Banjo players talk funny."

✳✳✳

The Hummer was just turning onto the narrow trail to the cabin when they spotted oncoming headlights and seconds later a dark van hurtled by, swerving just in time to avoid a collision.

"Crazy bastard," Black cursed, barely controlling the vehicle and looking back at the van which had screeched onto Route 50 and sped away. "Did anyone see who was in it?"

"Just a glimpse of the driver from your headlights," Saunders said. "Male. Dark complexion. Wearing a cowboy hat."

"Cowboy hat! 'The Cowboys'!" Black exclaimed, his mind racing to a split-second decision of whether to give pursuit.

"Our folks need help," he shouted over the roar of the engine. "We can always find those guys. We keep going."

No one disagreed as Black raced ahead. A minute later the Hummer rounded a bend and almost collided with the light blue Impala parked on the side of the road.

"Shit!" Black uttered as the Hummer's headlights illuminated two bodies slumped on the ground next to the Bureau car. The Hummer skidded to a stop and the four agents leaped out to huddle over the still forms, stunned by what they saw in the glare of the headlights. Anguished looks were exchanged, heads slowly shaking in sorrow. "No pulse on Sam," Black said.

"Same with Larry," another agent grimly seconded, gently rolling the stilled body on its side. "Three entry wounds in the back."

"Four here," Black reported. "All in the back also. The rotten bastards! Our guys didn't have a chance. Sam's cell phone is still gripped in his hand." He pried it loose, looked at it curiously, and pushed the redial button, surprised when a familiar sounding voice answered "hello."

"Mike! Is that you?" Black paused to listen to a response before nodding his head. "Just arrived at the creek. It's a grim scene. Sam and Larry are dead, shot in the back. We think we saw 'The Cowboys' escaping in a van. They damn near hit us. Where are you?"

Listening again, Black stared across the creek at the faintly visible trail on the other side. He directed the beam of the powerful flashlight in that direction. "Can't see you yet. Stay where you are by the road and we'll pick you up in the Hummer. I'm leaving an agent with Sam and Larry. We have some equipment that should help us dig out your friends. Damn, why didn't we get here sooner?"

Malloy disconnected and looked sadly at his wife. "No need to continue walking. Both gone. Must have been surprised by 'The Cowboys'."

"Oh Mike," Marie cried, falling into his arms, shivering from both the news and the cold night air. "Larry was just married, and Sam has a couple of children. What a shock. It can happen so fast."

He held her tightly. "We both know just how fast, honey. Let's not squander our time."

"I agree," she said, still shaking as the Hummer's headlights silhouetted them on the side of the road.

"Another Hummer is about ten minutes behind," Black told the pair as they clambered into the vehicle and he surveyed their abbreviated clothing. "New dress code up here, Mike? You two must be freezing," he said, handing Marie a field jacket. Another was handed to Mike from the front seat.

"We had a tight squeeze coming up a chute from the basement, Craig. I think it was an old wine and whisky passage for a former owner. We've got six people still in the cellar who can't make it out that way. What equipment do we have?"

"This is equipped for fire fighting. We have shovels, axes and rakes. Should be the same for the following vehicle. I think we can do the job."

"I've guaranteed it, Craig. Four of the folks are worth bare-handed digging if necessary. It would be no loss to society to leave the other two down there."

"You know we won't, Mike, but when I think of Sam and Larry, it's a temptation."

"Amen," Mike murmured, saying a silent prayer for the slain agents.

***

"Slow down!" Pedro pleaded, as the van careened around the repetitive curves of the narrow blacktop. "There aren't any headlights behind us. I don't think anyone is following us."

"We need to insure our escape," Ramon grunted, maintaining speed.

"But with all the stuff in the back," Pedro reminded, "you know what it can do! I think some of it shifted during that last turn."

"I know what I'm doing, little brother. Didn't I teach you the trade? Relax and start playing your fiddle again."

"Guitar," Pedro responded with a tone of futility.

"Play," Ramon repeated, "and don't forget your big brother knows best."

Pedro had just struck the opening chords of a melancholy song about unrequited love when they rounded a sharp curve and were washed with the brilliant sweep of oncoming headlights.

"I can't see!" Ramon shouted, twisting the wheel.

"Madre de Dios!" Pedro screamed as their tires lost grip with the tarmac and the van hurtled uncontrollably into space.

***

Black's Hummer had just pulled into the debris-littered parking area between the chute entrance and the demolished cabin when Kerry and Scannelli rushed up. "More nature lovers," Black said when he observed the scantily clad pair, focusing major attention on the striking woman. "We're running out of cover-ups," he was saying when a thunderous roar erupted in the near distance. Everyone looked at each other with startled eyes.

"Could justice have been done?" Malloy questioned, turning with the others to look in the direction of the explosion where a sustained flash of orange-white light briefly illuminated the dark sky.

"Wish I could believe we were so lucky," Malloy answered himself, "but our immediate task is to dig our friends out. Let's go," he said, grabbing one of the long-handled shovels from the Hummer's fire-fighting equipment.

Chapter Fifty-one

"I'm cold," Loose Louie grumbled, "and my back aches like hell from being hunched over with these handcuffs."

"I'm gonna file a fuckin civil rights complaint for the fuckin way they've treated us," Sulfur Sal responded. "Pure fuckin torture, that's what it is."

"Shut up you two," Wilhelm ordered from a distant corner. "You're lucky they didn't leave you up in the cabin. And watch your language. There are ladies present."

Loose Louie chimed in. "I agree. Your language offends me too, Sal."

"Jesus Christ!" Sulfur Sal erupted. "You got us into this fuckin mess, and you're offended! I fuckin don't believe it!"

Wilhelm approached the pair, carrying a two-foot section of a stairway two by four. "One more obscenity and you'll be out cold till you wake up in a jail cell." He moved the club menacingly. "Go ahead, you prick, give me an excuse," he challenged. The tone of voice was convincing, and he finally walked away after a prolonged period of silence.

Several minutes intervened before Loose Louie whispered to his accomplice. "Smell all that booze?"

"Yeah, I could use some now," Sal mumbled back.

"That's what I'm thinking, Sal. Ya know when all that shit fell on the floor when the place blew?"

"Yeah."

"Well, I can feel the necks of some bottles. They got those wires holding the cork, like champagne or Chianti bottles. I think I can unwind the wire. Then I shake the bottle and the cork pops out."

"So whatta ya gonna do then? They'd be behind your back."

"You roll over behind me and I pour some in your mouth. Then you do the same thing for me."

"Think it will work?"

"Worth a try, Sal. Ya said ya was thirsty."

"Okay, but don't make no noise. I don't want that big pig clobbering me."

***

"Don't let those pitiful souls bother you, Henry. They aren't worth the trouble. We'll be out of here soon."

"You could be out of here by now, Mary Agnes. You don't have to stay with my big carcass."

"I rather like your big carcass," Mary Agnes said, placing her arm around his shoulder and kissing his cheek at the same time a pop sounded in another corner. "What was that?" she asked.

"At first I thought it was my heart," Wilhelm said, "but I suspect our idiot prisoners have somehow managed to uncork a bottle. I'd better take it away."

The former nun chuckled. "Such wasted talents. Why don't you let them alone? At least they are not cursing."

"All right by me. I like the popping here better."

"Oh, Henry," she sighed, cuddling closer.

"Pop" came another sound a few minutes later.

***

"Tastes good," Loose Louie said, slurping a mouthful of wine. "Must be Chianti. Pour some more, but get it in my mouth. You're spraying it all over my damned shirt."

"Shit, Louie, how can I get it in your mouth if I can't even see it? Be thankful for small flavors. And it's my turn now. Uncork another one of them fuckers. Ya got one within reach?"

"Yeah, a big mother. Feels like a champagne bottle. Roll over and open your mouth."

"Keyriste, ya trying to drown me?" Sulfur Sal sputtered a minute later. "And you're getting it in my fuckin eyes."

"Hey, this ain't easy, asshole. Want me to stop?"

"No, just aim better. Do something right for a change."

"Up yours," Loose Louie said, splashing the alcohol all over his partner.

***

"How's your leg, Honey?" Anna asked from their position on the ground.

"Feels wonderful with you here, Anna. But I wish you would scoot up that chute. I can manage till they dig us out."

"We have not exchanged our vows in church yet, Del, but I already have in my heart. It's still death do us part for me."

Del sighed, moved with emotion. "Lord, I'm blessed," he murmured.

***

"Not a hell of a lot left," Black observed, pointing his shovel at the mounds of mangled debris. "Where do we start?"

Malloy located the remains of what he gauged to be the front entrance, and began to carefully weave through the rubble toward what he estimated had been the bedroom area where the trapdoor was located. "Watch for soft spots," he warned as the others followed cautiously behind, carrying rakes, axes and shovels. "Right around here," Malloy suggested, pointing at a waist-high pile of shredded lumber. "Let's start clearing this area. Push the debris to the rear."

Seven determined rescuers attacked with unrestrained zeal.

***

Shortly after the sound of another popping cork echoed around the subterranean chamber, Mary Agnes looked abruptly up at the dark ceiling. "Hear that?" she asked, tilting an ear upward. "I believe I hear some scraping and pounding."

Wilhelm strained to hear, a hopeful smile slowly engulfing his face. "Yes, it's faint, but persistent, some thumping and shuffling. I do believe our deliverance is at hand."

"I do too," she said, gazing into Wilhelm's eyes and squeezing his hand.

"I'm sure they're trying to find the trapdoor area," Wilhelm speculated, "so we should probably be as far from there as possible in case it caves in."

"Another smart idea," she complimented. "Let's move over by Anna and Del. They are about as far away as you can get. What about the hoodlums?"

"I'd just as soon leave them where they are," Wilhelm replied, standing up and motioning to Mary Agnes to head in the direction of Anna and Del.

She looked at him with curiosity. "Aren't you coming?"

Wilhelm cracked a slight grin. "Just saving a trip. I know you'd have me going back for them in about two minutes."

"My," she said with admiration, "we have gotten to know each other quite well, haven't we?"

Wilhelm looked at her with surging hope before picking up a flickering candle and heading for the source of subdued giggling.

★★★

"There are some bigger pieces of junk than I thought," Malloy admitted, his perspiration-covered face glistening in the light of the Hummer's headlights. "Let's take a break," he suggested to the others who had reached similar conclusions after a furious twenty-minute working spree that had cleared an area far less than hoped for. Even the best efforts of a small chainsaw had proved ineffective.

Craig Black nodded. "It's those big roof rafters that settled like spider's legs just over the section you indicated was our target. We need a small bulldozer or something to push the stuff away."

"How about something to pull it away?" Marie interjected, as the second Hummer pulled up and four figures disembarked. She pointed to the cable winch on the front of the vehicle. "I think our needs have been met."

"Damn," Black addressed Malloy with obvious admiration. "You not only married a beauty, you got one with brains."

Malloy grinned with pride. "Don't give her a big head. I've got to live with her."

"Poor bastard," another agent jested to everyone's laughter.

"Okay," Marie said, suppressing a blush, "let's put it to work. Who's our engineer?"

"The rambling wreck," one of the new arrivals said, pointing to the driver of the recently arrived Hummer. "Georgia Tech, he keeps telling us. Supposed to know everything about engineering. We call him 'Johnny Reb'."

A tall, blond-haired agent shuffled forward with a slow-moving "aw shucks" demeanor and scanned the group. "Gollee," he drawled in an exaggerated Dixie cadence before bursting into laughter. "Okay, comedians," he enunciated in a clear Midwestern dialect, "I tell you what to do, you do the work."

Kerry nudged Scannelli. "He sure doesn't sound southern."

The jolly engineer smiled in her direction. "Southern Michigan. Detroit to be precise. Attended Georgia Tech on a football scholarship. Now shall we get to work?"

Chapter Fifty-two

It was twenty minutes before 'Johnny Reb,' more properly known as Special Agent John Miller, had positioned his vehicle, stretched the one-inch cable around two sturdy fir trees near the edge of the parking area and wrapped the free end of the cable around the thick roof timbers that had refused to budge for the straining rescuers. Standing back to assess the alignment, Miller looked confident. "This should pull it to the side and clear the target area," he remarked to Malloy, "unless the damn cable breaks. It's marginal in that department. The winch is rated at 12,000 pounds. Too bad the other Hummer doesn't have one. It would be a cake walk then. Keep your fingers crossed."

With Miller at the wheel, and the winch cable extended its full length, the Hummer's 195-horsepower turbocharged diesel engine growled as he tried to move in reverse. After miniscule initial movement, the piled mass stubbornly remained in place, while the vehicle's engine roared, and its four-wheel-drive dug its sixteen-and-a-half-inch wheels into the soft ground. Mud splattered in every direction.

"Need more power," Miller conceded, disembarking to test the condition of the stretched cable. "Stay further back," he cautioned his audience. "If that sucker snaps, it could whip you to shreds. Time for phase two," he continued, calling to Craig Black. "Back your vehicle to the rear of mine, and connect the towing hitches. You move forward, while I try to back, and we may make it. Take it slow, and don't jerk so we keep the cable taut. Start moving at the count of ten."

Both engines were soon roaring, with the observers watching at a safe distance as the cable tightened to a laser-straight line. Spirits soared when they heard an encouraging creak and saw the pile beginning to move. Snapping noises escalated as the tent-like mass continued to move steadily sideways. With a low rumble, it reached the perimeter of the cabin's foundation and loudly collapsed into a mound of dusty rubble.

The cheers of the rescuers mixed with the victorious honking of the Hummer's horns as the group rushed forward with flashlights.

***

"Hear that!" Wilhelm exclaimed. "Sounds like major activity above."

"Not only that," Del added from his location with a better view of the trapdoor area, "but I see some flashes of light up there."

"I'll go take a look," Wilhelm stated, standing up.

"Be careful," Mary Agnes cautioned.

"Hic," one of the hoodlums sounded from his slumped position against a far wall.

***

"I can see the opening," Kerry yelled, rushing to the spot.

"Be careful of your footing," Malloy warned everyone, as shovels and axes clawed at the surrounding litter. "We're coming!" Malloy shouted into the spreading void. "Stand away from the trapdoor."

It took several minutes to clear an opening large enough to extract the cellar's occupants, using the ladders that had been strapped to the Hummer's roof. The women were helped first, followed by Del, who resolutely clasped a rectangular-shaped package wrapped in remnants of his parachute fabric. Wilhelm came up last, after pushing not too gently on the two bulky hit men, who wobbled unsteadily on their feet after being jerked unceremoniously to ground level. "Drunk as skunks," Wilhelm reported as he cleared the opening and looked with bemused contempt at the pair.

"So many bad habits," Mary Agnes remarked with a look of pity, watching Sulfur Sal slump to the ground and Loose Louie bend over to retch.

"Real tough guys," Del mocked, turning to Kerry. "They won't give you any more trouble."

"We have unfinished business," Malloy reminded, curtailing the celebration. He turned to 'Johnny Reb' Miller. "How about taking your crew and see if you can find the site of the explosion we heard. If the God's are with us, the murders of Sam and Larry may have been avenged. And Craig, I guess your Hummer is the best way to transport our dead comrades down the mountain. Marie, Chris and I will do a crime scene search at the shooting site and follow down with Anna and Del. Henry and Mary Agnes have a car at the creek, and can meet us in town with Kerry. Her Jeep was disabled by the cabin blast."

"I want to stay here with you," Kerry said, casting a glance at Scannelli. "I won't be in the way."

Malloy nodded approval.

"So what do we do with the dynamic duo?" Miller asked, pointing to Loose Louie and Sulfur Sal.

"Tie them to a tree and feed the bears," Wilhelm suggested.

"Oh, Henry," Mary Agnes protested. "You don't really mean that."

"Of course not," he smirked, winking at the agents. "We wouldn't want to deprive these misguided murderers of their rights."

She directed an uncertain look at the husky ex-policeman.

Malloy addressed Miller, "Hate to dump them on you, John, but would you take them with you when you check out the blast site? Might give them an idea of what lies ahead for them. I don't want them desecrating the memory of Sam and Larry by traveling in the same vehicle."

Miller nodded agreement. "Maybe we should strap them on the roof like dead deer."

The ex-nun looked unsure of whether 'Johnny Reb' was kidding.

***

A few miles away a small fire flickered on the edge of denuded underbrush in the narrow ravine, sufficient to ignite a forest fire in drier times. But the soggy ground that had cushioned the crashing van before the earth-shaking explosion had pulverized it into metal scraps contained the incipient blaze that continued to smolder.

Portions of the vehicle's engine block and transmission projected grotesquely from a still smoking crater. Bits of human and mechanical remains dangled from the swaying limbs of surrounding pine trees. Clinging to the tip of one tree limb was the seared remnants of a white cowboy hat. Lying nearby on the ground was the scorched metal frame of a guitar case.

***

Miller's crowded Hummer had left, and the others had retreated to the creek, using Black's Hummer to transport them across the still formidable span of water.

Wilhelm had collected the discarded clothes of the wine cellar escapees, and all were now more comfortably dressed against the chilly air, as the hour approached early morning. He also salvaged two bottles of aged scotch that he passed around to the survivors and their rescuers. "Takes the chill off," Wilhelm declared, demonstrating the technique. The others showed they were fast learners, if not previously schooled in the art.

The bullet-riddled remains of the two slain agents were respectfully loaded into Black's Hummer. The group solemnly saluted as the vehicle moved away at a hearse-like pace. Wilhelm and Mary Agnes followed closely behind.

***

The crime scene search was brief, but thorough, the casings of seven nine-millimeter rounds quickly found in two nearby locations at the edge of the woods. Using a crime-scene kit from the slain agents' car, Marie completed a detailed sketch of the scene, showing locations of their Bureau car, where their bodies had fallen, and the site of the recovered casings, a clear portrayal of how the attack had occurred. The agents' unfired weapons were tagged and retained as evidence by Scannelli, who looked particularly grim and sorrowful as he collected blood samples from the ground.

"Not much more to be done here," Malloy was commenting when a message came over his car radio from Miller.

"We found the place, Mike. A big hole and not much else. It's only about a mile down from where you turn onto Route 50. On the right. You'll see our vehicle on the edge of the road. You might want to take a look."

"Ten four," Malloy responded. "We were just preparing to leave. See you shortly."

Malloy turned to the others. "We have two cars," pointing to his and that of the slain agents. "Marie and I can check out the explosion site and the rest of you can head back to South Lake Tahoe in Sam's car. We'll join up there later. Lots of paperwork to handle, and we need to get Del medical attention for that leg, although it looks like he's had top-flight care here. You did a great job, Kerry."

"Just a friendly mountain courtesy," she replied modestly, directing an affectionate look at Del who was still clinging tenaciously to the wrapped ledger book. "He was a good patient."

"You have valuable cargo," Malloy addressed Scannelli. "In addition to these special people, you are transporting the evidence that can cripple a major crime family. Protect it well."

Scannelli nodded confidently. "I just came from New York City, as you know, and I am very well aware of that book's value. You can rest assured I will take every precaution."

Chapter Fifty-three

Malloy and Marie had just driven off, leaving the remaining four to welcome the first rays of the early morning sun that were beginning to filter through the towering trees of the thick surrounding woods. A chapel-like stillness enveloped the area.

Anna broke the silence, rising from the trunk of a fallen Douglas fir where she had been sitting with Del, witnessing the crime scene search. "I'm sure you are all happy it's about over."

"It's like the end of a nightmare," Kerry began to reply when a shocked look froze her face. "What are you doing?" she asked Scannelli, who had drawn his Glock automatic from his right hip holster and leveled it at his companions.

"Completing my mission," he said without emotion. "Give me the book, Del."

"What do you mean?" Kerry demanded in an incredulous voice.

"I mean I want the book, Kerry. Sorry, but that's the way it is."

"I can't believe this," she cried, grasping the meaning of his actions. "You're an FBI agent."

"I just resigned, Kerry."

"You rotten bastard," Del muttered.

"Now don't get carried away, Del. Everyone cooperates, no one gets hurt."

"You've betrayed us all," Kerry wailed through a torrent of tears. "Why? I thought you were something special."

Scannelli nodded. "Maybe we could have had something once. I wish I had met you before."

"Before what?" Del interjected. "Before you violated your oath and disgraced your badge?"

"I've thought about that, believe me. It hasn't been easy. But this is the only way out. What is in that book about me could get me twenty years or more in the pen. It's all there-- under my undercover name. Instead, I get a million for returning the book, and take a nice long vacation."

"You Judas!" Del spat.

"Hey, it can be two million if I finish off Kerry. That's what I was offered. Be grateful I'm not greedy."

Del continued to glare. "Where is your sense of decency, Scannelli? Have you no honor, no ideals?"

Scannelli looked reflective. "I had ideals when I went undercover, and then I saw how the corrupt officials and politicians cleaned up, while laughing at us 'Boy Scouts.' Dealing with them every day, I got caught up in their lifestyle, began to gamble, mess with drugs, and cat around. Before I knew it, I was in way over my head, owing a mint. Then there was a leak from a DEA informant and the mob found out I was a Bureau agent. I faced a swim with the fishes if I didn't cooperate."

"Christ, man," Del vehemently replied with an uncharacteristic oath, "the Bureau would have pulled you out. You didn't have to surrender your integrity."

"And do what?" Scannelli shot back, "spend the rest of my life running from the mob and working as a plant guard under an assumed name?"

"You didn't have to sell out, Scannelli."

"Easy for you to say, Del, but it's the way it is, and it's time for my departure. Give me the book."

"And if I don't?"

Scannelli waved his automatic. "You know what this baby can do. You're a pretty decent guy, with a beautiful girlfriend. It would be a shame to have to waste you both."

"How about me?" Kerry spoke up, her disbelief transformed to a simmering rage. "You said I'm worth another million to you if I'm dead. So, go ahead, kill me. You've about killed my soul anyway."

Scannelli's look was agonized. "I don't want to hurt you, Kerry."

"What do you think you've done already?" Kerry shrieked, bursting into tears again.

"How far do you think you'll get?" Del asked. "You know the Bureau's investigative capabilities."

"I've got a few of my own, Del. I didn't last almost two years under deep cover by being stupid."

"Well you're being stupid now, Scannelli. You won't get away with it."

"We'll see. I'll have a good head start before my old associates start their search. It will be some time before they realize I'm gone, and I know how to hide." His eyes scanned his stunned listeners. "You won't be spreading the alarm for awhile."

"You would leave us here alone?" Anna asked.

Scannelli smirked. "I don't think Del will mind. He will have his little harem. Your friends will eventually miss you and come back. By then I'll be long gone." He looked at his watch with impatience. "Enough of this true-confession session. I'm leaving with the book, one way or another."

Del addressed the increasingly nervous gunman. "You will do no more harm to anyone if I give you the book?"

"Word of honor," Scannelli assured.

"That's a strange word to hear from you at this stage," Del replied, "but you can have it."

"Don't do it," Kerry pleaded.

"We have no choice," Del responded. "I'm not going to be responsible for the deaths of you and Anna."

"Smart man," Scannelli said bending over and reaching for the book which Del lifted up with his left hand, stretching it out over his right leg.

"Here it is," Del said, whipping out his snub-nosed revolver from his ankle holster and firing two rapid shots into Scannelli's right shoulder.

The Glock fell to the ground, where it was immediately seized by Kerry. She leveled it at the astonished man who had been propelled backwards and was staring up with unbelieving eyes.

Stunned, and grimacing with pain, Scannelli's left hand was being saturated with blood as he held it against the freely bleeding wounds. "Damn, I forgot you had that thing," he wheezed. "Never knew it hurt this much," he added with a plaintive moan.

"You were thinking of doing the same thing to these people," Del reminded.

"Never would have," Scannelli gasped before passing out.

"Suppose we better get our ambulance headed out fast," Del directed, helping the women as best he could as they loaded Scannelli into the back seat. He was again impressed with Kerry's strength and resolve. The women then helped Del into the front passenger seat.

"You know the roads , Kerry, so you drive," he said. "And Anna, you'll have to be the nurse. How's the bleeding?"

"Pretty heavy, honey."

"Needs pressure," Kerry said, removing her jacket and handing it to Anna. "Press this down on the wound."

Del glanced from his awkward sideway position to the woman settling in behind the wheel, admiring her indefatigable spirit, and trying to ignore the overflowing black bra that seductively profiled her ample upper body. He looked back at Anna. "If he wakes up, remind him I've still got two .38 rounds in my snubby, and a fully-loaded nine-millimeter Glock. I'll handle the radio, and let them know we're coming in fast with a wounded prisoner. Let's go, Kerry."

"Can I do the siren?" she asked, heading down the trail.

"Oh, hell yes!" he grinned, looking from one beautiful woman to the other. "And the emergency lights too. The whole damn schmear. Let 'em rip. We're family, aren't we?"

Both women wondered what he meant. Upon reflection, so did he.

Epilogue

San Francisco was selected as the best location for a reunion of what the survivors had elected to call "The Big Mountain Blow." A private dining room at Rubinos was reserved for the participants who drifted in through the early evening fog of a fall Friday night. Fittingly, a large panoramic photograph of the 1906 San Francisco earthquake decorated one wall of the restaurant's "Earthquake Room."

Mike and Marie had volunteered to coordinate the affair, and welcomed arriving guests, presenting each with a glass of celebratory champagne. "We serve the first one. You help yourself to the rest," Malloy said, pointing to a corner table loaded with a variety of libations. The dress code was Bay-area casual, he in a dark blue blazer with white turtleneck, she in a pale blue cashmere dress that subtly enhanced her stunning figure. Her up-swept raven hair was held in place by glittering diamond clips that matched the pendant earrings dangling from petite ear lobes, emphasizing the swan-like grace of her delicate neck.

It had been a month since the explosive conclusion of the group's memorable adventure. Physical and emotional wounds were slowly healing.

Del and Anna arrived early, his cast-encased leg guided into the room by the aluminum crutches that had become annoying reminders of the tedious, desk-bound case he was working while his leg mended. The unexciting computer fraud inquiry provided surplus time to reflect on recent events, including the amazed reaction of orthopedic doctors over how well his fractured leg had been treated. That invariably prompted melancholy thoughts of Kerry and her many talents.

Anna was dressed in an elegant purple silk brocade sheath with pink piping that seductively emphasized her slim, well-proportioned figure. Her long, glistening black hair, gathered in a soft braid, draped gently over one shoulder. Hovering attentively over Del, who wore his favorite pearl-gray suit, she displayed her characteristic serene smile that seemed this night to harbor a trace of sadness.

Mary Agnes and Wilhelm arrived shortly thereafter, exuding good spirits on their first day back from New York City where they had spent the past month. They were eager to discuss their imminent trip to Hawaii, and the former nun made little effort to conceal the diamond engagement ring gracing her left hand. It stirred profuse congratulations, further elevating the already festive mood. Wilhelm looked resplendent in the new brown and white hound's tooth jacket selected by his partner, who looked equally stylish in a well-tailored beige suit that quietly defined her slight but pleasing form.

Kerry arrived next, escorted by a tall, trim, blond-haired man wearing an Army uniform with captain's bars. He also displayed Jump Wings above a cluster of service ribbons. "Meet Ted," she introduced. "He jumps out of planes, but doesn't land in trees." Her glance at Del was mischievous.

The officer approached Del to shake hands. "Hello again," he said to Del's questioning look.

Kerry smiled at Del's obvious effort to recall where he had seen the man before. "Dr. Bennett," the man said, extending his hand. "We met at the hospital in South Lake Tahoe."

A look of confused recognition flooded Del's face as he pondered the caduceus insignia on the officer's lapels.

"I'm on a two-week reserve duty assignment," the doctor explained. "Kerry heard I was going to be in San Francisco and invited me to your shindig. Hope you don't mind."

"Certainly not," Del assured, "we're honored. I owe you a lot."

The doctor shook his head, looking at Kerry. "All the hard work was already done. This young lady is a natural. I'm trying to talk her into exploring the medical profession."

Kerry kept smiling. "I know my limitations, but it's nice to have a doctor on call."

The doctor smiled back with obvious admiration. "And I make house calls."

Kerry took Ted's arm possessively. "Come say hello to my aunt," she said, leading him away. As they departed, Kerry whispered over her shoulder to Anna. "And he's single."

Assistant Special Agent in Charge Phil Whitman, and his wife, Norma, arrived a short time later. The party was soon seated around a large round table, savoring a tasty antipasto that presaged a multi-course Italian feast that would ultimately leave the guests groaning with overfed satisfaction. Conversation flowed as freely as the wine, and as the last of the Cannoli disappeared from the plates, Whitman stood up before his relaxed companions. "We have a little business to conduct," he announced, extracting a number of envelopes from the inside pocket of his well-tailored dark-gray suit coat. Opening the first one, addressed to Ms. Kerry Vita, Whitman proceeded to read a pro-fuse message of appreciation from the Director of the FBI, thanking her for her courage and outstanding demonstration of good citizenship in heroically assisting the Bureau in a major investigation. He read similar letters addressed to Mary Agnes O'Brien, Henry Wilhelm, and Anna Chen, presenting each with their letters and leading a rousing round of applause.

The ASAC then looked at Del, Malloy, and Marie. "Your letters of commendation will be presented at Monday's all-office conference, and I believe you will like the enclosures," an allusion the agents knew meant they would be receiving checks representing financial incentive awards.

"Now for a case update," Whitman continued. "Word today from New York is that a Federal Grand Jury is handing down indictments like confetti against 'family' members and customers listed in the ledger book. A lot of prominent people listed in the book have been singing like canaries."

"I know a canary who sings like an angel," Del offered offhandedly, glancing briefly at Kerry.

"And New York had another bit of information," Whitman resumed. "A body found floating in the East River a few days ago has been identified as that of the late Nicky 'The Nose' Vincente."

"May he rot in hell," Kerry interjected, a look of satisfaction brightening her face.

"Now, Kerry," her aunt counseled. "It's not for us to judge."

"He ordered the murder of Dad and Jeff," Kerry reminded. "But, okay, may he rest comfortably in hell."

Mary Agnes released a condescending smile and elected to let the issue rest.

"How about Loose Louie and Sulfur Sal?" Del questioned.

"I've been following that case," Malloy volunteered. "They are still in jail in California, awaiting extradition to New York. They want to try them there for murder, and, as twice-convicted felons, they should receive life without parole. The Federal charges have been put on hold, pending the outcome in New York, but can be resurrected if the State process somehow breaks down. They won't be going on any cross-country trips, except in chains. And, oh," Malloy chuckled, "they are sharing the same cell, with Sal regularly complaining about the smell from Louie's problem."

"Poetic justice," Marie commented.

Malloy turned to his wife. "Don't you have an update on your nudist buddy?"

"My bosom buddy, Charlie Simpson," she laughed, "pleaded guilty to a reduced charge of interfering with a Federal officer in the performance of her duty, and is serving two-to-five years in a place 'where the sun don't shine.' State authorities eradicated an extensive crop of weeds at 'Sunnyglow Slopes,' and will probably take over the property for a mess of unpaid back taxes. Julie, I hear, is still seeing strange things falling from the sky."

"The Morales Brothers," Whitman picked up, "or what few pieces could be found of them, were positively identified through DNA as leaving our world at the place where their van landed in the ravine."

"No more guitar music," Del remarked, adding, "it was good, but nowhere near as good as the music I heard from 'Golden Throat'." He turned to Kerry, "Do the rest of your fans know how good you are?"

Kerry's aunt chimed in. "Oh, she has a marvelous voice."

"How about a song?" Marie suggested. "We feel left out."

"Yes," Whitman agreed. "We need something to balance the sordid news."

"Please," Dr Bennett concurred, looking with enhanced interest at his intriguing new acquaintance.

"Well, if everyone promises not to throw the remains of their dessert at me, I'll try," Kerry said, standing up and stepping back. "I don't want to blast you from the table. I tend to sing loud."

Soon, the mellow words and rhythm of *Sentimental Journey* filled the room, and a growing cluster of restaurant servers paused at the door, tapping their feet. They joined in the applause, one calling out "more," before being dispersed by a smiling maitre d'.

Accepting everyone's accolades with professional grace, Kerry cleared her throat and drifted into a torchy rendition of a Tony Bennett classic.

"*Because of You,*" she sang with half closed eyes that seemed to shift between Del and Ted, "*there's a song in my heart.*"

"Because of you, our romance had its start."

She hesitated, visibly struggling to control her emotions, and continued.

"Because of you, the sun will shine, the moon and stars will say you're mine, forever and never to part."

As she continued through the song, she moved her supple figure, snugly encased in a low-cut, burgundy-colored velvet cocktail dress, ending on a plaintive note that left her audience momentarily silenced. She sat down quickly, as loud applause erupted.

"Wow!" her beaming escort proclaimed. "Another astounding talent!"

"Beautiful," Anna agreed, as others offered compliments.

"It's a shame," Whitman apologized with a serious look, "to follow such loveliness with a sour note, but you all deserve to know the status of our dirty linen."

"Scannelli," Wilhelm murmured to his partner.

"Most of you are aware," Whitman proceeded, "that Chris Scannelli was summarily dismissed with prejudice as soon as his treachery was discovered. He's been in the South Lake Tahoe hospital since, recovering from two well-placed ventilation holes. He has indicated a willingness to plead guilty to a series of charges that will probably get him out of prison in ten years or so. He has professed great remorse," Whitman was saying, when his cell phone rang. His look was grim when he disconnected. "I've got to call the office on a more secure line," he explained, excusing himself.

"Must be hot," Malloy murmured to Marie, "or they would have delivered the message on his cell phone."

"While we're waiting for Phil's return," Del spoke up, "Anna has received some potentially bad news that will require her immediate return to Taiwan. Her mother has suffered another heart attack, and we've agreed Anna should be with her at this time."

Anna nodded. "I'm her only child. She raised me by herself, and needs me now. I hate to leave Del, but feel I must go before it's too late." She squeezed Del's hand. "My heart remains here, and I expect to be back soon."

"We will be praying for you and your mother," Mary Agnes assured. "And for Del too," she added, noticing his forlorn look.

"Sorry to hear the bad news," Kerry was saying when Whitman reentered the room, his expression grave.

"The office just received word." He stopped and scanned the inquisitive faces. "Scannelli won't be serving any jail time. He tried to escape from the hospital jail ward this evening on a bed-sheet rope. Guess it wasn't as strong as the one you fashioned at the cabin. It broke while he was half-way down from the fifth floor. Broken neck. Died instantly."

"What a tragic waste," Marie sighed. "He had so much going for him."

"Tough way to go," Malloy added.

"At least he won't be living in disgrace," Wilhelm noted. "I wonder how accidental it was?"

"Good point," Del agreed, shaking his head sorrowfully. "May he rest in peace."

"I kind of liked the guy, despite what he tried to do," Kerry said with glistening eyes.

"Sorry to end our evening on such a somber note," Whitman stated, "but it is important to remember that the good guys came out ahead this time, minus a nice mountain cabin or so."

"Oh that wasn't such a loss at all," Mary Agnes said brightly. "My black-sheep brother had the cabin, and the wine cellar contents, heavily insured. Like they say in the Big Apple, 'he left a bundle.' As soon as Henry and I return from Hawaii, we are going to clear the rubble and build a new cabin, sans wine cellar. Kerry is going to help us design it."

"I like the location," Kerry said, flashing her dark eyes toward her escort. "I've sort of fallen in love with the area. And it's close to South Lake Tahoe."

Wilhelm raised his glass of Sam Adams in Whitman's direction and smiled. "Things are looking up."

Malloy then stood and raised his glass. "A final toast," he said, "to the intrepid survivors. As the old Irish blessing goes:

'May the road rise up to meet you, may the wind be always at your back,

May the sun shine warm upon your face, the rain fall soft upon your fields.

And until we meet again, may God hold you in the hollow of His hand.'"

Kerry sipped from her wine glass and stood, looking misty-eyed at each guest. "That was beautiful, Mike, and as Del knows, I have a hard time stopping once I get started, so if no one minds, I would like to say goodbye to you wonderful people the way I did with the band."

Her rapt audience sat motionless as she lifted her head and in a husky voice delivered her trademark farewell:

"I'll be seeing you, in all the old familiar places, that
this heart of mine embraces all day through.

In a small café, a park across the way, a children's
carousel, a chestnut tree, a wishing well."

Kerry paused, her eyes tearing momentarily. Breathing deeply, she continued:

"I'll be seeing you, in every lovely summer day, in
everything that's light and gay, I'll always think of you
that way.

I'll find you in the morning sun, and when the day
is through,

I'll be looking at the moon, but I'll be seeing you."

A choke of emotion accompanied her final whispered note. Few dry eyes remained. The room remained momentarily silent, until the guests rose in unison to applaud with gusto.

Whitman finally spoke for the group. "Now that, folks, is what I call Flying High!"

Coming Soon…

Bonus Feature 1st Chapter of

LUCKY DAZE:

FBI vs. MOB-REMATCH

Another Special Agent Del Dickerson Novel

Chapter One

South Lake Tahoe, California

"**R**un like hell!" Sulfur Sal Rinalti shouted to Loose Louie Milano in the suddenly darkened El Dorado County Jail.

It was shortly before midnight when the miraculous happened. A power failure in the energy-plagued State caused quirky electronic controls to fling all jail doors open. Startled inmates wasted little time in seizing the opportunity to race out of the facility. Generator-powered sirens immediately wailed, and feeble emergency lights began flickering. But the jail doors remained open, surrounding streetlights inoperative.

"It's our lucky day," Sulfur Sal puffed to his cellmate as they dashed for freedom.

Separating from other escapees several blocks from the jail, they pounded into an alley and paused for breath.

"But it ain't daytime," Loose Louie corrected.

"It's a figger of speech, dummy."

"Oh," Loose Louie grunted. He tightened the blanket covering his colorful inmate underwear.

"We gotta get rid of these shitty pink things," Sulfur Sal said. "The lights come back on , we're fish in a barrel."

"I don't see no fish," Loose Louie observed.

"That's another figger of speech," Sulfur Sal groaned. "Didn't ya learn nothin from all them books ya was reading?"

"They was love stories," Loose Louie retorted. "I like love stories. Didn't have no barrels. And no fish either."

"Unbelievable!" Sulfur Sal exploded. "I can't shake ya, no matter what I do. We go on a job together, which you royally fuck up. We get caught, and I end up in the same stinkin cell. And then of all the bright guys inside, I end up escapin with you. What'd I do to deserve this?" He looked heavenward.

"Thought we was buddies," Loose Louie said with a pout. "We been through a lot together."

"Don't remind me. But it was yur idea to grab the blankets, so I guess yur good for somethin."

"Thanks, Sal. We gotta use our wits to get outta this. Let's ditch the skivvies and make like we're Indians."

"Just what I was thinkin," Sulfur Sal replied, proceeding to discard his jail garments in a nearby trash can. "Now we gotta make tracks outta here."

Loose Louie frowned. "Ya think that's a good idea, Sal? Make tracks?"

Sulfur Sal glanced skyward again. "Let's go," he sighed.

Echo Summit, California

Kerry Vita slipped off her robe and stepped into the compact shower of her temporary RV home, her mind on her inadvertent introduction several months before to Doctor Ted Bennett, who had just telephoned. The attractive young orthopedic surgeon at South Lake Tahoe Hospital had eagerly accepted her invitation for dinner the following night at the construction site of her aunt's new cabin.

"Don't get many days off, and can't think of a better way to spend it than with you," he had asserted. "It's my lucky day."

Enjoying the sensation of the pulsating spray caressing her nubile body, Kerry thought of the night she had rushed into the emergency room with two wounded FBI agents, one of whom had parachuted into a tree on her Sierra Nevada mountain property. Bennett had marveled at her skill in setting the man's fractured leg and nursing him for several days. She shuddered, recalling how her cabin had been dynamited by gangland assassins, and how close two New York hit men had come to killing her. Her thoughts brightened in recollection of the warm bond of friendship that had developed with Bennett during their subsequent dates, both wondering where the unexpected romance might lead.

Kerry shampooed her wavy black hair, her thoughts wandering to the intriguing young agent she had rescued from the tree. Generous lips parted in a slight smile. They had spent some stimulating time together, including his heroic role in thwarting attacks on her life. Once again, she found herself troubled by the sensations invading her body whenever she thought of him. Spontaneously, she began singing a torchy ballad from her brief career as a Greenwich Village band singer:

"You'll never know just how much I love you,
You'll never know just how much I care..."

The words resonated sensuously around the steamy chamber. Then her dark brown eyes narrowed when she recalled the deferred disclosure of his semi-engaged status. Hope you're happy, you lovable bastard.

San Francisco

FBI agent Del Dickerson switched off his bedside light and reviewed the day's events, beginning with his early-morning conference with Assistant Special Agent in Charge Phil Whitman. The trim, sandy-haired six-footer had strikden triumphantly into Whitman's trophy-laden office, a broad smile defining his sunny mood. "Look, boss, no sticks," he had proclaimed, spinning completely around, bereft of the aluminum crutches which had been his constant companions for almost six months as his broken left leg slowly healed. "Cleared by the doc for full duty and raring to go." He remembered their conversation almost verbatim.

"You mean you don't want to stay on the computer fraud special?" Whitman said with a grin, as if he didn't recall Del's repeated pleas for a more exciting assignment.

"That's for the bean counters," Del responded dismissively. "I'm really itching for some action."

"Aren't we all?" Whitman cast a wistful glance at the row of marksmanship trophies crowding his credenza. "I haven't been able to compete in a tournament for so long I'm forgetting how to squeeze the trigger properly. We all have to make sacrifices, my boy, and by the way, don't you have an accounting degree?"

"I'm trying to live that down," Del remarked with a helpless shrug.

"From Yale?" Whitman pursued.

"I'm trying to live that down too, boss. You know all the ribbing I get."

Whitman chuckled silently, recalling the bizarre occurrences that seemed to hover over his precocious charge like a loaded storm cloud. He struggled to keep a straight face. "People rib you?"

"Yeah, and they keep ordering oriental carryout for me, because I studied Korean at the Language School in Monterey."

"You do have some world-shaking problems," Whitman commiserated with almost believable concern. "I'll see what I can do. And speaking of the Orient, how is that lovely lady from Taiwan?"

A frown furrowed Del's brow at the mention of his fiancée, Anna Chen, an Amerasian beauty who had rushed home to care for her critically ill mother.

"She's fine, Phil, and her mother is better, but neither of us thought it would be almost six months before she returned. It could be soon , though, according to her last letter. Guess that's something to be happy about."

"Right, count your blessings. Anna's coming back, you're off the crutches, and if your fabled luck holds, and I wake up tomorrow in a good mood, you just might get a more satisfying assignment. I'd say you should count this as a lucky day."

Del brightened, his characteristic smile reappearing. "Damn, you're right, boss. I need to think more positively."

Whitman returned the smile, dazzling white teeth emphasizing his smooth mahogany skin. Guess my Psychology degree pays off at times. "But remember," he emphasized to his young colleague, "no more parachuting into trees."

Del drifted into slumber, eager for a new challenge.

About the Author

Jim Healy is a 32-year FBI veteran who chased spies and bank robbers before directing the famed Ten Most Wanted Fugitives Program at J. Edgar Hoover's FBI Headquarters.

A Detroit native, Navy veteran, and Michigan State Journalism graduate, he writes with knowledge and humor about some of the colorful characters he encountered before retiring to his comfortable retreat on Virginia's Chesapeake Bay.

FLYING HIGH features some of his unforgettable acquaintances-whose names have been changed to protect the guilty.